By the same author

Novels

The Judas Code
The Red Dove
Angels in the Snow
The Kites of War
For Infamous Conduct
The Red House
The Yermakov Transfer
Touch the Lion's Paw (filmed as Rough Cut)
Grand Slam
The Great Land
The St. Peter's Plot
The Memory Man,
I, Said the Spy
Trance

Autobiographies

The Sheltered Days
Don't Quote Me But
And I Quote
Unquote

THE GOLDEN EXPRESS

Derek Lambert

STEIN AND DAY/Publishers/New York

For Julian Friedmann and Carole Blake

FIRST STEIN AND DAY PAPERBACK EDITION 1985
The Golden Express was originally published in hardcover
by Stein and Day/*Publishers* in 1984.

Copyright © 1984 by Derek Lambert
All rights reserved, Stein and Day, Incorporated
Designed by Louis A. Ditizio
Printed in the United States of America
STEIN AND DAY/*Publishers*
Scarborough House
Briarcliff Manor, N.Y. 10510

ISBN 0-8128-8184-2

ACKNOWLEDGMENTS

My thanks to the following for their help:

Lord Greenway, author of an excellent book on ferries. I have tampered a little with the facts he gave me in the interests of the narrative, and I hope he will forgive me, particularly as they were written on House of Lords notepaper.

The staff of Southern Railway's press office in their office among the pigeons in the rafters of Waterloo Station.

The staff of the Press Division of the Bank of England, who took me on a conducted tour of the anatomy of the Old Lady of Threadneedle Street but not, alas, into her vaults, an omission that gave rise to the speculation in this novel that perhaps the bullion stored there is illusory.

SNCF, the French railways; *Deutsche Bunaesbahn*, the West German railways; and D.E.R., the West German tourist agency.

John Harris, author of *Dunkirk: The Storms of*

War; Richard Collier, author of *1940: The World in Flames*; Alfred B. Gottwaldt and Eduard Bündgen, authors of *Der Rheingold Express*; Ray Vicker, author of *The Realms of Gold*; and Alan Wykes, author of *Hitler's Bodyguards* and honorary secretary of the Savage Club.

Mr. D. Withey of Johnson Matthey Ltd. for his advice on the chemistry of gold.

Derek Webb for the loan of his war books from his bar, El Galeon, in Denia, Alicante, Spain.

Denis and Pat French and Jeremy for access to their library at Old House, Denia.

Rupert Grayson, former King's Messenger and author, for the occasional divertissement during gestation. "It feels like leaving a maternity ward," he said on the day the book was finished. He should know. He's given birth enough times.

Hardy Schuch from Berlin, who helped me with German background, compiling the definitive work on Teutonic obscenities.

My wife, Diane, for her patience when every night in my dreams I stood on the footplate of the Rheingold, leaping from my bed whenever I saw a red signal.

PROLOGUE

1

S UCH WAS THE beatific quality of the smile on
the face of the young man wearing Walkman
earphones that it invited conjecture. What
sort of music was it that induced such appreciation?

The smile took on an almost wistful quality as
the voice on the cassette tape on the recorder slung
from his shoulder said, "Don't kill."

The warning, he reflected with a shrug of his
shoulders—interpreted by two sweating hikers as a
gesture of displeasure at some infelicitous chord—
should not have been necessary when all that was
contemplated was a straightforward burglary, but
when violence lurked inside you like an unstable
explosive it was an advisable precaution.

He kept the smile on his face, aesthetic, almost
saintly, framed with long blond hair, as he followed
the more mundane instructions he had dictated to
himself the previous evening during a conference
with the two accomplices who had visited the house
that was to be burgled.

"Turn left at the filling station."

The young man, Johann Hofer, from Bremer-haven, paused on the pavement of the road, the 462, as the morning traffic following the River Murg into the Black Forest streamed past him, exhaust fumes adulterating the August heat. When the lights changed he strolled dreamily in front of the shuddering bonnets and walked up the road leading to the house on a wooded hill overlooking the small town of Gernsbach in the Baden-Württemberg district of West Germany.

Hofer glanced at his digital wristwatch. Eleven fifty-seven. Three minutes to go.

"You should now be outside a house with two stone gnomes in the garden," his voice informed him.

Hofer, who hadn't been here before—he visited a location only once and that was the day of the hit—looked to his right. Correct. Like its neighbors, the house was big and somnolent, its garden exhausted from the unrelenting summer, and there were the gnomes gazing stonily into a dried-up pond.

"If there's anyone in sight, pause now."

An old lady being taken for a walk by a foraging dachshund passed by. Hofer smiled at her and touched the Walkman headset; Brahms, the smile said, or Liszt perhaps. He stopped the tape and waited until the dachshund had tugged its owner into a driveway two hundred meters away. He glanced up and down the road; there was no one else in sight. He switched on the recorder again, consulted his watch, and mentally added two minutes to the instructions. He would now enter the grounds at 12:02.

"A police car normally drives down the street at 10 A.M. It doesn't reappear until four in the afternoon," his voice reminded him.

Hofer, you're just killing time. There isn't any need to commune with yourself until you reach the wrought iron gates. According to his observant accomplices—one had represented himself as a mechanic who had come to replace the handset of Herr Schleicher's telephone, the other as an electrician who had called to fix the wiring damaged (deliberately) by the telephone mechanic—the gates were mounted with two rusting eagles. In case Schleicher reported the fault in the wiring, Hofer called the electricity authority in Rastatt to cancel any such complaint. It would never do to have two electricians arriving on the doorstep.

"One minute and you're there."

Hofer swung the canvas bag that contained his snack, his tools, and, beneath them, his gun, with exaggerated nonchalance. The familiar fever was on him now. How could anything ever compensate for what lay ahead? The intrusion into a stranger's life, a cough in a house presumed empty, the first sight of the plunder, tires on gravel, discovery, escape.

Or capture? The pendulum swing of the bag faltered as he thought that he had never considered such a possibility before. Then he rationalized that if the threat of capture didn't exist, then there would be no suspense, and he was comforted, although the fever had subsided a little.

Like a student worrying the bone of truth, Hofer sometimes asked himself why he was different from others. Why he could never be content with the rewards of honest endeavor. His childhood had been happy enough, hard-working parents and a small house with a pointed roof and a garden as neat as a postage stamp. After due consideration, professor Hofer informed student Hofer that he had been born out of his time: his genes had been generated for war.

He turned and looked at the rusting eagles.

For the second and last time the injunction reached him from the cassette, "Don't kill."

He had killed only once before, a fence who had cheated him and drawn a gun. He didn't want to kill again but if he was cornered. . . . You were conceived for battle, student Hofer, and in the Golden Years you would have been heavy with medals by now.

From the pocket of his jeans he took a key made from an impression obtained by the electrician and inserted it in the lock. It turned sweetly. Diffidently, as though he did this every day, Hofer walked into the life of Herr Kurt Schleicher.

On either side of the driveway roses grew, spindly with thirst, blossoms like crumpled tissues. So that was all right. The gardener hadn't been doing his job, which meant that, as anticipated, Schleicher and his wife were still on vacation on Lake Lucerne. Hofer was perpetually in debt to indolent gardeners.

"You will see a garden shed on the opposite side of the lawn."

There it was, a modest structure for so spacious a garden, leaning against a cedar tree. Hofer walked across the yellowing grass, took some gardening gloves from his bag, put them on, and opened the door. From the depths that smelled of creosote and manure he took a rake, a hoe, and a pair of shears. Then he returned to the beds of roses, thinking how much the house resembled a miniature fortress, with its robust gray walls and its two towers, except that from the rear it looked vulnerable with all those drains and water pipes clamped to the wall, an open invitation to a cat burglar. Hofer preferred the more militaristic frontage because, after all, the house contained relics of aggression, which were what he had come to steal.

He began to hoe the parched earth. The neighbor came crunching down the drive after he had been working for ten minutes. He was a slight man with a potbelly, a freckled pate, and a twitch in one eye. He wore baggy shorts and a white, open-neck shirt. He didn't look too sure of himself.

"Excuse me."

"*Ja?*" Hofer switched off his Walkman, removed the headset, and leaned on the hoe.

"Herr Schleicher didn't say anything about a gardener before he went away with his wife."

"Should he have?"

The good neighbor spread his hands. "He asked me to keep an eye on his house."

"Me too."

The neighbor looked nonplussed. "He didn't say . . ."

"Look." From the pocket of the old blue shirt, smeared the day before with mud, Hofer extracted a sheet of letterhead notepaper stolen from the house by the electrician, bearing the typewritten message, *To whom it may concern, This is to authorize Herr Hans Lorenz to obtain access to the grounds of my house in the furtherance of his duties as a gardener.*

The note bore the signature that the telephone mechanic had copied from the form he had got Schleicher to sign.

"Well it looks all right," the neighbor said, eye twitching.

"And he told me to check the doors, windows, et cetera, whenever I came."

"He's a careful man, Herr Schleicher."

"You can't be too careful these days," Hofer agreed, thinking of the farcical burglar alarm that the electrician had fixed so that it would abort after one snip with a pair of pliers. He began to hoe again.

"I wonder why he didn't warn me you would be coming."

"Perhaps he didn't think I merited a warning." The neighbor was beginning to annoy Hofer, and because his irritation was always on a short fuse, he replaced the headset. There were no more instruc-

16

tions for the moment, merely music, a group called the Police.

The neighbor began to speak again, but his words dribbled away. He walked slowly down the drive, shaking his head, and disappeared beneath the ravaged eagles.

Hoefer hoed carefully around a rose named Peace; as a child he had learned a little gardening from his father. A swallow dipped across the lawn, touching the stagnant contents of the pond; he remembered swallows dipping over a lake near Bremerhaven, beaks leaving tiny ripples on the water.

The alarm on his wristwatch sounded faintly.

His voice again, just like a policeman: "Gardening break over. Pick up your bag and proceed to the back door. Take your time about it."

He sat down on a dilapidated bench beside the kitchen door and the dustbins. From his bag he took a thermos of coffee, two wurst sandwiches packed in clingwrap, and a pair of pliers.

From the balcony of the house next door, just visible through a thicket of pines, he caught a flash of sunlight. Field glasses. He waved to the good neighbor. In thirty seconds, the neighbor, who lived by himself, would receive a phone call telling him that his antique shop in Baden-Baden, ten kilometers away, had been burgled.

The phone rang, a leisurely sound on a droning summer day. A car engine fired, tires squealed.

Hofer munched his sandwich. The Police again

on the tape. When his own voice replaced them, he removed the brick from under the kitchen window already loosened by the electrician. Snip. A wire parted, and the antique alarm system was breached, more of an invitation than a deterrent.

Why, Hofer wondered, was Herr Schleicher so lax? Perhaps he didn't appreciate the value of his collection; that was often the case with old people. They didn't realize the money the years had added to their treasures. No, that wasn't a satisfactory answer. Kurt Schleicher, by all accounts, wasn't the sort of man to have been tricked by the passing of time. He would know that the Nazi relics in his cellar were worth a fortune. The inconsistency began to worry Hofer; a single unsolved clue in a crossword puzzle.

He opened the back door with two more dummy keys, entered the kitchen, and took off the gardening gloves, replacing them with a latex pair. The kitchen was a display window bristling with electric appliances. So why the ancient alarm system?

"Go through the living room to the hall. The door to the cellar is located to the right."

He walked through the lounge, heavily Teutonic, with a beamed ceiling and stags' heads and guns on the walls. On the fireside table lay a copy of *Playboy*, a bottle of whisky, and a backgammon set. Hofer decided he might have liked Schleicher in his youth, now even. Perhaps the youthful Schleicher was like me, he thought, but lucky enough to have had a war. A shame I have to rob you, but perhaps you will understand.

18

The cellar smelled of whitewash and the past. Because he specialized in Nazi memorabilia, Hofer had visited many cellars and attics. He enjoyed them because you could share a life and come out still young.

He removed his headset and set the pygmy alarm on his wristwatch. He had half an hour until the van was due. There were three hefty trunks on the flagstones, each adorned with stickers from the watering holes of Europe. One was from America, Waldorf Astoria, 1952. Within a minute he was, with the aid of a bunch of tiny keys—you could have opened these locks with a nail file—burrowing into the life and times of Herr Kurt Schleicher.

Trunk Number 1. Photograph albums. A beautiful girl with braided hair who a few pages later became a bride. A little boy wearing too-long shorts kicking a football. A skiing holiday. A bundle of postcards written in ink that had faded to copper. A riding whip. A pair of patent-leather dancing pumps. An empty bottle of Krug champagne. *Yes, I would have liked Schleicher.* A brown, double-breasted suit with broad lapels, spotted with mold.

He closed the trunk and turned his attention to another. He guessed that there would be a missing period, circa 1936 to 1945; there always was with the wealthy, aging Germans he robbed. It was sad that they had to strike the Golden Years from their lives.

The contents of the second trunk were similar to those of the first, except that everyone in the photographs had aged and the Schleichers had visited Brazil.

So if the informant, who had told the fence, who had told Hofer, was to be believed, it had to be the third trunk. He felt his heart pumping as he turned the little key in the lock. The lid snapped open.

A black and silver-braided SS officer's uniform. Not Schleicher's, of course. They never belonged to the Schleichers of this world. "Just a collector's item, my dear friend." Hofer abhorred the duplicity, recognized its necessity. A cap with an arrogant peak. Inside the cap a 7.6 Luger that had been converted into a 9 mm Parabellum. The Treaty of Versailles, recalled Hofer, who knew about such things, had forbidden the Germans to manufacture 9 mm handguns, so they had made weapons of a smaller caliber that could be easily converted.

He picked up the gun, handling it with respect; beneath it a magazine containing eight rounds. The bullets were irresistible, and he loaded the pistol, curling his forefinger around the trigger. He found he was holding his breath. He felt like this when violence was expanding inside him, as though a bird of prey was trying to escape. Get a grip on yourself. He laid the gun on a flagstone and returned to the trunk.

Insigna worn by the crack *Totenkopf,* Death's Head, and *Das Reich* divisions of the SS; a steel helmet painted with runes like flashes of lightning, the band inside bearing the name Sepp Dietrich, commander of the *Leibstandarte SS Adolf Hitler,* the Führer's bodyguard and one of the finest fighting units the Third Reich had produced.

According to legend they had to place a primed grenade on their steel helmets during training and wait for it to explode. A Knight's Cross; a letter from Hitler to Dietrich—a find indeed if it wasn't a forgery; swastika armbands, buttons, badges; bundles of memorandums and battle orders; a bloodstained calendar printed in Russian.

He closed the lid. He heard the ring of jackboots on frosted cobblestones, smelled the cordite fumes of battle. *Then I wouldn't have had to become a thief.*

The present reasserted itself, whitewash instead of cordite. He sat on the chest worrying. An admirer of the SS, even if he *hadn't* been a member, wouldn't have been so sloppy: that alarm system went out with mantraps. A blind for a more sophisticated system operated with lasers? No, the electrician would have been too thorough for that. What then?

Then he had it. He had so far assumed everything Schleicher had wanted him to assume—that the alarm was so rudimentary that there was nothing more valuable to steal than the relics. A sophisticated alarm would have alerted his keenest predatory instincts. So there was something even more valuable to steal in this house.

Where was the safe?

Hofer stood up, excitement held on a leash by professionalism. Where would I have hidden a safe? Certainly not behind a picture or a mirror. Upstairs? Probably—he wouldn't hide all his loot in the cellar. Or that, rather, is what an ordinary housebreaker might deduce. Not this one. Hofer pulled a moth-eaten Wilton rug from a corner of the cellar; he took a short crowbar from his bag and tapped the flagstones; one had a hollow ring to it. He thrust the crowbar into the crack beside the stone and levered upward; the stone was only five centimeters thick. Underneath it the safe, dark green with polished steel fittings, snug and impregnable, a beauty, a bastard. No time now.

When he told the driver of the van, purporting to belong to the Rastatt sanitation department, that he intended to return, the driver, who had previously been the telephone mechanic, told him he was crazy. As they loaded the mothballed memories of the Golden Years into the van, Hofer thought, He's right—but I'll return just the same.

WITH A SURGICAL probe blunted with hard rubber, he forced the condom into the lock of the floor safe. He didn't like floor safes because they were awkward to handle, but they had one advantage: they made it easier to pour the nitroglycerine into the contraceptive. From the delicately sprung container in his bag, he took a bottle that had once contained linctus codeine and, with a steady hand, poured the liquid into the condom, thinking that there was a whole range of sexual suggestion to the operation: delicacy of touch—one rough overture and it could be blown—the condom itself, mounting excitement, final plunge, explosive orgasm.

22

He slid two copper wires attached to a detonator containing fulminite of mercury into the sheath; then he went up the stone steps, uncoiling wire behind him. The two strands of the wire, positive and negative, he clipped to the final instrument of destruction, the Beethoven Box in the living room. (Why it was called that he had no idea; perhaps there was some connection with Ludwig's deafness.)

Somewhere in the house a clock chimed. Midday. This time he had no Walkman. He knew the layout and he had no accomplices—neither of them had wanted anything to do with a return heist because it broke all the rules. But the cunning of Schleicher had to be confounded. The safe had to be blown.

The police entered the house just as he was about to press the plunger on the Beethoven Box. They came in through the front door (Schleicher must have left the key at the police station) and made straight for the cellar without even looking into the living room.

Inside him the bird of prey stretched its wings.

There were fifteen steps. They would be descending cautiously. He gave them eight seconds before pressing the plunger.

The explosion reminded him of an express train hurtling through a small station. The blast came straight up the steps, blowing out a window in the hallway, bringing flesh and clothing with it.

He gave it a couple of seconds before going down, Walther P 38 pistol in one hand. One policeman—

they had both been in plain clothes—had been torn to pieces; his companion was crouching at the foot of the steps, hands masking his face.

Hofer pointed the Walther at his head. "Who?"

"I don't understand. Please help me."

"Who told you I was coming back?"

"I can't see," the policeman said, letting some light through the mask of his hands.

"Meyer?"

"Yes, Meyer." His voice wet and slurred.

"Take your hands away from your face."

When he did Hofer shot him, out of kindness, between what was left of his eyes.

Poor bastard. But they were the enemy, and when they became policemen they invited death and violence into their lives. Poor dead bastards just the same.

He turned his attention to the safe. It had been a neat job, and he was proud of it. The contents of the safe surprised him.

A small gold bar and a leather-bound book.

HE REMOVED THE blond wig as he drove the van down the hill. He accelerated along the riverside road, the embankment railings hung with pots of bright blue and red bedding plants by an enlightened council, but he took care not to exceed the speed limit.

Obviously the tipoff had been received shortly before the two policemen arrived, otherwise there would have been more of them. They must have been cruising when they were alerted on the radio. But others were already homing in on the house—a green and white police car had just raced past him in the opposite direction—and they would find the bodies. Pretty soon the whole area would be crawling with police looking for him, and there would be roadblocks on all roads leading from Gernsbach. But would they know whom they were looking for? Meyer would have mentioned the wig. They wouldn't be on the alert for a young man with crisp black hair cut military style. He glanced in the driving mirror to reassure himself. But a search would give the game away, gun, gold, book—he had left his tools and the nitro behind. And the van. Someone may have spotted it in the driveway; fortunately the good neighbor was spending the day at his antique shop. Hofer had checked this out earlier.

Should he get rid of the van? Well, the police speeding in the opposite direction hadn't taken any notice of it, but that didn't mean a lot because they were merely acting on the original tip from Meyer. Meyer. It was always the fences who betrayed you, always, since crime began. He decided to risk keeping the van because the theft of another vehicle would waste time and a van owned by the sanitation department wouldn't arouse suspicion, only distaste, if anything.

He turned left over the bridge spanning the small, cheerful river, and drove at a sedate speed past shops and old timbered houses with alpine

25

roofs leaning against each other. He took the Baden-Baden road, cocking his head to one side with the predictable interest of any good citizen as a police car and an ambulance hurtled past. The bodies must have been found. He opened the window and heard the braying of police sirens, as though a flock of alien birds had descended, he thought, as he swung the van into a lane rutted with baked mud.

He took a black plastic bag from the back of the van and dropped the gun, gold ingot, and book into it. Instinctively he felt that the book was more important than the ingot, that this was what Scheicher had been trying to hide.

The spare wheel was kept under a section of plywood. He removed the wood and the wheel and dropped the bag into the cavity beneath. Then he replaced the wheel and the plywood. As he backed out of the lane, a police car hurtled past, swaying with speed; he braked to avoid it. A crash with a police car was all he needed.

The first roadblock was three meters ahead beside a picnic area on the crest of one of the Black Forest's pine-covered hills. Hikers who had been about to plunge into the cathedral-quiet depths of the forest leaned on their sticks and watched curiously as police motorcyclists, theatrically tough in their leather armor, stopped each vehicle.

"Name?"

"Reiss. Hans Reiss."

"ID?"

The policeman, who looked very young and

fierce, drew his gun when Hofer stretched out his hand to the glove compartment. He put it away when Hofer handed him the papers forged in Stuttgart; a sanitary engineer was an unlikely public enemy. One day the young policeman would learn that there were no such pigeonholes in crime.

"Where have you come from?"

"Gernsbach."

"Doing what?"

"Sewers," Hofer told him. The policeman took a step back.

"Rear doors, open them please."

He stood aside as Hofer climbed out of the driving seat. Obviously at college they had told him about the old trick of knocking a cop flying with one jerk of the door. He watched warily while Hofer unlocked the doors, as well he might. On the other side of the road another policeman was questioning the sleek-haired driver of a Mercedes 320 SL. The driver looked worried; perhaps the Mercedes was stolen.

"Okay, step back."

The young policeman peered into the interior of the van, which was littered with tools that performed unspeakable functions. Hofer watched him. If he lifts the plywood and the wheel I'll have to get to the gun.

The policeman lifted the plywood.

Hofer stepped forward.

The policeman replaced it and said, "On your way, Herr Reiss."

As he climbed into the driving seat, Hofer asked

what it was all about, but the policeman, who took secrecy very seriously, said, "Nothing that need concern you," and dictated the registration number of the van into a handset.

Hofer drove away. Five minutes later he had reached the pastoral approaches to Baden-Baden, that elegant seat of wealth, with casino and spas handily placed for the dispatch of its riches.

It was just the place for Meyer, a snob whose father had been a sheetmetal worker in Duisburg. Meyer had abandoned metal and become a dealer in Nazi memorabilia, a market that had expanded steadily since 1945. Today items such as Sepp Dietrich's helmet were worth their weight in.... Where the hell had Schleicher got that gold bar from? And what was written in the leather book?

By now Meyer would have had ample time to value the proceeds of the first robbery at Schleicher's house. He would appreciate the haul because he was a connoisseur as well as a dealer, although in Hofer's view he groveled rather than worshipped at the altar of the Aryan creed.

Well, Hofer reflected, glancing at the dashboard clock, he had better make the most of it because he had barely 30 minutes to live.

He pulled up at another roadblock, more businesslike this time, with a police car pulled across the road. This check was cursory because, he supposed, they had already got his number from the young zealot up in the hills.

"What's this all about?" he asked, exactly as any law-abiding citizen would ask.

"There's been a double killing in Gernsbach." This policeman, who wore a thick macho mustache, was older and had long ago shed his cloak of secrecy. "Two detectives blown up. Just wait till we get the bastard who did it."

Hofer drove past a *gasthaus* called, incongruously, Don Quixote. Now he was coming into Baden-Baden. He kept a tight rein on his hatred of Meyer, but it was difficult when he visualized the terror on the fence's insignificant features. Meyer, he realized, looked a little like Himmler. Hofer had never admired the onetime head of the SS. With his pince-nez and sneak's features, he was the antithesis of the Aryan dream and, because he interfered with his ideals, Hofer didn't dwell on him.

Why had Meyer betrayed him? For the usual reasons, he supposed. Police pressure. Give us the thief who's been tormenting the forces of law and order throughout the Federal Republic of Germany and we won't ask questions about your stores in Duesseldorf, Hamburg, and West Berlin.

Hofer left the van in a parking lot near the Augustabad and, carrying the black bag—you didn't leave gold ingots around so that humble car thieves could get lucky—walked toward the center of the city. He had one fear: that the police would have alerted Meyer. And one hope: that with the deaths of two of their kind uppermost in their minds, they wouldn't have spared a thought for the fence.

Swinging the bag briskly, he reached the avenues and parkland of the city center, a work-soiled artisan on his way to perform some mundane task. The people here, even the tourists, had the gloss of wealth about them, but they didn't look at Hofer with contempt. They didn't look at him at all. I don't exist, he thought. Wonderful.

He crossed Leopolds Platz and the diminutive River Oos and walked across clipped lawns threaded with mauve clover, past the colonnaded portals of the casino, and the Trinkhalle, where invalids took the waters, hot, salty, and unpleasant. A man in shorts with a base-drum belly lay on a white lounge with a glass of the stuff in his hand; beside him sat a top-heavy woman blinking into the sunlight. Prosperous and elegant Baden-Baden might be, but it was also a tired place, as though everyone was doing everything too late.

When he neared the ancient block of luxury apartments where Meyer lived, Hofer slowed down. There was no one around except a debonair old man walking along the street with marionette movements, his eyes staring into the past.

Here I come Meyer, you *fotze*.

He paused outside the marble-floored foyer. Three floors above lay the greatest obstacle to the killing of Meyer, the Judas Eye in the door of his apartment through which he could study any visitor.

Hofer stopped a youth of seventeen or so with water-slicked fair hair.

"Do you want to earn a fast ten marks?"

"How fast?" looking at him as if he were a gay on the prowl.

"Very. Two minutes. Say twenty marks. Here's the first installment," handing him a ten-mark note and telling him what he had to do.

Together they went up in the caged elevator to the third floor. Hofer stood back while the youth pressed Meyer's bell.

"*Ja*, what is it?" By now Meyer would be peering through the Judas Eye.

"A message, Herr Meyer."

"Who are you?"

"The concierge's son."

"A message from whom?"

"I don't know, Herr Meyer, but it could be the police, it looks official."

Grumbling, Meyer opened the door.

"Good afternoon, Willi," Hofer said as the youth scuttled down the corridor clutching the second installment of his payment.

"You!"

"Me. You seem surprised."

"Not surprised exactly, but you do usually come at night, don't you." He tried to slam the door in Hofer's face.

"Sorry," Hofer said, taking the blow of the door on one shoulder as, Walther in his hand, he entered the room.

"What do you want?"

"You," Hofer said pleasantly.

He surveyed the scene. Chandelier sparkling with the colors of the spectrum, molded ceiling, green, gold, and cream walls and, across the balcony, vistas of dignified composure. The only inelegant touch was the pile of booty on the white carpet.

Hofer pointed the barrel of the Walther at it. "I assume you've taken Dietrich's helmet and Hitler's letter and anything else of value?"

Meyer said, "Yes, of course, the wheat from the chaff. Why do you ask?" a throaty catch to his voice.

"Because I assume you were going to keep the good stuff and hand over the rubbish to the police."

"Police? Why should I hand over anything to the police?" Hofer had to admire his composure; in a way it drew the teeth of his own fury. Then Meyer broke, "Look, I know what you think, but you're wrong." Hofer's fury intensified because it was what he had expected.

Now all he wanted to do was to end it before his rage exploded.

Curling one finger around the trigger of the Walther, he said, "You squealed, Meyer, you know what to expect."

"Did *you* know what to expect?"

Hofer frowned. "What?"

"This." Meyer delved into the heap of swastika armbands, Death's Head penants, and silver runes and from beneath them fired the 9 mm Luger that had been converted so cunningly from a 7.6. The gun had been well cared for so, despite its age, the mechanism worked with oiled precision, and the bullet went straight into Hofer's heart, spinning him around in such a way that, as he fell, the arm of which the Walther was an extension shot up into a semblance of a Nazi salute.

Then he pitched forward into the jetsam of the Golden Years and, as he died, found comfort from it.

FOUR DAYS LATER an American journalist named Story—like a detective called Holmes he had long ago wearied of jokes about his name—paused beside the statue of the Duke of Wellington on a bronze horse and stared across Threadneedle Street at the Bank of England.

Even though he was a financial correspondent, based in Bonn, he was assailed by something akin to awe every time he came face to face with the Bank's blind, sand-colored screen walls. This exaggerated reverence irritated him because in his opinion the Old Lady was a fraud. Like most financial institutions.

He had come to this devastating conclusion years ago when, after a decent but stifling upbringing in the Bronx, he had triumphantly majored in journalism at Columbia, turned his sights away from his confined origins, and set them on Wall Street. He had quickly mastered the intricacies of high finance but had found that the financial district was overpopulated with journalists. Besides, he didn't want to settle anywhere as yet. There was a Teutonic strain in the family on his mother's side, so what better place than West Germany with its highly respected currency? He applied himself to learning German and, with the application of an intruder trying to assert himself in realms in which he believes he isn't accepted, soon mastered it and took himself to Bonn as a free lance.

It was during this quicksilver advancement that, bearing the resentment he had brought with him from his humble origins like a haversack on his back, he discovered that wealth had no foundations, that it was all a matter of manipulation. Witness the fluctuation of the dollar, the pound, the mark—all manipulated, a global confidence trick.

And what happened when the manipulators in New York, Tokyo, London, got their figures wrong? The Wall Street crash was what happened, and the terrifying thing was that it could happen any day because even the most consummate con man in the world could slip up. So could his computer.

So the Old Lady across the street, matriarch of what was still arguably the most potent financial center in the world, had no cause to look so smug. One ill-timed run on a currency could precipitate a panic against which those walls, 14-foot thick in places, would be as effective as tissue paper. The figures on the central portico representing strength, security, and abundance would look pretty silly, too.

Nevertheless Story, thirtyish with thinning fair

hair and an interrogator's eyes that constantly disbelieved, couldn't dispel his awe. It was, he supposed, because the Bank was one of the headquarters of the caste of which he had never become a fully qualified member. Although his markets included such illustrious journals as *The New York Times*, *The Times* of London, and the *Wall Street Journal*, he was still treated with respect that was somehow condescending, and he could always detect the deprecating gesture, the tightness of a smile. These attitudes sometimes made him pursue an interview beyond its proper limits. Sensing his power, that of the knowledgeable intruder, he became vulgarly intrusive and knew it. No breeding, that's my trouble, he thought as he crossed Threadneedle Street to take his revenge on the Bank, the citadel of financial breeding.

He dodged a red Number 11 double-decker bus. A few drops of rain fell from a hot sky. Thunder rumbled from somewhere behind the mirror-glass skyscrapers in which the reflections of the old City, the true City, could be seen.

Keeping a tight hold on the briefcase containing the leather-bound book he had bought from Meyer, Story walked into the Bank.

INSIDE THE FRONT hall, Story approached the pink-liveried head gatekeeper, scarlet and gold robe discarded because the temperature was more than 70 degrees, and told him he wanted to speak to someone from the Information Division.

While he waited at the desk in the corner he looked around. Above him was a carving affirming that the Bank was founded in 1694 during the reign of William III and rebuilt in 1930 in the reign of George V. The inscription was in Latin, which Story didn't understand, but he knew the dates anyway. During the past four days he had done his homework on the Old Lady. He knew, for instance, that the rebuilding wasn't finished until 1939. One year later the leather book took up the tale. And what a tale!

At his feet sprawled elaborate mosaics. Those in the inner hall, beyond the black Belgian granite pillars, included a map of the south coast of England, set with a single red stone, like a drop of blood, pinpointing the town of Cobham, where the architect of the reconstruction, Sir Herbert Baker, had lived. Story wished he wasn't so impressed by it all.

Beside him a beefy young man in shirt sleeves was saying into a telephone, "A Mr. Story. Representing? No, a free lance."

"Tell him," Story interrupted, "that I'm representing *The Times*," that always got to them, "and *The New York Times*," sometimes that even more so; the combination was a major offensive.

While the young man relayed this information, Story's attention strayed to the spiral staircase, without visible means of support—all the books made a point of that—leading from the heights of the seven-story building to the depths where the

Old Lady kept her purse. Her paper money was produced in Loughton, Essex (eight million notes printed daily, about the same number burned), but her ingots were here below his feet. Or so it was said.

The young man put down the phone. "Someone is coming to see you," he said and turned his attention to another visitor, an Arab.

The two gatekeepers in pink looked everywhere except at the visitors. Apart from them and a couple of older men in dark suits there didn't seem to be much evidence of security; but of course that was part of the great British deception. How many prime ministers had been assassinated in comparison with the death toll of American presidents? He assumed that he was being observed on closed-circuit television.

Footsteps tapped briskly on the mosaic and the representative of the Information Division was with him to repel assault. Some hope.

"What can I do for you, Mr. Story?" She had fair hair, a determined face, good figure, and a voice from the London suburbs, with nice sooty vowels. "You should have let us know you were coming," giving the impression that he was one of the correspondents foremost in their thoughts.

"It's not really you I want to talk to."

"I see," by which she meant she didn't. "Then why . . ."

"Did I call you? Because I would have got you anyway. You know that, Miss . . ."

But she didn't fall for that one. Perhaps she had

been caught before, seen her name leaping at her from the pages of a tabloid. "Then whom *do* you wish to see, Mr. Story?"

Story said, "The Governor," and enjoyed the moment.

It took her a few moments to summon up, "I'm afraid that's quite impossible. Please tell me the nature of your inquiry, and I'll see if we can arrange an interview with another official."

Someone else from the Information Division in other words. The Division was useful, no doubt about that. It was also the Bank's first line of defense.

"I'll tell you what I'll do. I'll settle for the head of security."

"I'm afraid that . . ."

"Will NOT be impossible, Miss Fairchild."

"Forrest," she corrected him, and almost swore. He wanted to say he was sorry because he liked this girl with her London voice and her determination to be correct, but in this sort of encounter you had to retain authority. "Mr. Story," she said tightly, "I think the best thing for you to do is to go away and write a letter stating your requirements."

"I haven't come all this way to write letters, Miss Forrest." He took her arm, and she was so surprised that she allowed herself to be led out of earshot of the receptionists and gatekeepers to the passage leading to one of the banking halls.

"Now listen to me carefully," his voice more gentle. "I want you to contact Mr. Shaw"—that surprised her too—"and tell him who I am, and tell him that I've unearthed some intriguing information about the bank at the beginning of the last war, and I would like him to elaborate. Tell him I came upon it in Germany."

"First of all, Mr. Story, if you don't let go of my arm I shall summon help." *Summon* help, he liked that. He released her arm. "And secondly, such a query could be dealt with quite competently by the Information Division."

"Sure it could, but just tell him, okay?" He smiled at her. "I promise you won't get bawled out."

She edged away. "It's quite ridiculous."

Lovely, where would the English be without their *quites?* "But you'll do it?"

"If you insist."

He wouldn't bet on it, but he thought she would. As she crossed the hallway her heels rang with indignation, and when she spoke to one of the receptionists he guessed she was saying something like, "It's your job to protect us from lunatics like that."

Then she disappeared at speed. The flunkies in pink moved closer, actually looking at him, and a big man in a too-tight suit came up the spiral staircase from the depths and stood between the black pillars looking quietly menacing.

What did they do with nuts here? Throw them into Threadneedle Street? That surely wouldn't do, this wasn't a beer hall. Perhaps I shall find out soon enough, he thought, if my instincts about Miss Forrest are wrong. Perhaps even now she is standing in front of a mirror repairing the ravages of her anger, grimly determined not to pass on the message to Shaw. Miss Fairchild indeed!

A young man with pale hair, wearing a beautifully cut pinstripe —too well-cut for him to be a thoroughbred aristocrat—materialized from the direction of the Garden Court and said, "Would you like to follow me, Mr. Story."

AFTER THE YOUNG man had departed Shaw said, "Can I get you a drink, Mr. Story?"

He was lean and trim, in his mid-sixties, with a clipped gray mustache and lines on his tanned face that smiled although he didn't. He wore a light gray suit, blue shirt, and knitted navy tie, and he made Story in his charcoal gray and white shirt feel like an undertaker.

Shaw was standing beside a liquor cabinet with a rosewood door, the only extravagance in his functional office: desk covered with scuffed red leather, three chairs, filing cabinet, three governors—two past and one present—exuding business acumen from photographs on the walls, a view staring into the mirrored eyes of a skyscraper, and that was it.

Story consulted his wristwatch. It was 11:58 A.M. The timing so far was perfect. The Governor would still be conferring with the Court of Directors, as he did, whenever possible, at 11 A.M. every Thursday.

"It's a little too early for me," Story replied. A lie but he had found in the past that abstemious piety gave him a little edge.

"Really?" Shaw didn't believe him; the edge was blunted. Shaw started to make himself a pink gin, taking his time about it. "Take a pew and tell me how I can help you."

Attack. "I want to see the Governor," he said.

"Really?" He could invest *really* with a scale of inflections, another *quite*. "Don't you think you'd better tell me what this is all about first?"

You know what it's all about, Story thought, or you wouldn't have seen me in the first place. The knowledge encouraged him; they understood each other. And for a fleeting moment it was borne in on Story that neither of them belonged here, that Shaw's mannered ways weren't natural, that there were flints left in his voice that he never quite managed to dig out.

"It's all about World War II," Story said, "and the Bank's role in it."

"I understood from Information that you're a journalist. Isn't all that rather old hat?"

"The past is part of the present, Mr. Shaw."

"Perhaps." Shaw swilled angostura bitters around his glass and poured the surplus into a cut-glass bowl. "But I don't think the editor of the Old Thunderer, or *The New York Times* for that matter, would thank you for giving him a story that was 45 years old."

"On the contrary, Untold Secrets of World War II always make headlines."

"I suppose you're right. Wraps off the Official Secrets Act. Now it can be told. All that sort of stuff," tone indicating what he thought of that sort of stuff.

He unscrewed the top of a bottle of Beefeater's and splashed gin into his glass. "Are you sure you wouldn't like a little something?"

Smelling the scented fragrance of the gin, Story almost weakened. "Quite sure."

"Very well." Story heard ice cracking in the gin.

Shaw brought his glass around the desk, sat down, and made himself comfortable. Although he looked casual he had about him an air of concentrated competence, as indeed he should. He was guardian of the billions entrusted to the Bank by the British government, the national banks, the overseas central banks, foreign sisters of the Old Lady, and other customers as formidable as the International Monetary Fund. If the Bank of England collapsed, then so would Britain and probably the rest of the Western world.

Yes, Shaw needed those distilled capabilities of his. Even now, knowing that *I know*, he was handling himself well. But I'm in the driver's seat. Reassured, Story stared at Shaw across the desk. Shaw's eyes were very blue.

"I know what happened, Mr. Shaw."

"In World War II? Well, if you know I really can't understand why you're causing all this fuss. And we do have a Museum and Historical Research Section, you know."

Shaw, Story understood, was making his last contact with the cozy sense of security that had existed until a few minutes ago; he had to admire him for it.

He said, "Candidly, Mr. Shaw, I think it's time we cut the crap."

"Whatever you say."

"The period I'm talking about is 1939 to 1940. Your gold was shipped to North America, right?" He detected a flicker of hope in Shaw's expression. Shaw was thinking, praying, *Is that all he knows?* "But it never got there, did it." The hope was extinguished. The lines on Shaw's face were still genial, but the muscles in his jaw were working.

"Are you asking me or telling me?"

Story opened his briefcase and handed Shaw the leather book. "It's all in there. In German. Do you want me to translate?"

Shaw shook his head and began to read the handwriting, once a bold hand but now, with loss of pigment, infirm as though it had aged with its author.

Story knew it page by page:

Page 1. The call from Reichmarshall Hermann Goering.

Page 2. Planning in Berlin, Munich, and Hamburg.

Page 3. Assembling the cast.

Shaw obviously knew the story if not the script

because he was skimming the pages, nearing the end.

Page 30 or thereabouts. Pursuit.

Page 31. Attack. Hijack, to use today's parlance.

After page 38 the rest of the sheets were empty. Shaw closed the book; Story didn't think he'd even bothered with the last two pages of writing.

Shaw said, "In circumstances like this I believe I'm supposed to say, 'You don't expect me to believe all this, do you?' Well I won't, because I do. Satisfied?" He sipped his drink.

Story wasn't sure that he was. Even though the chips were down Shaw should have looked more aghast. Is there some ultimate catastrophe that I don't know about, he wondered. Surely nothing could be more catastrophic than the loss at sea of most of Britain's gold reserves; nothing more humiliating than its capture by the Germans.

"I've had it copied, by the way. So now do I get to see the Governor?"

"Why? You've got your story. Like that gentleman once said," pointing in the direction of Wellington, "'*Publish and be damned.*'"

"I'd like some sort of comment. A denial even. After all, the Germans never claimed the capture of the bullion."

"We both know why that was, don't we. Goering wanted it for his own coffers, not Germany's."

And you, Story thought, are being altogether too cool. Publish and be damned! Shaw should have been leaning across the desk pleading with him not

44

to write the story for the sake of Britain, the free world. Then he thought, Perhaps he doesn't think I've followed this thing through to its logical conclusion, and he smiled.

When, aloud, he followed it through for Shaw's benefit, the head of security finished his drink and sat for a moment staring into his empty glass as though mourning its passing.

Then he asked Story to excuse him while he went to make a private call. When he returned he said, "The Governor will see you in half an hour."

THE COURT ROOM is one of the most beautiful rooms in the world, noble without being aristocratic. Its colors are gentle, pale green and gold mostly, and its chandeliers, fireplaces, and columns have an air of elegant permanence about them. Such a setting does not encourage violent debate, and the only reminder that decisions of immense fiscal moment have been reached here is the great table, forty feet long. The Wilton carpet, Story remembered reading, weighed half a ton and had been laid in 1939.

When he entered the room with Shaw, the Governor was standing beside one of the Venetian windows staring down at the garden. Why are we meeting here, Story wondered. Did they hope that his brash intent would lose direction in such surroundings, like a blasphemous voice in a cathedral?

"I thought it better that we talk here," the Governor said, half turning, "because no one can hear us from the outside. The room is fitted with double doors."

He moved from the window and sat at the head of the table, and Story thought, If he thinks I'm going to sit at the other end forty feet away he's got another think coming.

"Here." The Governor pointed at the two chairs on either side of him. Apparently there weren't going to be any introductions—you don't exchange niceties with unwanted guests. Well, I don't intend to be intimidated. Firmly Story smoothed his sparse hair, a habit of his; as he did so he felt sweat running down his chest inside his shirt.

The Governor, another trim figure, with the sort of fine fair hair that turns silver imperceptibly and aesthetic features saved from dull refinement by a foraging nose, looked cool by contrast.

Shaw spoke first. He seemed assured enough; Story couldn't imagine him any other way. He said, "As I told you, sir, Mr. Story has a theory about our gold reserves and would appreciate your views on them."

"Not a theory," Story said. "More of a conclusion." He placed the leather book on the table between the three of them.

The Governor ignored it. "Are you sure it's my views you want, Mr. Story, or do you seek some more substantial reaction?" His voice, deep and resonant, went straight to the heart of the matter with one rapier thrust. How much to keep quiet?

Well, it wasn't going to be like that. Story was a

journalist. His materials were facts and words, and he liked to use them. He also needed to consolidate his authority, gaining strength by the moment, by airing his knowledge.

"First," he said tapping the book, "I think you should appreciate how much I know."

"Mr. Shaw has already appraised me of the salient points."

Story continued as though he hadn't spoken. "At the outbreak of the last war it was decided to ship the Bank's bullion and other securities to North America, ostensibly Canada, in case the Germans invaded Britain and captured London. The decision was kept under wraps because it wouldn't have done to let the people know that defeat was even remotely considered. Some of the assets did reach their destination and the title documents of Britain's foreign investments were stored in the vaults of the Sun Life Building in Montreal."

"I think," the Governor interrupted, "that all this is common ground." But Story stormed on, a kind of exultancy upon him. So many momentous matters had been debated at this table and here he was, the boy from the Bronx, with the key to the most awesome of them all.

"But the gold didn't reach its destination, which in any case wasn't Canada; it was the States. And the reason it didn't get there was because Goering heard about the shipment through his own intelligence service, the *Forschungsamt*, and decided to get his fat little hands on it."

The Governor sighed but didn't speak. Shaw picked up the book and Story noted that he appeared to be searching for something. That was odd because to all intents and purposes he knew the whole story.

Story went on. "The bullion was loaded onto an American ship, the *Alaska*, because it was thought that the Germans wouldn't risk attacking a United States vessel. Right, they wouldn't. Wrong, Goering would. He sent in the Luftwaffe, which sunk or crippled the escort vessels when they were still within range of his bombers. Then he sent in his pirate ship, the *Countess of Cork*, flying the colors of neutral Ireland but manned by Germans. At the helm was an adventurer named von Ritter."

Story paused and the Governor spoke. "I think you have made your point, Mr. Story. You *do* know the alleged facts." He poured himself a glass of water. "To cut a long story short, the *Alaska* was boarded by the Germans. The alleged events"—he had the lawyer and policeman's penchant for *alleged*—"took place in the spring of 1940 before the invasion of the Low Countries."

Shaw said, "We mustn't forget that the *Countess* was holed. As it was sinking, one of the escort vessels managed to let fly a torpedo."

"I realize," Story said, "that you don't want to ignore the resourcefulness of the British in such a situation. The fact remains that German pirates got away with all Britain's gold."

"Not all of it," the Governor corrected him, and

Story was prepared to accept the correction because as it happened he wasn't sure on that point.

"Well, most of it," he said, hoping for elaboration.

The Governor inclined his head toward Shaw. Governors liked to talk about profits, not losses.

"Probably about 500 million pounds," Shaw said.

"A bit dumb, wasn't it, laying on escort vessels for an American ship? Even if Goering hadn't known about its cargo, it would have aroused the suspicions of German patrol boats."

"They were deployed at a distance, and they were disguised. Nothing was as it seemed that day, neither the *Alaska*, nor the *Countess of Cork*, nor the escorts."

Story returned to the value of the hijacked bullion just in case the two of them thought they had succeeded in minimizing it. "Of course we're talking about billions of pounds at today's values. What are Britain's gold reserves at the moment?" he asked the Governor.

The Governor said, "So at last we are reaching your conclusions, Mr. Story. It's taken a long time. The last figures were 4 billion dollars."

"And the gold held by you on behalf of foreign interests?"

"That's a figure we don't divulge."

"You know what I'm suggesting, of course?"

"One doesn't have to be an Einstein to follow your train of thought."

"I'm suggesting that your figures are false. That the gold stolen by Goering was never replaced. That if the true value of the ingots in your vaults was ever revealed the Bank of England would go bust."

Silence. But neither the Governor nor Shaw seemed as devastated as they should have been; it was as if they were more outraged by the impertinence of the suggestion than its implications. From the outset their attitudes had been puzzling. They shouldn't have been so ready to concede that the gold had been stolen in the first place. And the Governor, wasn't he even interested in the authorship of the revelations?

"I understand from Mr. Shaw," the Governor said, picking up the book with distaste, "that this account was written by someone who took part in the raid."

Shaw said, "He makes no secret of it."

The Governor opened the book and let the thin, war-starved pages slip through his fingers like a fan closing. He made no attempt to read them. Then he closed the book, snap. "Do we know the identity of the author?"

Story appraised Shaw. The chronicle wasn't signed and there was no obvious reason why Shaw should know who wrote it. But there was nothing obvious about Shaw. Shaw said, "If you know you might as well share the secret."

"His name is Kurt Schleicher."

"Is?"

Story thought, I should be asking the questions, and said, "Is, was, it doesn't matter. What matters is what's in that book."

"I should have thought," the Governor said, "that it mattered a great deal. If he's alive then it's surely the duty of any self-respecting journalist to interview him. To check the facts."

But not if the book had been stolen!

The Governor went on. "May I ask, Mr. Story, how you came by this document?"

"You may. I bought it from a German dealer named Meyer."

"Dealer?" Shaw pursed his lips, tasting the word, then swallowed it, reluctantly. Fence, said Shaw's expression. "Did this *dealer* appreciate the supposed value of the book?"

"You're assuming I got it for peanuts. In fact it cost a small fortune."

"Did you check to see if it had been stolen?"

Oh no you don't, Story thought. This is my interrogation. "Have you checked your gold lately?"

The Governor said, "I wonder if you could be persuaded not to publish your story."

Could he? Have enough money to join the ranks of those who patronized him? He heard himself saying to an eager reporter, "No comment." He waited; he didn't know the answer to the Governor's question.

"As you have gathered," the Governor was saying, "we do not contest the facts documented by

Herr Schleicher." He took a gold pen from the inside pocket of his dark jacket and began to tap the table with it. Was he going to write a check there and then? "But I'm afraid your conclusions are flawed."

The measured certainty of the words cast shadows across the sunlight of Story's future. But he had come prepared for a denial, and he used the ammunition he had brought with him.

"Are you saying that all the bullion was accounted for?"

"I am making no comment whatsoever, Mr. Story."

"Because if that is what you are saying then you shouldn't have any objection to letting me see for myself."

The Governor almost smiled. He left Shaw to answer such a preposterous inquiry.

"I'm afraid that's out of the question," Shaw said.

"Then I shall go right ahead and write the story. I don't have to state categorically that your balance sheets aren't what they seem. I shall leave the readers to draw their own conclusions, and when they do, gentlemen, the lines to get money out of the Bank of England will stretch from here to Land's End. I don't have to tell you what effect that will have on the West."

The two men were silent. But again Story got the impression that it was audacity rather than the plausibility of his words that had silenced them.

The Governor's pen tapped the table, a few blobs of rain hit the windows. Lightning flashed but its thunder was still trailing far behind.

"You think anyone would publish such a story?" the Governor asked after a while.

"You bet your sweet life they would. *The Governor of the Bank of England said yesterday, 'We do not contest the facts documented by Herr Schleicher.'*" Story enjoyed the expression on the Governor's face. He felt he had achieved the first penetration of his defenses. "And I shan't confine myself to a couple of papers. I shall spread myself all over the world. In this country the *Telegraph*, the *Mail*, the *Express*. I can just see the tabloids now: BANK OF E BUST? OLD LADY OF THREADBARE STREET?"

"But I *do* contest your conclusions, Mr. Story."

"Too bad. I shan't be reaching any. But as sure as God made little green apples the financial editors of the papers will. And then . . ." Story spread his hands.

"They'll be dancing in the streets of Moscow, eh, Mr. Story?" The Governor examined his pen. Where was his checkbook? "And will you feel very proud of yourself?"

"At exposing the greatest fraud ever perpetrated? Why not? Isn't there an inscription above one of your doorways, *Let no one bring us fraudulent devices?*" He was glad he had done his homework.

"It's in Greek," Shaw said enigmatically.

The Governor said, "Your zeal does you credit."

He rubbed one side of his patrician nose. "And yet you have implied that you could be persuaded not to write the article. I find it a little difficult to reconcile those two viewpoints."

Story shrugged. "It was your inference." To hell with him, he wouldn't accept a bribe.

The Governor and Shaw exchanged glances. Story sensed that whatever was about to happen had been prearranged.

The Governor pointed his pen at Story. "I have a request to make."

Excellent. An unexpected and uncharacteristic display of humility. Suddenly the omens were looking good again.

The Governor asked, "Can you spare, say, two hours of your time?"

Story frowned. He had nothing to lose, he supposed. "Okay. But can you rustle up all that missing gold in 120 minutes?"

The Governor didn't smile. He put away his pen, pushed back his chair, and said, "I'm going to leave you with Mr. Shaw; he has a lot to tell you." He walked toward the main door, footsteps silent on the magnificent Wilton.

When he had gone Shaw also stood up, saying, "I can't stand this place much longer, I feel as if I'm being suffocated by our heritage. I have an apartment in the Barbican."

No, Shaw didn't belong here: he had adapted. Which wasn't so surprising, assuming he was an ex-policeman of some sort. Or was he? I will have to question him about his background, Story decided as he followed him out of the Court Room.

By the time they reached the front hall the storm had burst. Lightning leaped across the sky, thunder cracked, and the rain bounced high on the road.

"*'Hard pounding this, gentlemen. We will see who can pound the longest.'* Wellington at Waterloo," Shaw explained, pointing his umbrella at the glistening equestrian statue of the Iron Duke. "I'm a great admirer of his."

"So I gather."

A taxi drew up and Shaw's umbrella blossomed. "Ours, I believe," although how he knew Story couldn't imagine.

Five minutes later the taxi deposited them outside the modern gray penitentiary that contains the much-sought-after Barbican flats. In contrast to his office, and the exterior of this bleak place, Shaw's apartment was sedately comfortable. The leather easy chairs sighed when you sat on them, and there were rich tapestries on the walls.

Shaw picked up the telephone and ordered smoked salmon sandwiches. "What will you have to drink?" Not, "*Will* you have a drink?" Such hypocrisies, he implied, were in the past.

Story said he would have a beer.

Shaw poured cans of beer frothing into two pewter tankards. "You must have a lot of aggravation with that name of yours. Good story, Mr. Story. That sort of thing."

"I do," Story said.

"Well, what I'm going to tell you is a good story. But, make no mistake, it's not fiction. And in its way it's *A Battle of Giants*." He smiled, and for the first time his eyes smiled with the lines on his face. "Wellington, of course."

"Of course," Story said.

"And like so many adventure stories it begins on a train. . . ."

I

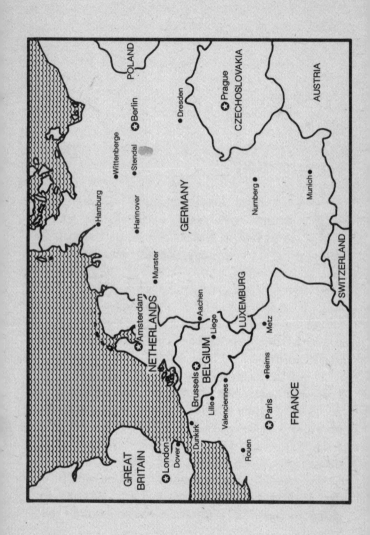

2

May 10, 1940

THE IRON HORSE galloped through the Dutch countryside at breakneck speed. Sparks and embers flew from its nostrils into the night; its carriages, purple, cream and gold, swayed with speed.

And on the footplate, the floor of the locomotive cab, the fireman grumbled. "What's the hurry?" he shouted as he shoveled coal into the ever-hungry mouth of the engine, a Bavarian S 3/6 Pacific, black and beautiful.

The driver, Hans Vogel, didn't reply. He looks like a man possessed, the fireman thought. But he always did when the locomotive got up a really good head of steam, eyes wild behind his goggles, red scarf tossing like a mane, peak of his cap pulled down over the back of his neck.

The fireman, bandy-legged from the weight of the coal-carrying years, tried again. "Aren't we going too fast?" The question was so insolent that he felt it would somehow reach Vogel even above the pounding of the driving wheels and the voice of the engine. Not that the fireman was too worried. Vogel was the best in the business, which was why he was on the footplate of the Rheingold. The truth of the matter was that the faster they went the harder the fireman had to work.

The fireman consulted the water-level indicator and the steam pressure gauge on his side of the firebox. My God, but they were traveling. He adjusted the injectors to keep the boiler filled with water. Rule Number 1: Never let the water level drop below the top plate of the firebox.

A whisper reached him above the exultant noise of the locomotive. It was Vogel's shouting. The fireman lip-read, "You do your job, I'll do mine." The fireman grinned. They understood each other, these two. He opened the door of the firebox and shoveled coal from the tender evenly on the grate.

Vogel tugged the whistle cord and the call of the engine across the flat countryside was heard in children's dreams.

One hand on the regulator, the other hovering near the brake lever, Vogel leaned out of the cab window and stared down the moonlit rails. He had heard the fireman the first time asking, "What's the hurry?" and he wished he knew the answer. Still, what was important was the fact that *he* had been chosen for an obviously vital mission. "You must be over the Dutch frontier into Germany by dawn," the director of *Deutsche Reichsbahn* had told him. The director! And there had been a veiled hint that the order had come from an even higher authority than German Railways.

Destination Duisburg, just across the border. There he would await further instructions. He hoped that these would take him down the Rhine to the Rheingold's usual destination, Basel in Switzerland, the familiar route that he had taken every working day of his adult life before the service had been suspended in September 1939. He knew every curve, every gradient of the track, and he loved the river with its broad brown waters and robber barons' castles in the vineyards high above it.

But there was another reason for wanting to reach Basel and her name was Margarethe. She was plump and compliant and, unlike his wife in Emmerich, who complained constantly about the oil and smut he brought into the house, she thought train drivers were glamorous, especially the driver of such a crack express as the Rheingold.

"You look like a buccaneer," she had told him last time, as she lay naked on the bed waiting for him to strip and bathe, when he had arrived in Basel on a lesser substitute express. Nothing about oil or smut.

The train charged Utrecht and left it behind. Next Amersfoort. Normally a Dutch crew would have taken the Rheingold on this stage of its journey, from the Hook to Arnhem, but plainly this mission could only be entrusted to Germans.

The Rheingold had been laid up in Holland since September last year with the old Bavarian— like other footplatemen Vogel preferred it to some of its progeny—and ordered back into service only a couple of days ago.

But why dawn? On the rim of the countryside Vogel noticed a faint glow of green light. He increased speed to 170 kilometers an hour and shrugged elaborately at the fireman. Normally the Hook to Basel took 10 hours, 36 minutes, but at this rate they'd be there in 10 hours flat if, as he hoped, that was their destination. And I will catch Margarethe in her dressing gown, unbraiding her flaxen hair and scenting her body. She had once said that there was something very sexual about a train thrusting its way through the countryside. "But it doesn't always have to be an express train," she had whispered into his ear.

He tugged the whistle cord again.

As the train, slowing down, took a restricted curve, Vogel was able to see coaches curling behind him, colors muted in the moonlight. Purple, what an inspiration that had been, regally extravagant, as befitted the queen of the German railroads.

The track straightened: the Rheingold gathered speed. Windmills sped past. The light on the horizon grew brighter.

And who were the passengers in the coaches? There were forty or so of them. The men were mostly on the dignified side, speaking with Berlin accents, although a couple were out-and-out thugs. Vogel's guess was that they were diplomats and their families, the thugs being bodyguards of some sort. He hadn't asked questions. You didn't these days.

The Rheingold swept through Arnhem. The frontier was twenty kilometers away. Signals glowed green. They had been green all the way from the Hook. The trip was important all right.

The skyline grew brighter.

What happens if I don't make the frontier by dawn? But you will make it, he admonished himself. You and the Rheingold are as one.

Beside him the fireman, sweat streaming down his blackened face, shoveled more coal into the firebox. Poor sod. But a good man, strong and reliable; they had spent many an evening together in crowded hostels for railwaymen, drinking beer and playing *skat*. Still, even if his responsibilities were just as exacting, he wasn't the stuff of what drivers are made.

The frontier was only eight kilometers away now, a mere nothing the way the Rheingold was eating up the track, but to the east the light was gaining strength.

As the first rays of the sun lit the land, the Rheingold passed over the frontier into Germany. At the same moment, along a front stretching 175 miles from the North Sea to the Maginot Line, Nazi troops launched *Sichelschnitt*, Sweep of the Scythe, the invasion first of three small and neutral countries, Belgium, Luxembourg, and Holland, and then of France.

VOGEL EASED THE Rheingold into Duisburg *bahnhof*, sixty kilometers inside the German border, thirty minutes later.

A squadron of Stukas flew low over the steel town, and a detachment of troops in field gray stood at ease on a platform on the far side of the station. So it was on. He had realized as much when, as he crossed the frontier, Dorniers and Heinkels had swarmed into Dutch airspace. After Poland, Norway, and Denmark, the Low Countries; then France, then Britain, and at last Germany would be great again. An end to the sacrifices endured by 70 million Germans—*wurst* that tasted like sawdust and houses that in winter were like refrigerators—to equip the war machine.

And trains will play a vital role in the victory. Communications, that was what war was all about, and we Germans are good at them. Wiping his hands on an oily rag, Vogel waited to see what his immediate role would be. He suspected that the Rheingold had been chosen for diplomatic missions. He had been right, his passengers *had* been diplomats, German Embassy staff evacuating The Hague before the hammer fell. He imagined himself transporting statesmen to neutral Switzerland for negotiations. Perhaps the armistice would be signed in one of his *wagons-lits*; the armistice that had humiliated Germany after the last war had been signed in a railway carriage.

"Here comes the big cheese," said the fireman,

who was leaning out of his side of the cabin smoking a cigarette.

Down the platform came the stationmaster. He always had an important walk but today's events had invested it with a military strut. As he strutted he sharpened his waxed mustache with his fingers.

"He thinks he's Goering," Vogel said. He had no love for stationmasters. In their fine uniforms, they tried to take all the glory earned by the real railwaymen. This dislike was reciprocated by the stationmasters, but they treated him warily—Vogel was Vogel.

He pushed up his goggles on his forehead and leaned out of the cabin. "*Guten morgen*, Herr Rimmer. A great day in the history of the Third Reich, eh? Have you any news?"

The stationmaster looked up at Vogel. "Only that we've marched into Holland, Belgium, and Luxembourg to safeguard their neutrality against an imminent invasion by the French and British."

Vogel looked at the fireman. Does he really believe such crap, the look said. "And do you have any news for me, Herr Rimmer?"

"Yes indeed." The stationmaster took a buff envelope from an inside pocket of his blue and gold uniform. "Perhaps you would be good enough to come down here and read it."

"Hand it up," Vogel said. He enjoyed the advantage of high ground.

The stationmaster hesitated, then handed him

the envelope. Obviously he had read its contents because he was quivering with anticipation. Well, whatever it is I won't give him the satisfaction of reacting.

Expressionlessly he read the cable. So the prick knew about Margarethe. Why else would he be bursting with suppressed joy at an order directing Vogel to take the Rheingold to Hamburg?

THREE DAYS LATER Hermann Goering, Commander in Chief of the Luftwaffe, took a short break from his mobile headquarters in the Eifel mountains in Germany and flew to Berlin to visit Carinhall, the extravaganza that was his home.

The brief visit was quite justified in his view. *Sichelschnitt* was proceeding better than anyone had dared to expect. Thanks to his Stukas the enemy was already punch-drunk, and stunning victories had been won by paratroops and glider-born units—the *impenetrable* Fort Eben Emael, for instance, had been captured by eighty-five men. If the Dutch didn't throw in their hand soon, then Rotterdam would be razed like Warsaw before it.

Even now the British and French didn't seem to comprehend that all this was a diversion. As anticipated, they had come scuttling to the aid of the Low Countries, leaving the way clear for the panzers to storm west over the Meuse and cut them off. As for the impregnable Maginot Line, it was a folly to be outflanked.

As he shaved in his marble bathroom, Goering smiled into the mirror, not that there was much to smile at there. His face looked pale and flabby, and the red silk dressing gown did nothing to disguise his girth—at the last weigh-in he was 252 pounds. What people didn't realize was that the pallor was caused by insomnia, the obesity by a glandular disorder, not overindulgence. Well, not entirely.

He was young enough, forty-seven, to become a hero again—Iron Cross First Class and the *Pour le Mérite* in the last war—but he had been betrayed by his body. Even his indulgence in morphine, not an addiction any more, had physical roots: he had been shot full of the stuff when he had been wounded in the abortive *putsch* in 1923.

But if he couldn't lead his armadas through the skies, he could embark on other adventures that had their compensations. It was just such an adventure that had brought him back to Carinhall.

Goering loved trains. He had a 26-meter-long model railway in the attic, so what better adventure than one involving trains? He loved gold, so what better adventure than one involving gold? And what better prize than a fortune in bullion that would probably make him the richest man in the world?

Goering took off his dressing gown and turned away from the unpleasantness in the mirror. Then he lowered himself ponderously into the bath and, as he soaped himself, considered the next moves to be made.

If Hitler ever finds out, he thought as he massaged the hummock of his belly, he'll put me in front of a firing squad.

He floated a loofah in the water. That was the *Alaska*. An American freighter loaded with ballast, if you believed the explanation assiduously circulated around Greenock docks but not if you had had an intelligence source at a much higher level. He dropped a sponge into the water. The *Countess of Cork*, ostensibly a cargo ship flying the colors of neutral Ireland, but armed to the teeth and crewed by a gang of cutthroats led by Max von Ritter, the biggest cutthroat of them all. Von Ritter was seconded from the SS Liebstandarte, despite Sepp Dietrich's protests, to Goering's own intelligence organization, the *Forschungsamt*. Goering sighed. If only he could be there on the bridge instead of von Ritter.

He searched the ledge beside the bath for some escort vessels. He tried an enamel soap dish. It sank immediately. Excellent, because Junker 88s were at this moment flying across the eastern reaches of the Atlantic, skirting the north of Scotland and its islands, to attack the disguised British warships shepherding the *Alaska* at a discreet distance to give the impression that she was none of their concern. When they were crippled or sunk, the *Countess of Cork*, a streamlined Polish cruise vessel beneath her disguise, would home in on the prey.

According to Goering's source in London, the

Bank of England bullion on board the *Alaska* being shipped to North America was valued at 500 million pounds. Could any man claim personal wealth, not merely assets on paper, on such a scale? Goering wondered as he heaved himself out of the bath. He doubted it.

He toweled himself and powdered his face to forestall the shaving rash to which he was prone. A few splashes of cologne on his torso and he was ready to dress. He padded naked into the changing room and surveyed his wardrobe, more extensive even than his wife's. He had granted himself an eight-hour absence from the war. As he could still afford two more hours at Carinhall, he dressed in cavalry twill trousers, white silk shirt, and waistcoat made of soft brown leather.

Then he went to the attic to take command once again of Operation Argo, code named after the ship in which Jason had sailed to seek the Golden Fleece. Sitting in an armchair beside the control panel for the model railway, he picked up a telephone and on a direct line called Lieutenant Fritz Becker at the headquarters of the *Forschungsamt* in Berlin.

A good man, Becker. They had flown together when Goering had taken over Manfred von Richtofen's squadron in 1917. But a bullet from a Spad had taken away some bone from his spine—and his nerve. Goering had appointed him fellow conspirator because he was loyal and a good administrator, and because he remembered him in the brave days in blue skies over the fields of Flanders.

Becker said, "Good morning, Herr Feldmarschall. Are you well?"

"How's it going, Fritz?" Really, this was no time for pleasantries.

"According to plan, Herr Feldmarschall."

Goering pictured him standing, frozen-featured and stiff-backed beside the telephone, one hand exploring the ache in his spine.

"Feel free to be more explicit, Fritz."

"Two *gruppen* of Junker 88 dive-bombers took off from an airfield at Sola, in Norway, and from an improvised strip near Trondheim as planned. They were making a rendezvous north of the Orkneys prior to the attack on the *Alaska,* which is now west of the Hebrides. The *Countess of Cork* is ten miles north of her. The attack was timed for 1200 hours, twenty minutes ago, that is."

"Conditions?"

"A little sea mist but nothing to worry about. As you know, the Rheingold has already arrived in Hamburg." His voice faded. When it returned full strength he said, "Fresh information coming in. I'll call you back in thirty minutes."

"Very well, Fritz, as quickly as you can." Goering cradled the receiver.

The Rheingold, he felt, was the touch of class that distinguished an entrepreneur from a mere operator. It was also practical. The express had to be rescued from the German blitzkrieg; so did the

German diplomats in The Hague. It was logical that the Rheingold should be used to bring the stuffed-shirts to Germany.

Goering pressed a button on the control panel. A light glowed green and a diminutive Rheingold set off around the attic, the pride of his miniature rolling stock.

It was also logical for the Rheingold to go to Hamburg, the home of the German ambassador to Holland. It would be used to transport the components of a captured secret weapon—not unlike the missile von Braun had been working on, or so Goering had put it about—which the British had been shipping to the United States to be developed there. The components would be taken to Berlin for analysis and, as his passion for trains was common knowledge, no one would question the fact that Goering had appropriated the Rheingold in the interests of preservation. When you had forged such a heroic bond with the Führer in the early days, when you were first in line of succession, then no one questioned your actions. Except the Führer himself, and he was too engrossed in *Sichelschnitt*.

Just in case anything went wrong on the way from Hamburg to Berlin, in case other marauders came hunting the gold, he had given orders for an armored car to be coupled to the rear of the train. Not that anything could go wrong.

At that moment the Rheingold at his feet came off the rails.

It took a walk in the grounds to banish the disquiet caused by the derailment. Here in the environs of the baronial residence he had bought in 1933 and named after his first wife, Carin, he always found peace. The inner tranquility of a man of means and property, all 100 thousand acres of it.

He strode briskly across the heathland and the woods of pine, oak, and beech, hoping as always that the exercise would shake a few ounces from his bulk. By the time he returned to the portals of his palace and had stopped to contemplate his coat of arms, a mailed fist grasping a bludgeon, his confidence was fully restored.

He went down to the cellars where already his *objets d'art* were accumulating. Soon it would be a world-class museum of the fine arts; but then it would have to be moved to divert attention from the vaults beneath the cellar, where the Bank of England's bullion would be stored.

Goering went down another flight of stairs. Water dripped icily from the ceiling. He consulted the combination in his wallet, 98563214, and rotated the handle on the lock of the steel-plated doors. They swung ponderously open. Inside nothing, but Goering saw neatly stacked piles of ingots, soft, heavy, indestructible, giving off the serene glow imparted when the earth had been a cauldron.

His mouth watered.

He closed the doors and mounted the steps. Above him the phone rang. Becker?

His wife's theatrical voice was as seductive as

ever, but, just this once, he was disappointed to hear it. "I called your headquarters but they said you had taken a break. I was worried. You know it is the thirteenth today?"

Goering smiled indulgently into the receiver. Emmy, who was on holiday in Bavaria, was very superstitious. If she knew about the gold she would have even more cause for concern. He doubted whether he would ever tell her; he was extremely fond of her, not perhaps with the same passion he had felt for Carin, who had died in 1931, but with a tolerant devotion that brought him much happiness. How could knowledge of the bullion benefit her? She already had everything.

"There's absolutely nothing to worry about," he told her. "We're winning the war, romping through, that's all that matters."

"They said you were taking a *well-earned* break. You haven't been overdoing it have you, Hermann?"

You could hardly be *underdoing* it when you were in charge of the greatest aerial assault force ever mustered. He said, "No, everything's fine. I just thought I'd come home for a few hours. You know how this place relaxes me."

"Would you like me to come home?"

"No," Goering replied hastily. "No, don't spoil your vacation. Just go on listening to the radio. It's going to be all good news." Faintly he heard the other phone ringing upstairs. "I've got to go now, my car's just arrived."

"Goodbye, Hermann, take good care of your-self."

"And you," he said, hanging up the receiver and running up the broad staircase. When he arrived in the attic he was out of breath. Collapsing into the armchair, he picked up the telephone.

Becker said, "I've read all the latest reports."

"And?"

"The attack went off as planned."

"Good." But the exultation that should have been blossoming inside him was restrained. There was something about Becker's tone. "Get on with it, man."

"We lost a few planes."

Only to be expected. It had always been an over-ambitious project to make a dive-bomber out of the Junker 88 but, unlike its venomous little sister, the Junker 87 or Stuka, it had the range.

"And was the *Alaska* successfully boarded?"

"It was."

So why the hell was Becker less than enthusiastic. "And?"

"You remember I mentioned sea mist, Herr Feldmarschall? Well a British destroyer that the Luftwaffe crews thought was out of action managed to get within range of the *Countess of Cork*. She *was* sinking but she didn't go before firing a torpedo." A pause; Goering could hear Becker's breathing. Then, "The *Countess of Cork* was hit."

"With the gold on board?"

"Yes, Herr Feldmarschall. We don't know how badly yet."

Goering hung up. The thirteenth, he should have more respect for Emmy's superstitions.

He sat down and replaced the Rheingold on the rails. He pressed the button on the control panel. The train disappeared into a tunnel.

3

March 16

TWO MONTHS EARLIER, one of the two *giants* to whom the head of security at the Bank of England would refer forty years later in an interview with a German thief arrived in the small town of Redditch in England, thirteen miles south of the industrial sprawl of Birmingham, to commit an act of sabotage.

His name was Miller, but he wasn't physically a giant. He was slim in fact, without the tapered mold of the natural athlete. Nevertheless, he exuded strength as if he had taken his muscles to the gym, and his face had the pale tautness of the keep-fit fanatic who has overtrained.

He had also spent a lot of time training his mind, converting it from its original specifications. Born the son of an out-of-work printer in the East End of London, he had, with the help of an elocutionist, extracted the Cockney flints from his voice. He spoke some French and a lot of German. He wore neat suits and his sleek black hair was stylishly barbered.

He could have been mistaken for a young stock-broker—he was 23—or, perhaps, a slick accountant. Such an assumption would have been a mistake. Charles Miller was a safe-cracker specializing in the theft of gold. But he was a patriotic one: since the outbreak of war he had been an agent working for the Fifth Branch of the Luftwaffe, its espionage division, and for the *Forschungsamt,* Goering's own private army of spies. He was also working for British Intelligence, with whom his true loyalty lay.

He had volunteered for normal military service but had failed his medical because of his lungs, a family weakness on his father's side. So, through his Member of Parliament, he had offered his services as an explosives expert to the government and within 24 hours of the offer he had been approached by a man who looked more like a pub landlord than a master spy and enrolled into MI5.

He was dispatched to burgle the home of a known Nazi agent. He executed the crime with uncharacteristic clumsiness. He was caught by the agent and given two choices: spy for Germany or be turned over to the police. He chose the former and became a double agent in Britain's embryonic Double Cross System.

His mission in Redditch, he had been told, was to further enhance his already glowing reputation with Goering and to consolidate the position of all the turned German spies in Britain.

"No damned good always sending useless snippets of info," the publican had said. "We've got to give the swine a few pearls. Then we can follow up with bloody great lists of phony military targets so that when the buggers start bombing us in earnest they'll be destroying acres of fuck-all. By the time that happens we should have a battalion of turned agents. I have my own patented method of unmasking a suspect," the publican said modestly. "I shout Heil Hitler and they near as dammit dislocate their shoulders."

When Miller had asked the publican what particular pearl he was going to cast to the swine, he had been told that it was a factory at Redditch that, until 1938, had made needles. It had then been converted to produce components for the hub of the Spitfire's Rotol propeller, and there was nothing more calculated to bring joy to Goering's heart than sabotaging Britain's triumphant answer to the Messerschmitt 109.

Two days before Miller, journeyed to Redditch by train, the plant had been secretly moved, according to the publican, to Castle Bromwich, where the Spitfires were being produced. "So all you have to do, old man, is destroy a sodding great shell."

In fact, the factory was very small. Sewing rather than knitting needles, Miller thought as he surveyed the building through fieldglasses from a copse of beech trees. It was also shoddy looking, red bricks sloppily cemented and a corrugated iron roof that, from inside, would give raindrops the impact of machine-gun bullets.

It was raining now as the day faded into blacked-out night. Miller turned up the collar of his greasy raincoat. He was dressed like a factory-hand—toolmaker, according to his identity card—a cover that had the additional advantage of dissuading formidable ladies from asking why he wasn't in uniform. Apparently artisan noncombatants were more acceptable than those from the professions.

The site of the factory, surrounded by plowed fields, was protected by a high wire-mesh fence capped with barbed wire. It was guarded—to preserve the illusion of its importance, according to the gamekeeper—by three morose soldiers wearing rubber capes and carrying ancient Lee Enfield rifles, 1902 issue by the look of them. If Hitler could vault over France and the Low Countries, Miller reflected, Britain was there for the taking.

He replaced the field glasses in the bottom of his tool case and, leaning against the streaming trunk of a beech tree, waited for the darkness to settle. In case there were any unwanted observers in the vicinity, the act of sabotage had to be carried out professionally and credibly and that meant after dusk.

Not that Miller intended to be particularly sophisticated. The interior of the factory had been doused with gasoline and a pile of saturated wood shavings had been piled under the third ground-floor window from the entrance, the one with adhesive antiblast netting missing from one of the top panes. All Miller had to do was cut his way through the fence—the soldiers had been warned to expect him—and toss a Molotov cocktail through the window, which had been left half open. The rafters and supports were made of wood and there was sufficient debris left behind from the move to Castle Bromwich to make sure the building went up like a torch.

In the tool case were two cocktails, copies of the crude weapons used so effectively by the Finns in the war with Russia that had ended four days earlier. The Finns, fighting bravely but hopelessly against overwhelming odds, had knocked out hundreds of Soviet tanks with bottles filled with a mixture of tar, kerosene, and gasoline, which was fired on impact by an ampule of sulfuric acid.

When the day had quite gone, Miller set out across a plowed field. The darkness seemed to have opened up the clouds, and the rain coming from the west drove at him, finding its way inside his raincoat and overalls. The turned sods of earth under his feet were as slippery as seaside rocks, and he felt more like a Finnish foot soldier than a supposedly sophisticated cracksman. He hoped the publican appreciated what he was doing; more important, he hoped Goering appreciated it.

This mission would be a feather in the cap of the Feldmarschall's Fifth Branch. But Miller was becoming increasingly aware that Goering valued him more for his work for the *Forschungsamt*.

Although it was small and select, the *Forschung-samt* was reckoned to be the most effective espionage network in Germany, far more canny than the intelligence division of the SS, the RHSA—of which the Gestapo was a section—or the Abwehr, military intelligence. The word *Forschungsamt* meant Research Office but it was a misnomer: it monitored the world's diplomatic channels, cracked codes, and kept surveillance on every embassy in Germany, and on the homes and offices of every Nazi boss, including, quite possibly, Hitler's.

The *Forschungsamt* had always been Goering's private army, but lately it had become more private than ever before. He was using it to earmark Europe's treasure troves for his own collection, which was another reason why Miller was valuable to him: he was a thief and a good one. And it was through the *Forschungsamt* that Miller had learned that if and when Germany invaded Britain, Goering intended to get his hands on as much of the Bank of England's gold as he could.

He was close to the fence now. The rain was easing off and rents of star-filled sky showed through the scudding clouds. He could do without moonlight, although the soldiers wouldn't bother him. He took a pair of powerful wire cutters from the tool box and screwed in handle extensions to give him leverage. The blades sliced through the strong wire with satisfying noises, clip-clip.

The opening was almost big enough to squeeze

through. A few more snips, a good accurate lob with a cocktail, a sheet of flame leaping ravenously from one end of the factory to the other as he ran for the copse. Despite everything, he was enjoying himself.

He bent the wire back so that it resembled a small door. Big enough now. He took the bottle that had once contained a soft drink called Tizer and stepped through the opening into a blaze of white light that blinded him. Instinctively he put up one arm to shield his eyes; the arm holding the cocktail hung limply at his side.

"Don't move."

The voice came from inside the window, which had suddenly swung wide open. From either side of the factory figures came running. He blinked tightly to try and focus his eyes. Soldiers. Five, six of them, without capes, but holding rifles.

He stepped back toward the gap in the fence but was stopped by the voice from the window. "Another step and you're dead."

He heard rifle bolts clicking. The soldiers closed in, one behind him. Through the window climbed the owner of the voice, wearing a belted raincoat and carrying a hat in his hand. He was followed by another man similarly attired, also carrying his hat. Unmistakably Special Branch. Miller decided to wait until he was alone with them to explain the mistake that had been made.

The first detective out of the window put his hat on and said, "Now put that bottle down on the ground, the right way up, very gently." When he followed the instructions, the detective picked it up gingerly by the neck, a handkerchief in his hand.

"Okay, turn around, hands against the fence." To the other Special Branch man he said, "Search him, Wilson."

While he was being expertly frisked, Miller remembered the times when he had anticipated capture, had eluded the frisking hands by minutes, seconds. If he had been caught, so he had assured himself, he wouldn't have resented it. Like it or not, it would have been justice. But this, serving king and country. It was laughable, but he didn't laugh.

Wilson said, "He's clean."

And always had been. He'd never carried a gun, although recently the publican had taught him how to use one.

The publican, that was it. He would tell these bunglers to telephone him on the number that was only to be used in emergencies.

The other Special Branch detective snapped, "Right, turn around." When he did, Miller found himself facing a square, bleak-faced man with tufted eyebrows who said, "My name is Macdonald," and read out the charge.

Powdered rain hung above him in the white glare of the floodlights and his breath smoked on the cold air as he spoke, but Miller didn't take in the words because, for the first time since the floodlights had blinded him, the terrible possibility had occurred to him that maybe this wasn't some bureaucratic mixup, that no mistake had been made.

"... that your words may be taken down and used as evidence against you."

Miller didn't reply. The rifles the soldiers were holding weren't 1902 models: they were lethally new.

Macdonald handcuffed him to Wilson, and Miller thought, This is some sort of elaborate deception. In the back of the Wolsey taking them in the direction of London he said, "You know, of course, that I'm working for MI5."

But there was no *of course* about it. Macdonald, who was driving, merely said over his shoulder, "MI5, is it?" and put his foot down on the accelerator.

"If you stop at a phone box you can check it out."

"You'll have every chance to prepare your defense when you get back to London," Wilson told him.

Defense. It was then that another possibility, an extension of the first, occurred to him, chilling his mind: he had been framed and was going to die.

When Wilson finally called the telephone number from a room at Scotland Yard, it turned out to be a disconnected line. "Sorry, sir," said Macdonald, but his tone said he wasn't sorry at all, not where traitors were concerned. It was a tone that Miller was to recognize many times during the next two months.

He was committed for trial at the Old Bailey, and

after proceedings held *in camera* and briskly conducted because really he had no defense at all, he was convicted and sentenced to death by a black-capped judge. He took his case to the Court of Criminal Appeal, where the judges appeared mildly surprised at his impudence. As for the plea that he was a double agent working for Britain, well, they had heard that one before.

As he sat at a table in the green-walled condemned cell in Wandsworth Prison on May 15, with 20 hours and 29 minutes of his life left, he tried once again to work out why he had been double-crossed, but as before his reasoning was dissipated by lurches of fear and gusts of anger.

The fear was terrible, worse than he had ever imagined it could be on the rare occasions when he had considered mortality. A mixture of incredulity that the hanging could take place, in this building, Cell Block F, and awareness that for him the world would cease to exist.

The anger was an explosion of self-pity and frustration. He had always accepted that one day there might be retribution, but, naively, he had never anticipated injustice.

He screamed but no sound issued from his lips. And when a formation of aircraft flew overhead he didn't go to the barred window because he didn't want to see the sky, which he knew would be blue and high and free.

Vaguely he heard the turn of a key, the sliding of a bolt. The door opened and a guard with an institutionalized face and hands with outsize knuckles came in carrying a mug of tea.

"You're bleeding lucky to get that," he said. "More than the poor bastards in Holland will get from now on. They surrendered today. They didn't have any option. The Krauts gutted Rotterdam."

So Holland had fallen. Soon it would be the turn of Belgium and France, and then Britain would stand alone. But I shall never know whether we survive.

As the terrible fear visited him again, he took the mug from the guard and took a gulp of the luke-warm tea that tasted of metal polish. The guard hated traitors more than he hated child molesters, and he had deliberately let the tea get cold before bringing it in.

The guard said, "If Europe hadn't been riddled with traitors then Holland wouldn't have been done for. But make no mistake, matey, the BEF will have the Krauts on the run soon enough and then all your double dealings will have been for sweet Fanny Adams."

The fear was replaced again by impotent anger. Double dealing was certainly what he had been perpetrating. For Britain. And with premeditated ruthlessness he had been double-crossed.

Why?

"The hangman arrives this afternoon," the guard said. "You know, he likes to have a look at a body before getting to work. Height, weight, et cetera to get the length of the rope right. Then he hangs a bag of sand on the end of the rope to stretch it so that it doesn't jump around. He sleeps here overnight, you know. Comes to the cell just before eight in the morning with the sheriff, the governor, and the quack. They pinion your arms, then it's off to the scaffold as quick as a frog up a pump. Bag around your head, noose around your neck, and through the trapdoor you go. Record is seven seconds."

The guard waited for Miller to recoil in horror but he was disappointed. "Quicker than some of the poor sods in Holland," he said. Then, "You've got a visitor in five minutes."

Immediately Miller knew who it was. It had always been like that with Vic. Born within an hour of each other, he and his twin brother had always been able to anticipate each other. And in a way Vic was the reason he was sitting at a table in the condemned cell with 20 hours, 29 minutes—no, 27 minutes—of his life left.

Admittedly he had been introduced to injustice as a child on a day outing to the seaside, and subconsciously that had probably set a new aim to his life, but it was Vic's wheezing lungs that had finally called him to crime.

"Hallo twin," Vic said from the other side of the grille and gave the mock military salute, American style, with which they always greeted each other. And then he was silent because what do you say to someone who has got 20 hours, 22 minutes to live?

Miller said, "I'm glad you came," conscious of

the guard behind him making sure that between them they didn't find a way of relieving the hangman of his burden. "Mum and dad, they're not coming?"

"You said you thought it would be better that way." A pause. He looked much the same as always, did Vic. A little bewildered, thick suit buttoned with the wrong button, hair unevenly cut and slicked down with water. Like their parents, Vic had never quite learned how to spend the money *he* earned from stealing. In fact, telepathy apart, they had only one factor in common and that was bad lungs. Vic's were much worse than his. "So they stayed at home," Vic said as the pause yawned between them.

"It's better that way." Miller could imagine them now, sitting at the kitchen table covered in the same oilcloth that, as kids, he and Vic had disfigured with their forks making railway lines. They would be staring at their lunch, a ration of boiled beef and new potatoes from the allotment perhaps, wondering how they had come to produce a traitor. Bewildered. Hopeless. Ashamed. "Much better."

"Anyway," Vic said carefully, "I want to thank you. You know, for everything."

For the treatment in Switzerland. For the cash in his pocket when he was out of work. For a lot he didn't know anything about. For everything.

Miller said, "You know I didn't do it."

"I know."

"And mum and dad?"

"They don't understand."

"How's the job?"

Vic was in munitions, something to do with bombs. He never talked about it—*Careless Talk Costs Lives.*

"It's okay." He hesitated. "There's a girl there."

"Pretty?"

"Some broad," Vic said trying to smile the way they did when they borrowed dialogue from American movies.

"That's swell, just swell," Miller said in his George Raft voice.

Vic leaned forward and said, "Why, Charlie?"

Miller ran his finger under the collar of his coarse prison jacket. Fear lurched inside him again. "I don't know," he said. He stood up. "Time to go, Vic."

"But . . ."

"Tell mum and dad I love them." *And you, I love you.* "Tell them I'm sorry." He managed a wink. "I'll beat these dirty rats yet," in his James Cagney voice.

Then he turned away so that Vic couldn't see the tears in his eyes.

Why?

AT THE SAME time that Miller was talking to his twin, five men were conferring urgently in the Court Room of the Bank of England.

It was around the forty-foot table, or rather at one end of it, that the five men were discussing a topic of more moment than anything that had been debated since the Bank had been founded 246 years earlier.

At the head of the table sat the Governor, an ingenious, energetic man with a small wagging beard.

On either side of him sat the head of the British Secret Service, a calculating Scot named Logan; Commander Nicholas Weaver, a sleek destroyer from Naval Intelligence; an American named Grover, serious and bespectacled but built like a fullback, who worked for the information department of the United States Embassy in London but who was more precisely employed by President Roosevelt to keep him in touch with the realities obscured by Ambassador Joe Kennedy's defeatest views about Britain; and the Bank's own security adviser, Jack Munnion, a former chief of the City's fraud squad who, because he smoked a pipe, was invariably labeled *capable*.

Weaver was addressing an appalled but receptive audience. "Despite the sea mist that was getting thicker by the minute and despite the fact that she was sinking, the *Woodstock* managed to score a direct hit with a torpedo on the pirate." Managing, Munnion thought, to make the whole disastrous fiasco sound like a victory.

"And the other escort vessels?" asked the Governor.

"We must assume the worst," Weaver said. He sleeked smooth brown hair from his temple with the palm of one hand. "We have lost radio contact," he explained for the benefit of the morons around him.

"So the greater part of Britain's gold reserves, not to mention gold held on behalf of some eminent clients, is now in the hold of an enemy vessel that may or may not be sinking in the North Atlantic. Is that the position, Commander Weaver?"

Weaver, deputizing for the Director of Naval Intelligence, who was in New York to supervise that end of the operation, tapped a cigarette on a slim platinum case with unwarranted vigor. "That's just about it, sir."

"So what's to be done, gentlemen?" The Governor pulled his wagging beard as though trying to still it. He turned to Logan.

Logan also lit up, a Churchman's Number 1 from a packet that had been in the pocket of his tweed jacket. He had just returned from Number 10 Downing Street—and the wrath of Churchill, who on May 10 had replaced Chamberlain as Prime Minister. Logan was in a mood of controlled intensity. He was not accustomed to being spoken to the way Churchill had spoken to him.

He said, "We have, of course, instigated a search and other Naval ships have been sent to the area." He inclined his head toward Weaver, whose responsibility that was. Naval Intelligence was a department of the Secret Service, but Weaver gave no indication that he was aware of his subordinate status. "All ports to which the *Countess of Cork*, or whatever her real name is, might try to limp to are being kept under observation by aircraft from Coastal Command. But, of course, they do have other commitments at the moment."

The Governor's voice snapped back. "I am quite aware that Europe is in flames. I am also aware that if France and Belgium fall"—*when* they fall, his tone implied—"Britain will stand alone. But she can't remain upright for long without her foundations."

Grover spoke. His voice was slow and deep and he seemed to be testing his words and approving them. "So what happens," he asked, looking first at Logan then at Weaver, "if your planes or ships get a sighting? No way can they sink her because if they do the bullion will fall straight into Davy Jones's locker. If it's not there already," he said, taking off his spectacles and frowning at them.

No one spoke until Munnion, pointing his smoking pipe at the gold-fingered wind vane on the wall, which had once helped directors estimate when a ship would reach the Port of London, remarked, "The wind here is blowing from the south. Theoretically, if the *Countess* is west of the Hebrides, that could help her on her way to Iceland, or the north coast of Norway."

Weaver smiled indulgently. "*If* the winds are the same here as they are there." He and Munnion had taken an instant dislike to each other.

"I assumed you would have had that information," Munnion said. He stood up and walked over the new Wilton carpet, which reputedly weighed half a ton, to the Venetian windows, ashamed of himself. Weaver brought out the worst in him. Through the windows, taped with antiblast adhesive, he looked down into the sandbagged garden. One big bomb dropped down there by the Luftwaffe and goodbye to our sterling heritage. That is, if it still had any meaning.

The Governor's beard wagged impatiently. "There must be something more that can be done. I entrusted the gold with you," contemplating them one by one, "and you've lost it. Now you've got to get it back."

Munnion fought the temptation to say, "Weaver lost it," and turned to Logan to come up with something. He usually did, that tweedy landowner with the frosted soul.

"If the *Countess of Cork* has gone down, then the gold is in God's hands," Logan said. He was a very religious man, Logan. "If it hasn't, then we must establish its destination."

They waited because Logan wasn't normally given to flashes of the blindingly obvious.

Logan lit another Churchman's with a Swan Vesta match and said, "When we have established that, we can act. One act of piracy deserves another." He smiled faintly through the lacework of cigarette smoke. "I don't think I need elaborate at the moment."

Grover replaced his spectacles, blinked, and said, "With respect, sir, what should be occupying us at this minute is *how* to establish the *Countess*'s destination. And I don't see how the hell you're going to do that with the North Atlantic blanketed in fog. Or sea mist as you choose to call it."

"It is pretty bad," Weaver admitted.

Logan said, "There is a way." He paused, pained by the need to embroider, Munnion, who knew him well, realized. "It all depends," he continued, "on one man. A man you know about, Jack," nodding at Munnion. "His name," he said, turning to the Governor, "is Miller."

OH YES, MUNNION knew all about Miller. Logan had discussed Miller with him over dinner in the annex of his club, the Carlton, sharing his guilt, Munnion had thought at the time, or what in Logan's case passed for guilt, but showing no inclination to reverse a decision that was, in Munnion's opinion, a clear-cut case of murder, justified or otherwise.

Miller, apparently, was an early victim of the Double-Cross System—in Miller's case the Double Double-Cross—that relied on the use of double agents to supply the Germans with misinformation.

Miller, Logan had revealed over the port, had been the leader of a ring of spies supplying information to the Fifth Branch of the Luftwaffe and Goering's *Forschungsamt*.

Logan gave Munnion a rundown on the *Forschungsamt*. It had begun in 1933, the brainchild of an anti-Semite named Gottfried Schapper, and operated from an attic in one of Goering's offices.

94

Like Topsy, it grew and grew and was now situated at Schillerstrasse 116-124 in Berlin.

Munnion was glad he didn't have a mind like Logan's: it must get very boring mentally photographing everything in sight. He could probably recite the menu.

A relative of one of Goering's friends had been put in nominal charge, but Schapper was still the man that mattered. Up to a point. These days, although the *Forschungsamt* was supposed to be a national network, all paths led to Goering, who used it to rob the treasure houses of Europe of their jewelry, paintings, and tapestries, and then to transport the booty to Carinhall, his palace.

"Doesn't anyone ever protest? Goebbels, Himmler, Ribbentrop?"

"Goering is Goering," Logan said. "He was at Hitler's side during the bad times so Hitler lets him have his fling during the good times. He's also got access to all the other Nazi leaders' secrets, so they let him get on with it. God knows, perhaps he's found out that some of them have Jewish blood."

But surely, Munnion queried, spies and code breakers weren't the sort of operators to commit grand larceny on Goering's behalf.

"When he first fancied himself as a collector," Logan said, "Goering merely used them to ferret out the loot and then subcontract for the theft. But now he's recruited some pirates into the organization. And when he's setting up a good old-fashioned robbery, he doesn't work through Schapper. He consults a man named Becker, a former pilot who flew with him in the '14 to '18 war. He's totally loyal to the Feldmarschall.''

"And was Miller one of his pirates?"

"Not exactly, but he was a thief, a housebreaker to be precise. It was he who first discovered that Goering intended to help himself to as much of the Bank of England's gold as possible if the Germans reached London. So indirectly he was the one who first warned Chamberlain that they should ship it to North America in double-quick time.''

"But if he was so valuable, why did you decide to murder him?''

Logan frowned. "Sacrifice," he murmured, "not murder." Sipping his port, he offered an explanation that boiled down to: alive, Miller was valuable, dead he was priceless.

Goering, Logan said in his Sunday school voice, had become suspicious about the ease with which his agents operated in Britain and irritated by their lack of concrete success.

"So why not kill two birds with one stone?" Munnion asked, searching Logan's face for some sign of remorse and finding none.

"Exactly." Logan told Munnion about the incident at Redditch when Miller had been framed. Goering must have been exultant at the prospect of crippling the Spitfire and distraught when the operation was blown. "But Miller's capture and execution," Logan's voice passed smoothly through the hangman's noose, "will enormously improve our chances of survival."

Munnion poured himself some more port.

"Because, you see, it will convince Goering that his agents are genuine, that they haven't been turned. Surely, he will reason, the British wouldn't hang one of their own men. So the double agents can go on providing the Luftwaffe with false information. As you will appreciate, it's absolutely vital that, when they start to bomb Britain in earnest, they hit the wrong targets."

"And you're going to allow Miller to be hanged?"

"I have no choice. If I saved him from the gallows it would put the whole misinformation operation in jeopardy. After all's said and done, Miller is only a thief."

Munnion gazed at Logan in awe. They had never been close, only acquaintances who used each other as sounding boards, and now he knew why friendship had never developed. Logan, in his British way, was as icily inhuman as Heinrich Himmler.

Logan, who sometimes read the lesson at his village church on Sundays, took to the pulpit. "Before this war is over, thousands of decent, honest citizens are going to be killed in the line of duty. In that context, surely the life of one crook is expendable?"

Sickened, Munnion supposed he was right.

Then he considered Miller alone in his cell awaiting death.

Was he so right?

"What disturbs me," Munnion said, "is that by

doing this we're sinking to the same loathsome depths as the people we're fighting."

Logan said, "Eye for eye, tooth for tooth, hand for hand, foot for foot," and closed the good book. "If we're going to win the war, we've got to," he said tersely.

Right, of course. Munnion thought of his own family. They had to be saved.

Then he again thought about Miller in his cell. What had haunted him since that dinner at the Carlton until the conference at the Bank of England was that the poor bastard didn't even know why he was being killed.

AND SO, LOGAN was explaining in the Court Room, that although it had once been imperative to hang Miller, it was now imperative to release him to discover the destination of the gold on board the *Countess of Cork*. And he listed the reasons: Miller had worked for the *Forschungsamt* and could therefore discover their intentions; he had become a martyr for them and would thus be embraced by them; he had in the past specialized in the theft of gold and was therefore an expert in the commodity involved; his outlets as a burglar had been German and, consequently, he had a passable mastery of the German tongue.

There really was no one else better qualified to track down the Old Lady of Threadneedle Street's bullion. No one in the Court Room demurred.

But obviously, Logan pointed out, Miller could

not be released from Wandsworth "just like that" because his credibility with the *Forschungsamt* would then be destroyed. No, he would have to escape.

Tonight.

"With respect, sir," said Weaver, no doubt impressed by Logan's coldbloodedness, "I should have thought you were the last person Miller would have wanted to help after he's been allowed to escape. After all, you were going to have him topped tomorrow morning."

"He'll cooperate," Logan said. "There are certain factors of which you aren't aware. Nor will it be necessary to elaborate at this juncture." Logan looked around the table, challenging them.

Grover said, "Perhaps you could tell us, sir, just how Miller is going to escape."

"I can go that," Logan conceded. He opened his briefcase and took out a copy of that day's *Daily Mail*. The headline read, DUTCH ARMY SURRENDERS. Logan had ringed a two-paragraph item at the bottom of the page in red ink. He read it out.

"Germans threaten to bomb England . . . 'German planes are already within reach of the important English port of Harwich,' said the announcer on the German radio last night referring to the German advance into the Low Countries.

"'But even more, they have bases for direct attack against the whole of England, especially against the highly important southeastern coast. Britain, which started the war, will now begin to feel it on her own body.'"

Logan put the newspaper down and said, "I think, gentlemen, that Britain will begin to feel it tonight. In Wandsworth."

MILLER BELIEVED THAT he had exactly twelve hours to live when Munnion visited him in the condemned cell.

At first he treated Munnion as if he barely existed. You don't share your last hours with a policeman and that plainly was what Munnion was. What did he want? A list of all the jobs he'd pulled so that he could balance his books?

Eleven hours, 59 minutes. Fear moved inside him.

Munnion held up one hand. "Yes, I am a copper in a sort of way, and I've come to offer you a reprieve."

The evening froze. The barred windows receded. Cold filled his skull.

When he raised his head from the table and the evening reassembled, Munnion handed him a silver hipflask. "Take a pull on this," he said, sitting opposite Miller, "but not too much, mind, because you've got to have your wits about you."

And he began to explain. First about gold. And because he couldn't see how the Bank of England's bullion could possibly concern him, Miller began to wonder if he was the victim of some monstrous hoax.

Munnion told him that it was Chamberlain who had decided to ship the gold to Canada. Churchill, picking up the wreckage of Chamberlain's policies, had decided to divert it to the United States, "for reasons that we needn't go into now."

An intuitive glimmer of understanding reached Miller. "But it never got there?"

Munnion packed his pipe with Player's Airman and told him what had happened. Miller wondered what the deal was. When a policeman was being reasonable there was always a deal. What had Munnion meant, a policeman *in a sort of a way?* With his center-parted hair, sensible suit, sturdy physique, and pipe he looked like a well-heeled superintendent.

When Munnion mentioned Goering, Miller knew what the deal was. "And you want me to find out where they're taking the loot?"

Munnion nodded. "You're the only man who can do it."

"In exchange for my life?"

"Exactly. But we can't let you walk out just like that. If Goering found out that we'd sprung you, he'd know what you were up to immediately. So you'll have to escape."

Munnion produced a plan of the prison. He brought it around to Miller's side of the table and prodded it with the stem of his unlit pipe; he held the pipe, Miller thought, like a pistol.

"The star-shaped complex in the middle contains the main blocks, A to F. You're here, F, the smallest of the six. Luckily it's opposite the main gates."

"So what am I supposed to do? Turn the key and walk out?"

"As soon as it gets dark there will be an air raid. One bomb will drop here," prodding the area outside Block F. "Another here," indicating the space between Block F and the gates. "A part of your wall will be blown out, but only *your* wall because we don't want a mass exodus, and the gates will be blasted open. Across the road from the gates there's a parking lot. You'll find a black Austin Seven with a doll hanging in the rear window. The driving keys are under a rubber mat in front of the driver's seat. I think you know where to drive to."

"These bombs, they'll be planted?"

Munnion nodded. "A small amount of explosive will be used to blow your wall—it's being put there now. The rest will be up to Maskelyne, an illusionist who's offered his services to MI5. He's very good with smoke bombs, I'm told."

Outside, Miller could see the daylight fading on the gray old walls of the block opposite. As a condemned man, he had anticipated death with incredulity; now he felt the same about the life that had been given back to him. He began to shiver.

Munnion handed him the hip flask again. "One swig, no more." Miller swallowed another mouthful of whisky and wiped his mouth with the back of his hand. "So," he said, "what sort of a copper are you?"

"A Bank of England copper."

"So why didn't the bastards who set me up come to tell me they'd changed their minds?"

"I suppose," Munnion said levelly, "that they thought you'd trust me. You know, safe as the Bank of England."

Now that he knew about the deal, Miller wondered what Munnion was holding back; police always held something back. Munnion still hadn't lit his pipe. Miller wished he would.

Miller said, "The fact that I worked for the *Forschungsamt*, was that the only reason you came to me?"

"The main reason. But there are others."

"Tell me about them," Miller said.

"For one you know about gold. It was your speciality, I believe."

"If the law knew so much about me why didn't they ever arrest me?"

"Because you were too clever by half. And that's another reason for coming to you. You're a resourceful man. Once you've tracked down the gold, we want you to help us get it back."

So that was one little item he'd held back.

"And you're patriotic."

"*Was* patriotic."

"It was a terrible thing they did to you. I don't expect you to believe me, but I was sickened by it."

"But not so sickened that you decided to tell the world about it."

Munnion didn't reply.

"You can show me how sorry you are if you like."

Munnion looked at him inquiringly.

"Lend me that gold hunter of yours. The seal on a gentleman's agreement."

Munnion took the watch from his waistcoat pocket, unclasped it from its chain, and handed it to Miller. It was smooth and warm. Miller cradled it for a moment in the palm of his hand. "A gold hunter," he said. "Appropriate. When all this is over I'll let you have it back." He placed it on the table beside the hip flask. "Now tell me something else, what made you think I would go through with this?"

"Because you want to live."

"I don't think you understand what I'm getting at. What made you think I would go through with it once I had escaped?"

"I'm not proud of what I'm about to say."

"But you've been told to say it? You're breaking my heart."

"Your parents are still alive. They live in Chadbourne Street, Stepney, I believe. And your twin brother, he lives with them, doesn't he?"

"You bastard."

"But there's no need to worry, is there? If you cooperate with us nothing will happen to them." Munnion avoided Miller's gaze. "I'm sorry," he said, and at last he lit his pipe.

BLACKOUT WAS LATE these days. The clocks had been

put forward so that war workers could have an extra two hours of daylight in the evening, and there had been a cartoon about it in *Punch.* A housewife calling out to her husband who was working in the garden that he ought to come in now because it was nearly midnight.

In the cells blackout was a simple matter: they put the lights out. In the condemned cell, however, the light was left on, and a frame on which black felt had been tacked was fitted over the barred window. It might, Miller supposed, be out of compassion, or it might be to enable the hangman to take a look at the prisoner through a spy hole and make his final calculations.

The patriotic guard put the frame up. "Not long now," he said.

"No," Miller said, "not long now."

The door closed behind the guard.

How long?

A little while ago I would have been holding onto the minutes trying to slow them down, now . . . He picked up the gold hunter and watched the minute hand creeping around the dial.

The air-raid siren broke the silence with a deep-throated groan that rapidly gained power, soaring and dropping in eerie warning. Miller went to the window and stared through a slit at the edge of the felt. Searchlights moved across the sky as though trying to sweep the stars from the night.

He heard the drone of aircraft, the muted explosions of antiaircraft guns.

A searchlight caught an aircraft in its beam, a silver fish suspended high above London. A British aircraft, he supposed.

Tracer shells took to the skies.

He remembered Munnion's warnings. One, don't touch the cocoa or anything they give you to drink—it's drugged so you don't put up a fight in the morning. Two, when the warning sounds, get around the corner out of the way and keep low.

The explosion came as he threw himself to the floor around the corner of wall abutting into one side of the cell.

The wall groaned and fell aside. He smelled explosive and fresh air.

He heard glass tinkling.

Then another explosion. Smoke poured into the gap in the wall. Maskelyne's smoke.

He picked up the gold hunter and cautiously approached the gap. He was one story up, not a great challenge to a professional burglar but the sort of jump that, carelessly done, could put an end to a job. In this case my life.

Clutching a steel support beam that ran the length of the cell, he let himself drop. He imagined a rope jerking his neck, breaking it.

He landed safely on the asphalt below.

He straightened up and saw two figures running toward him, but the smoke was very thick. They didn't see him.

Crouching, he ran toward the gates. They had

swung open, the massive lock ruptured. A guard was trying to close them. Miller hit him at the base of the neck with the blade of his hand, he hoped not hard enough to kill him.

There was a lot of shouting going on as he ran across the road, dodging the traffic and cutting through the beams of the smoke-dimmed head-lights.

He found the Austin easily enough, the doll grinning at him in the moonlight. He took the keys from under the rubber mat; the engine fired first time.

He stopped outside a public lavatory at the junction of Wandsworth Road and Nine Elms Lane and, taking the suitcase that Munnion had told him would be in the trunk, went into one of the cubicles. He stripped off his prison clothes and put on a single-breasted Fifty Shilling Tailor tan blazer with silver buttons, gray flannels, brown shoes and black socks, cream shirt, and a tie with stripes running vertically from the knot. Munnion posed no threat to the fashion industry.

Outside he heard a air-raid warden shouting, "Put that bloody light out," to some careless householder. Someone came in and used a stall, the warden perhaps. On the wall were the words *Mosley for Prime Minister*.

As Miller left the lavatory, the all-clear sounded, a single blaring note. He put the suitcase filled with his prison clothes into the trunk and drove along the Albert Embankment, crossing the Thames at Lambeth Bridge.

He was flagged down by a policeman in the Strand. "Excuse me, sir, just a routine check." He had a graying mustache and looked at Miller with the distaste reserved by some older people for any young man not in uniform. "Can you identify yourself?"

Miller took his identity card from the inside pocket of his blazer. He was Ronald Alfred Spears. He also handed the policeman a fawn envelope stamped OHMS. He wondered if, despite the letter in the envelope, the policeman would ask to look in the trunk. If he did, Miller would drive away, dump the Austin, and mingle with the tramps in the Victoria Embankment gardens.

The policeman read the letter. Miller had checked it in the lavatory. "To whom it may concern, Mr. Ronald Alfred Spears is engaged on important work for the government and should be given every assistance." Signed Oliver Stanley, Minister of War.

The policeman became conspiratorial. "If there's anything I can do . . ." Shaking his head, Miller put the car into gear. "Just keep on doing your bit, officer." And he drove away.

Traffic was sparse. Blacked-out, sandbagged buildings silent. Fleet Street was busier. The debacle in Europe would be the headlines but, if Munnion and the others had done their job, there would be another prominent item: JAIL BOMBED, CONDEMNED SPY ESCAPES.

108

He drove up Ludgate Hill. Nearby was the Old Bailey. He heard the voice of the judge, as dispassionate as an auctioneer's, sentencing him to death. And they expect me to help them!

The citadels of the Square Mile, the City of London, loomed around him. To the left St. Paul's. On the far side, in the great spread of high streets and pubs and squat terraces of houses that comprised the East End, stood Chadbourne Street, Stepney.

Vic and their parents would now be sitting in the kitchen, sipping their cocoa, joined in bewilderment. Vic wondering if, when his brother was hanged, he would feel the rope on his own neck. There had always been a kind of telepathy between them.

Would Munnion and the others carry out the implied threat if he didn't cooperate? It didn't matter. He couldn't take the chance. They knew that.

He drove to St. Stephen's in Walbrook, the Lord Mayor's Church rebuilt by Wren. Personal prayers written on folded sheets of paper had been pinned on a notice board covered with green baize in the entrance. He removed a prayer, the second from the right at the top of the board, and read it.

The prayer asked God to spare the life of a soldier named Frank Rivers who had been wounded in the fighting in Norway. Using the simple memorized cipher employed for drops like this, Miller decoded the prayer.

Then he drove to Etheldene Avenue in Muswell Hill, North London, the current address for emergencies, according to the prayer.

The man who opened the door of the semidetached house, Robert Kemble, a clerk at the Air Ministry code named Serpent by the Fifth Department of the Luftwaffe, said: "You!"

"Yes, me. Let me in." Miller shouldered his way past Kemble into the living room.

Kemble followed him. "How . . ."

"First get me a drink. A Scotch."

Miller watched him while he poured whisky from a small bottle of Johnny Walker. He had probably been saving it for Christmas. Kemble was that sort of man, a gray squirrel who hoarded. Everything in the room with its chintz curtains and varnished furniture had an unused air about it. Most spies he had met were nondescript; that was probably why they became spies.

He drank the whisky in one swallow and held out the glass again. Reluctantly, Kemble replenished it, lips in his fussy, bachelor face pursed. With his free hand he smoothed the long hair plastered across his bald head from ear to ear.

When Miller told him how he had escaped, Kemble said, "You shouldn't have come here." He poured himself a Christmas whiskey.

"And where was I supposed to come? This was the address in the prayer."

"You should have telephoned."

"So you could make yourself scarce? Come off it, Kemble."

"What do you want?"

"What do I want?" Miller stared at him incredulously. "What the hell do you think I want, the loan of a few bob? Escape, that's what I want. And you're the one who's going to arrange it."

"But I'm not sure . . ."

Miller put down his glass, stood up, and grabbed the knot of Kemble's tie. "No buts. You and I both work for the Fifth Branch. Radio them and they will get me out."

Because I'm a member of the *Forschungsamt*, Miller thought, letting go of Kemble's tie, and Goering won't want blown agents of his personal intelligence service wandering around Britain. Miller didn't know whether Kemble was aware of such niceties; Kemble was new. He didn't even know that MI5 was onto him.

"Goering will assume you blew everything when you were arrested, to save your skin."

Miller took the bottle of whisky from Kemble's hand and poured some more into his glass. "Perhaps that's what you would have done. I didn't. Goering knows my reputation."

"How do I know this isn't a setup?"

"An air raid, a bomb on Wandsworth. Do me a favor, Kemble."

"Those clothes, where did you get them?"

"In a suitcase in the trunk of a car I borrowed. Not much of a fit, are they?" pulling at the waist of the flannels to show the slack.

"Supposing Goering decides to kill you between here and Germany."

"He won't. You haven't studied him. Forget the

111

flab. In the last war he was a brave man, and an honorable one."

"Supposing you've been followed?"

"I wasn't. If I had the police would have knocked your front door down by now."

"They'll be looking for that car," Kemble said.

"Which is why I parked it half a mile away. Come on, Kemble, you don't want me to tell Goering that you wouldn't cooperate, do you?" He took Kemble's arm, fingers digging into the flabby bicep.

Kemble led him into the hall; it smelled of stale food and furniture polish. Kemble opened a door beneath a photograph of the king and queen at their coronation and led Miller down a flight of stone steps.

The cellar was very dark. Kemble flicked a switch, and it was filled with salmon-colored light from a red-paint bulb hanging from the ceiling. On a workbench littered with developing and printing materials lay a photograph of a young man wearing swimming trunks that sagged at the crotch; he was smiling. Kemble turned the photograph over.

He opened a cupboard stacked with photographic equipment and took out a Kodak camera case. From the case he removed a small radio transmitter, an old Philips set with a Morse key. Attached to it was a code disk made from white cardboard.

"Okay, make contact," Miller said.

Kemble activated the set. He called three times,

waited, listening intently into his bakelite earphones. Then he began to transmit; afterward he scribbled a few coded words on a pad.

When he took off the headset he said, "They're going to call me back."

"When?"

"In an hour's time." He looked at his watch. "0100 hours. Let's go upstairs, it's sweltering down here."

But Miller felt cold. He said, "You know something? I'd have only seven hours to live if things hadn't turned out differently."

In the greasy kitchen Kemble cooked bacon and eggs and smeared margarine onto slices of stale bread. A flypaper stuck with corpses, as though someone had thrown a handful of currants at it, hung from the ceiling.

Kemble sliced the rind from his bacon—perhaps he intended to hoard it—and said, "What will you do when you get to Germany?"

He wasn't really interested, Miller understood, merely wondering what might happen to him one day. But it never will, Kemble, you'll be hanged long before that.

Miller said, "They'll debrief me first. Then, God knows. Become a thief again, perhaps." He bit into his bread and margarine; it tasted terrible. "So," he said casually, "any big coups been pulled off lately?"

He thought he caught a flicker of wariness in

Kemble's eyes but he couldn't be sure. Kemble always looked wary and in his profession he wasn't alone in that.

"Usual stuff," Kemble told him. "In my case routine. Position of new airfields that sort of thing."

And all wrong, Miller thought, fed to you by MI5. He said, "Anyone else pulled anything off?"

"Not that I know of."

And Kemble probably wouldn't know, not if the bullion job was exclusively *Forschungsamt*. So I will have to wait until I reach Germany to get a lead.

When they had finished their meal and drunk their tea they returned to the cellar. What a miserable life, Miller reflected, hiding in a cellar that smelled of chemicals and decay. But at least it was a life. And that was precious.

Kemble put the receiver on the workbench and waited. Precisely at 0100 hours the Fifth Branch made contact.

"Let me talk to them," Miller said. After writing a few words on the pad, Kemble handed the headset to him. Miller, using the code disk, began to tap out a message.

Back came the reply, terse and exact. He was to drive to Bradwell Bay on the estuary of the Blackwater on the east coast of England. An ordinance survey map reference followed. He was to be there at 2330 hours the following day. A motor dinghy would pick him up and transfer him to a U-boat.

"Understood?"

"Understood. Over and out."

He said to Kemble, "And now some kip."

"You'll be gone by dawn?"

"I would have been gone *at* dawn."

"That's not an answer."

"I'll be gone, don't worry."

The least of your worries, he thought lying down on the sofa and closing his eyes.

They were outside the door. The door was opening and the hangman was behind him pinioning his arms and they were manhandling him out of the condemned cell into the execution chamber and he cried out and Kemble, who was shaking him, said, "It's time to go."

He reached Maldon in the Austin in two and a half hours and was stopped only once, by a corporal in the military police who, as an army convoy rolled past in the opposite direction, asked to see his papers. His letter from Oliver Stanley produced a crisp salute. He lunched at a pub in the town on bread and soapy cheese and a pint of bitter. He borrowed the *Mirror* from the landlord. He was on page 3, so Vic and their parents would know, the *Mirror* was their paper. He tried to picture their reactions. Would they have read it before or after 8 A.M., execution time? Before, with luck, because the paperboy usually got to the house at seven. Whether they would have read it under the circumstances was another matter, although the neighbors, the

Seeleys, would probably have come banging on the door with the news. For a while it would be too much for them to comprehend. He heard Vic coughing and ordered another pint, but the beer had run out.

Then he rented a room at a terrace house down the road because he didn't want to be seen hanging around. "Ten and six a night for a double and no questions asked," the landlord of the pub had leered. At 7 P.M. he set off on the last stretch to Bradwell. When he arrived the tide was just beginning to cover the warm gray mud.

He went to a pub in the center of the village and ordered cold meat sandwiches. Just before dusk he made his way toward the marshes, leaving the Austin outside the pub.

The dinghy nosed its way through the reeds at 2330 sharp. A voice whispered to him in German-accented English. He climbed into the dinghy.

The flare burst above them turning night into glaring day when they were about a quarter of a mile from the shore.

Immediately Miller thought, Another betrayal. Then, when the first gun fired and a spout of water reared up a long way ahead of them, he realized that the dinghy wasn't the target.

Staring across the bright water he spotted the sharklike silhouette of the U-boat and beyond it, prow thrusting its way through the swell, a British patrol boat, a development of the CMBs used in the last war. The Navy and MI5 had got their lines crossed. The Navy hadn't been told to let this particular *Unterseeboot* escape.

"Shit," said one of the two submariners in gray leather jackets and white sweaters who were manning the dinghy.

"Don't worry," said his colleague, who was in charge of the outboard, "it's no match for *U-47*." He turned to Miller. "You're honored. That's the baby that torpedoed the *Royal Oak* in Scapa Flow. What have you done to be so important?" He was speaking in German now.

"Escaped the gallows," Miller said.

The patrol boat fired again and another shell hit the water nearer the U-boat.

"Prien will get it with the cannon," the submariner on the outboard said. "You watch."

Fatalistically, Miller watched the barrel of the gun mounted on the deck swing toward the cocky little patrol boat. Another shell exploded in the water so close to the U-boat that Miller could see waves breaking over its torpedolike bows.

"He'd better hurry up," the other submariner said.

"No need to worry about Prien," his colleague said, and indeed there didn't seem to be a shred of doubt in his voice. "One shot and bang, no patrol boat."

But the next explosion came from another shell from the patrol boat and the U-boat rocked. Had it been hit? Miller hoped it had and knew he should hope it hadn't. Good shooting, he thought. *But if you hit it then I'm a dead man.*

"Christ," exclaimed the first submariner. "The toy ship is getting close."

"Don't worry," said his companion.

The U-boat's cannon fired and in the light of the flare Miller saw the patrol boat disintegrate.

The two submariners cheered, and as they did so the flare died and the only light came from the stars and the moon riding high above small motionless clouds.

It was Miller who noticed that the angle of *U-47* had changed. "It's diving," he shouted in German. "Either that or it's been hit."

"Prien wouldn't dive without us," the submariner on the outboard said, but for the first time his voice was smudged with doubt. "Not old Gunther," he said trying to find reassurance with familiarity.

"Then she's been hit," said his colleague. "Can't you make this thing go any faster?"

"Why don't you get out and push?"

"The shore batteries will open up in a minute."

When they bumped against the hull of *U-47*, the drill for diving was already in effect. The bridge watch were leaving their posts to take up positions below on the hydroplanes. The watch officer was standing by to clamp down the hatch.

As he scrambled onto the slippery, heaving deck, helped by two bearded members of the crew, a heavy

118

gun on the shore opened up. He heard the shell pass overhead with a soft, slithery sound. It hit the sea fifty yards ahead, exploded, and showered the U-boat with water.

Miller was thrust down the hatch. As though I were being bottled, he thought. Signals were transmitted to the engine room, a whistle blew. Because no one shouted, the urgency of the dive had a controlled intensity.

By now the exhaust and air intake conduits would have been shut off, diesel engines immobilized, E-motors engaged to drive the propeller shafts.

The commander, Prien presumably, wearing a peaked cap at a rakish angle and a white scarf, gave the order: "Flood."

The next shell from the shore battery must have been very close. The *U-47* was pushed to one side and began to shake. Miller was reminded of a dog shaking water from itself.

The commander glanced at Miller. So you're the cause of all this, the glance said. He had a pale submariner's face and tired eyes. He said, "We're lame, and you're going to be late."

The air that had kept *U-47* afloat roared out of her lungs and seawater whooshed in. As the hydroplanes were adjusted, the sleek predator began to slide into the depths where only the select few find balm.

The tower was below the surface when the last shell exploded. The *U-47* shuddered and then dove into the cold silence to lick her wounds.

4

May 18

*T*HE RHEINGOLD LOOKED beautiful in the May sunshine, as indeed she should, Hans Vogel reminded himself, considering the work he had done since he had driven her onto the quay at Hamburg.

The engine, Number 18 547, black and brutal with a bronze swastika and eagle on its prow and a red and white ring around its chimney, gleamed. The heat rising from it smelled of new oil and metallic cleanliness. Behind the tender and the two head-end cars that had seen service as mail vans, the three Mitropa coaches in their purple, cream, and gold livery, had an air of pampered somnolence about them.

Rag in one hand, Vogel, accompanied by the fireman who was carrying an oil can, walked up and down the length of the train dabbing at invisible specks of dirt. Cranes towered above them. At the far end of the quay an Italian cargo ship was being unloaded, making its small contribution to the teeming coffers of the docks.

"So," the fireman said, bending his already bandy legs still further to drop a globule of oil onto one of the engine's coupling rods, "when do we leave?"

"Soon." The question irritated Vogel because he felt he should know the answer and because it wasn't the first time the fireman has asked it.

"How soon? My wife wants to know why we're spending such a long time in Hamburg."

"Tell her there's a war on."

"Not in Hamburg," the fireman said.

"Don't belittle the part trains are playing in the war. Where would Guderian, von Kleist, any of them be without trains to bring them troops and guns?" And before the fireman could revert drearily to Hamburg, "Don't forget we're being kept for something special."

"A trip to the French Riviera by the look of it," the fireman remarked, pointing the long thin spout of his oil can at the three luxury coaches resting in the sun.

"Something very special," Vogel said enigmatically. "Something from the very top."

"From Goering," the fireman agreed. "I know that, everyone knows that," waving the oil can.

Vogel wiped a spot of oil from the purple paintwork on one of the coaches. He was fond of the fireman but really his outlook was very pedestrian. "You must be patient."

"You make it sound as if you know why we're hanging around here. Personally, I think Hermann has forgotten us."

"You are hardly in a position to judge anything," Vogel said, turning and marching back toward 18 547.

"And you are?"

As the driver, yes. That's what he wanted to say, although it wasn't strictly true. All he knew was that he had to drive the Rheingold to Berlin, which, as everyone knew, wasn't all that far from Goering's magnificent folly, Carinhall. So it was reasonable to suppose that Goering was appropriating the Rheingold and at the same time using it to transport some trophies from occupied territory. Which would suit Vogel fine. He would be a fellow conspirator, admittedly of minor rank, but surely in a position to press his claims to become the Feldmarschall's personal driver, and to seek his permission to get Margarethe installed in the servants' quarters at Carinhall.

Vogel smiled catlike in the sunshine. "You look like a buccaneer," she had said, and he supposed she was right. He adjusted the knot in his red and white spotted scarf and smoothed his freshly cleaned blue serge jacket.

"Well, are you?"

Vogel stopped in front of the bronze swastika and gave it a zigzag wipe with the rag. The fireman had an inflexible peasant mind, that was his trouble. He smelled a saline draft coming downriver from the open sea, sixty or so miles away; the smell of victory—Belgium would fall soon, then France, then Britain.

"You must understand that I was given the information in confidence," he said.

He paused; it took the peasant mind a long time to react.

The fireman said, "Then you must keep it to yourself."

Really, such lack of curiosity was unnatural. Just then, before Vogel could say another word, a small tank locomotive materialized, pushing an armored car on which an antiaircraft gun was mounted.

"Hey," Vogel shouted to the driver. "What the hell's that?"

"What does it look like?" the driver shouted back. "Anyway, it's all yours, to be coupled onto the end of your grand coaches."

Vogel frowned and then glanced at the fireman, who he realized was watching his expression. "Well, you must understand our freight is top-secret," he said to him.

"That's obvious."

But *how* secret, they both wondered. The sun went behind a cloud, and the air was suddenly cold.

SO THE GOLD wasn't on the bed of the ocean, it was still in the hold of the *Countess of Cork*, which, after running repairs, was limping across the North Sea.

That much Miller had discovered with ease after

the damaged U-boat had docked at Hamburg and he had been taken to an apartment overlooking the Outer Alster, the larger of the two lakes in the center of the city, in the keeping of Lieutenant Albert Wessel.

Wessel had been seconded from the Luftwaffe to the *Forschungsamt* because, like many others who became members of that august body, he was a crook, a forger of paintings, and thus invaluable to Goering who liked his *objets d'art* to be genuine. Wessel could spot a forged Renoir a mile off.

He and Miller, having a lot in common, had immediately hit it off, and Wessel, in charge of the apartment for the night, had opened several bottles to celebrate Miller's escape from the gallows.

It was while Wessel was downing his fourth schnapps that Miller said casually, "Kemble told me you've pulled off some kind of coup involving the Bank of England. You haven't stolen their gold have you?" He laughed.

Wessel spilled a few drops of the pilsner beer, the chaser for his schnapps. "Hardly anyone's supposed to know anything about that, not even me. How the hell did Kemble know about it? He's not even *Forschungsamt*."

Miller shrugged. "God knows. He said that it, whatever *it* is," almost but not quite winking at Wessel, "was at the bottom of the sea."

"Well, he's wrong there," Wessel said with the alacrity common to, but immediately regretted by, those in the know. "At least I think he is," he added with the qualifying instinct that is equally common.

Miller replenished Wessel's glass from a frosted bottle of Korn and topped up his own. He could drink but, although he had paid many visits to Hamburg to launder his stolen gold, he had never quite managed to find an answer to the depth charge which is schnapps.

In the hope of provoking another involuntary response, Miller said, "I suppose it's being taken to Norway." But this time, despite the Korn and the pilsner, Wessel said, "I don't know where the hell it's going," smiling with pride at his evasion.

Miller sipped his schnapps and assessed Wessel. Aesthetic features but secondhand, like his art, which he could copy but never originate. Eyes an honest gray but wet; hair a dry brown; an expression that said he could be tempted.

"Why don't we go out on the town?" he asked him.

The call to duty, or more accurately the penalties involved if he didn't answer the call, confused Wessel's adaptable features. "I'm supposed to be keeping you here until Becker arrives."

Becker, he explained, was a *Forschungsamt* officer on his way from Berlin to debrief Miller and report back to Goering, who was at his battle headquarters in the Eifel mountains. He owned the apartment and he was an *arschloch*.

"We could get some girls."

That did it. "Okay, the pompous *arschloch*

125

won't be here until tomorrow anyway." As he put on his tweedy jacket he pointed at a portrait on the wall. "Do you know what that is?"

Miller said, "I could probably identify a gold coin of the Sassanian dynasty of Persia, but I'm not so hot on paintings." He studied the portrait. "Gainsborough?"

Wessel shook his head delightedly. "Wessel. But you're right about the original. For a thief you seem to know a lot about art."

"I went to night school," Miller said.

"But you have a certain polish."

"Self-taught."

"Me, too." He touched the portrait. "I had to bake it, varnish it, and roll it around on a cylinder to fake the cracks. That's polish for you."

They walked in the direction of St. Pauli. Miller knew Hamburg well. He liked its elegance and the urgency, all those devout church spires and, at the docks slotted into the banks of the Elbe, the restless masts of the world's shipping fleets.

They left the Outer Alster and entered the Alter Botanischer Garten. It was late afternoon and the gardens were blooming with victory. It was on the tongues of the homeward-bound office workers, in their stride, in the newspapers tucked under their arms.

An old man wearing a green Tyrolean hat with a feather in it was listening to a portable radio on a park bench. Wessel translated the newscast for Miller. Antwerp had fallen. To the south von Kleist's panzers were sweeping through France toward the Channel to trap the British Expeditionary Force in the north.

"Some expedition," Wessel said. "They misread the whole of Hitler's strategy. Holland and Belgium, they were just the feint before the left hook. Good news, eh? Soon we'll both be back in business for ourselves."

Good news? After France they'd attack Britain. Miller grieved for his country. Then he remembered what Munnion and the others had done to him. "Good news," he said.

"A good day for girls, too. The scent of victory will make them abandoned. A pity we aren't in uniform. These days a civilian has to take what the warriors discard. Oh, for an SS uniform. All that black and silver, they can't resist it. Second best, a Luftwaffe officer, pilot preferably. My uniform's hanging up in my wardrobe," Wessel mourned. "Then the army and lastly the navy, because in this city the girls are sick of sailors."

Near the St. Pauli subway station workmen had dug a gaping hole in the street to repair a water main. Signs had been erected to divert traffic. A wag had scrawled across one sign, JEWS KEEP STRAIGHT ON.

We mustn't let these people win, Miller thought. And then, But my people would have let me die jerking on the end of a rope.

They went into a bar in Grosse Freiheitstrasse, just off the Reeperbahn. It was dark inside but the small dance floor was brightly lit, and on the floor, which was made of mirrors, you could see that the girls dancing with their partners were not wearing pants.

Wessel ordered schnapps and beer chasers and stared at the mirrors.

Miller said casually, "Of course the gold could be coming here; it's the obvious place."

"I told you, I haven't the slightest idea." His attention concentrated on the reflection of a blonde who patently wasn't blonde at all. "Forget the gold," he said, pointing at the brown mouse at the top of the girl's legs. "You wouldn't have seen much of that where you were going after they had strung you up."

"You never know, heaven might be full of it."

"But not the other place," Wessel said. He smiled at the blonde, who had left her partner and was sitting by herself at a table with a red telephone on it.

The phone on the bar rang. The barman picked it up. "It's for you," he said, handing the receiver to Wessel. Miller noticed that the girl Wessel had been smiling at was speaking into her red telephone.

Wessel put down the receiver. "Mirror, mirror on the floor, who is the loveliest of them all?" He bowed to the girl.

When they had been on the dance floor for a couple of minutes, Miller finished his beer and left the bar. He ran down the street, emerging in Simon von Utrecht Strasse. Then he turned and headed toward the apartment overlooking the lake. On the way he stopped at a hardware shop and bought some tools, including a pair of long-jawed pliers.

The beauty of the apartment was that it was unobtrusive and that meant no guards, no elaborate security. Miller now believed Hamburg was the destination for the bullion and the apartment was going to be the nerve center for its reception and dispatch, which was why Goering had made sure that it didn't attract attention.

It was the name Becker that had alerted Miller. He was the *Forschungsamt* officer directly responsible to Goering and he wouldn't have been dispatched to Hamburg for anything as mundane as a debriefing. No, he had acquired the apartment for much more ambitious motives, and Wessel had let the cat out of the bag.

Miller applied himself to the main door of the small, stubby block of flats. Behind him, across the lakeside road, the water was winged with white sails returning in the warm evening to their moorings. What war? they seemed to say. We've won it, relax.

As he had expected, the door, although a snug and chic yellow, was vulnerable; he opened it within a minute. Up two flights of chip-marble stairs to Number 7. Here the lock would undoubtedly be more of a challenge; it was, but far from insurmountable.

Miller, with the help of the long-jawed pliers, was inside the apartment within two minutes. There on the glass-topped coffee table in the lounge were the smeared schnapps and beer glasses; there above the four-bar electric fire was the print of Herr Hitler, hand Napoleonically at his breast, toothbrush mustache bristling.

Miller had known as soon as he had entered the apartment that the safe was behind Hitler. He stuck a chisel in the back of the Führer and levered him aside. And there it was. Obvious, at least to a cracksman, but then, Wessel aside, it could never have been anticipated that anyone in Hamburg would be looking for secrets in this discreet apartment. No one could have dreamed that he had been sprung from a British jail for just such a purpose.

Hands on hips, he stared at the safe. Smallish, khaki colored, brass fittings, embedded snugly and tightly in the wall. Easy.

Of course a small explosive charge would have been preferable but only a bungler, and he had never been that, would have stopped on the way to buy the ingredients. What he now needed was the combination. Although the movies always depicted a burglar with a stethoscope to his ears, the message of the tumblers could be detected by the naked ear, if it was trained to receive such intelligence.

With his head pressed against the cold steel, he rotated the numbers, listening to the snug clicks from within. Click. He turned the handle of the safe. Click. The door swung open. Inside a fat wad of Deutsche marks and a sheaf of papers. He pocketed the money and began to examine the papers.

Another click. Outside. Another apartment or

the main door two floors below? He waited as he had waited many times before for footsteps. Sometimes they materialized, sometimes only thickening silence followed the click, the cough, the crunch of gravel. This time silence.

He went to the window. Daylight was fading and the sails of the yachts had folded for the night. Church spires probed the dusk looking for the stars and the city relaxed, waiting for victory.

The papers were a disappointment. Bills, deeds, a will—Becker's—nothing more. He put them back inside and shut the safe.

The noise startled him. He froze. At first he couldn't identify it. Then he recognized it—a teleprinter. He traced it to a study next to one of the two bedrooms. Frowning, he watched the chattering figures spelling out gibberish. Code.

The voice from the doorway said in English, "I suppose you're Miller. Where the hell is Wessel?"

Miller turned. Becker was just like the photograph he had been shown months ago in London. Stiff-backed, bleak-faced, like a stand-in for the film star Conrad Veidt. The monocle was missing but not the long leather topcoat, despite the warm evening.

Whatever happened now, Miller knew that he had one factor in his favor: Becker was a coward, a mental victim of the last war. He had been told that in London.

Miller said, "He went out to buy a newspaper, to see if we had won the war yet."

"We?"

Miller shrugged. "You, us. Does it matter?"

"Not if you're a double agent, I suppose. A blown one at that."

Plainly Becker, whose shining principles were still suspended over the shell-pocked fields of Flanders, didn't have much time for spies. Then he shouldn't have been in charge of the *Forschungsamt*, and that was Goering's mistake, trusting an old comrade, stupid but admirable just the same.

Miller said, "He'll be back soon."

The teleprinter stopped chattering.

Becker said, "Why are you in here?"

"The teleprinter started talking. I wondered what the hell it was."

Becker stepped past him and tore off the coded printout. "Interesting," he said, scanning it. "It's about you. A radio message sent to Berlin from London and relayed here."

MILLER'S ESCAPE FAKED STOP TRYING LOCATE B OF E'S GOLD—something like that.

Miller held out his hand. "I'll take that."

As Becker's hand moved inside his leather coat, Miller leaped at him and grabbed his arm. He could feel the shape of the gun beneath the coat. Becker struggled but his reflexes were slow. He winced as his back twisted and stopped struggling. Miller pulled out the gun, a Luger, and aimed it at Becker.

The teleprinter began to chatter.

Miller told Becker to turn around, and Conrad

Veidt said, "You're crazy, you'll never get away with this."

Miller backed away and with one wrench pulled the cord from the curtains. He bound Becker's wrists behind his back and, with another length of cord, his ankles. He pushed him back into the swivel chair at the desk and gagged him with his tie, maroon silk adorned with a biplane embroidered in silver.

When the teleprinter had finished its garbled chat he tore off the message and slipped it into the inside pocket of his blazer along with the information about himself.

He said to Becker, "Don't be hard on Wessel, he only wanted to read about the glorious victories of the Luftwaffe," wondering, as he let himself out of the apartment, if one of Wessel's last memories would be the reflection on the dance floor. There were worse things.

Outside he began to walk. The contact address Munnion had given him was in Blankenese, eight miles down the river in the direction of the sea. He didn't want to take a taxi because, although his German was good, it wasn't faultless and he didn't want to risk encountering a zealous cab driver who would take him straight to the Kripo or, worse, the Gestapo.

He headed for the Elbe and began to follow its course. Ships and barges churned past in the fast-fading light; on the opposite bank the docks glittered and reverberated with activity. If his reasoning was correct, the *Countess of Cork* would berth over there somewhere. When? He hastened his step.

It was a pleasant evening with a breeze blowing down the river from the coast. The smell reminded him of the Thames and Southend at low tide; he wished he could enjoy it. A big woman with a chest like a bookshelf stared at him. He would have to get rid of these ridiculous English clothes.

He glanced behind him but there didn't appear to be anyone following him. Why should there be? Professional caution he realized, would be with him for the rest of his life, like his shadow. He smelled Southend again, the day it had all begun. Gray mud and cotton candy and a small boy in shorts.

Who, he wondered, was Hessen, the agent in Blankenese who was in radio contact with London, and why was he a spy? Was he seeking the same furtive escapism that Kemble sought? Miller decided that he would be pallid and nervous with a damp mustache.

Blankenese looked quite grand, big houses reaching down a wooded slope to the river, which was now silver in the moonlight. He climbed the hill and entered the driveway of one with an alpine-style roof. He made his way to the back door. He rang the bell as instructed by Munnion, three long rings and one short. V for victory.

The door opened. "Herr Miller?"

Miller nodded.

"I've been expecting you."

So right to the end Munnion had been holding something back: he hadn't told Miller that Hessen was a woman.

FIRST THINGS FIRST.

After he had identified himself—the Fifty Shilling tab on the inside of his jacket, brown shoes and black socks, password Croesus—Gisella Hessen took him upstairs, where they climbed a ladder to the attic. She produced a radio transmitter, also a Philips, from the false bottom of a chest of old clothes.

When she lingered, Miller smiled at her and said, "Like Greta Garbo, I prefer to be alone." After she went down the ladder, he related everything he knew about the bullion to London.

When he returned to the kitchen she had prepared a meal, ersatz coffee, wurst, cheese, and pumpernickel bread. While he ate hungrily, she picked at her food and watched him, assessing his capabilities, he guessed, for whatever lay ahead.

He also assessed her, melding his own first impressions, always the most acute, with what Munnion had just told him on the radio and what she was telling him.

The most important key to her was *motive*. Munnion, whose knowledge had been scanty, had said only that her hatred of the Nazis stemmed from bereavement. Now she inked in the black letters of death. She had been engaged to a student. He had been tortured, convicted of treason, and executed.

What sort of treason? She spread her hands. Was precision so important? Did you question the details of a fatal illness? He had been a critic of National Socialism and therefore a Communist and therefore a traitor.

If she had been consorting with a traitor, then wasn't she a natural target for Gestapo suspicion? Not, she explained, with a father as influential as hers, especially as he was in charge of the import of luxury goods from occupied countries and could keep the Hamburg commanders of the SS, SD, Gestapo, and Kripo even, supplied with the little extravagances their stations required.

And here the conversation began to embrace *character*, close relative of *motive*. "Life in those circles is totally corrupt," she said. "That's why the Nazis are so frightened of ideals: they could spread."

"And you're an idealist?"

"What goes on around me disgusts me. That's why I help people like you." *Like you*. He was placed firmly outside the boundaries of idealism. He was a means to an end.

"But this house . . ."

"It belongs to my father although he doesn't use it. And it's a good headquarters, it enables me to do what I have to do. I have no compunction about using it. You see I know it was my father who reported Otto to the Gestapo. Otto used to come here . . ." She put a hand to her face, shielding her feelings from his prying eyes.

When she had recovered she said, "Would you like to see Otto?" And before he had time to answer, "Let's go into the living room."

It was a big room with fragile graces, but the past lingered thickly like smoke from a snuffed-out candle. She took a framed photograph of a baby girl from a bookshelf. Gisella Hessen, he guessed. She removed the backing and turned the photograph over. A girl who was indisputably Gisella Hessen, aged about eighteen, looked at him; proud, the look said, of the young man standing beside her, a young man with a crusader's face.

Miller compared the girl with the woman holding the photograph. The woman was the more interesting of the two. Bereavement had given her premature knowledge of the human condition. Whereas the girl's blonde hair moved in a breeze, the woman's was combed back with severity. "But you still don't trust me. I understand that." Her English was accented but fluent, her eyes gray.

"How old are you?"

"Twenty-one." A bereaved twenty-one.

She sat down in a Regency-striped easy chair; he sat opposite. She was wearing pearls at her throat and a powder blue dress. She had dancer's legs, he noticed as she crossed them. "Cigarette?" She offered him a slim gold case.

Shaking his head, he tapped his chest. "My lungs."

She scrutinized the cigarette between her fingers, replaced it in the case. The snap of the case closing sounded like a twig breaking. "And now you," she said.

When he had finished she said, "And you're still loyal to them after what they did to you?"

He told her about Vic and his parents.

"And the gold's coming to Hamburg?" she asked.

"I didn't say that."

"Why else would you be here?"

"Because this is where the U-boat dropped me. But it could have been Wilhelmshaven or Bremerhaven or Denmark or Norway even. I was given a list of agents to contact wherever I got washed up. You were one of them."

"I know you don't trust me, Herr Miller, but the gold is coming here, isn't it. It's commonsense. You've found me, you've made contact with London and you're in no hurry to leave."

"Okay," he said, "it's my guess that the gold's coming here."

"We're supposed to be on the same side. I presume you're not going to tell me where or when?"

"I could do with another cup of coffee," he said.

When she returned she was smoking a cigarette. She gave him the coffee and sat on the window seat, cigarette smoke turning into lace around her. "And what are you going to do now?"

He said, "Stay here."

She took it calmly enough. "Are you now?"

"Where else can I go?" He took the printouts from his blazer pocket. "I can't tell you where or when the gold is arriving because I don't know. But these might help if we had a way to decode them."

She glanced at the two strips torn off the teleprinter. "I think I can decode them. I have access to many of the secrets in Hamburg, including the codes the *Forschungsamt* uses."

It took her five minutes to decode the messages with a typewritten key. "The first one's all about you," she told him. "You're blown."

"I guessed as much."

"Becker has a source in London. High up."

"And the other?"

Gisella Hessen said, "The *Countess of Cork* is due to dock at 1800 hours on May 23, in five days time, at Bremer Quay."

"Far from here?

"In the heart of the docks in Hamburg."

"You know all the quays?"

"I should," she said. "I used to work for my father on the docks, helping him take care of his goodies when they were unloaded. I still do when it suits me."

"Is that all you do?"

"I've got another job," she said, but showed no inclination to elaborate. She blew out a thin jet of smoke, and when it reached him it seemed to be scented with her perfume. To his surprise he found himself imagining the perfume on her naked body. She was looking at him, and the look said, "I know what you're thinking," as though she was accustomed to arousing such images.

"Will my presence here embarrass you?"

"Embarrass?" She laughed. "Very English. It could get me shot. That would be extremely embarrassing." She came and sat opposite him in front of the cold, empty fireplace. "Tell me something, if *they* hadn't got your family would you be doing this?"

"After what *they* did to me? Not on your life."

"If they hadn't double-crossed you. If they had just come to you and said, 'Look, you can save us from defeat. Will you do it?'"

"I don't know," Miller said. "War has a strange effect on values. Before it's declared there are barriers all around us. Class, accent, position. . . . In my case the law. Then all of a sudden we're supposed to 'all pull together' until the war's over. Then the barriers are put up again. Why should I suddenly help the forces of law and order? After all, it was they who were the enemy until September 3 last year."

Her gray eyes regarded him steadily, but she didn't speak.

He finally said, "Yes, of course, I would have helped them. A weird commodity, patriotism. But I would have helped myself to as many ingots as I could lay my hands on."

"Once a thief always a thief?"

"That's right."

"Mmmmm. Our motives are very different, aren't they."

Idealist or not, she was betraying her country.

She must have read his thoughts again, she said, "You don't understand how it is with me, do you?"

"I understand about Otto."

"And how I feel about the people who've debased my country?"

"I don't think," he said carefully, "that we should get involved in a discussion about ethics."

"You're right." She tossed her half-finished cigarette into the hearth. "I despise thieves, you despise traitors. Let's just listen to the news," and she switched on the radio.

The voice of the newscaster rang with the glory of it all. The German Army was storming across France, and the days of the beleaguered British forces were numbered.

"Can they escape?" she asked him.

He shrugged. "God knows. We're always supposed to be at our best with our backs against the wall—or the sea. But I'll tell you this, if we muddle through this one we're going to need that gold. And not just to rearm. Can you imagine what the world would think if it got around that we'd cleaned out all the loot from the Bank of England—some confidence in final victory—and then we'd lost it? Who would support us then?"

"I'm afraid no one may support you. Britain may have appeased and fed Hitler's arrogance far too long."

"That was because no one in Britain wanted another war." Certainly, he thought, no one in Chadbourne Street, Stepney.

"All that gold," she said. "How will you move it?"

"I was in the business," he said enigmatically. "First of all, however, I need help. Clothes, money, papers."

"Yes, you certainly need clothes," she said, looking at his brown shoes and black socks. "Everything can be arranged."

"And a bed?"

"That too. You'll find the sheets very soft. Nothing but the best for my father and his daughter. He's got an SS colonel lined up for me, I believe. An Aryan dream in black and silver."

She put a camp bed in the attic near the transmitter, and she was right, the sheets were soft, much better than those at Wandsworth.

When he went to sleep he had no idea how the bullion could be moved. When he awoke in the morning he did. It was frightening.

MIDDAY.

He acknowledged the call sign Croesus and, alone in the attic and surrounded by maps, began to transmit in code: IF GERMANS CAN STEAL SHIP WE CAN STEAL TRAIN.

He paused. Then his hand gained courage as the plan unfolded in stuttering dots and dashes.

An assault force of nine or ten men, one of them a trained locomotive driver, to be parachuted into the Saxon Forest fifteen miles east of the center of Hamburg. As the Rheingold steamed through the forest on its way to Berlin, one man would capture the signal box and display a red signal. Train to be boarded and continue in the direction of Berlin. Goering not suspicious at this stage.

Then a diversion at Stendal to Hanover via Wolfsburg. From Hanover to Munster and through the industrialized Ruhr into Belgium. From the railway crossroads of Liege a long plunge to Lille in France and then a last dash to the Channel.

At some stage the Rheingold would, he hoped, pass into Allied-held territory.

Then Miller dealt with the two question marks looming over the plan: (1) Who would authorize the free passage of the Rheingold? Answer—Colonel Fritz Becker. At gunpoint. (2) How would the bullion be transported across the Channel. Here Miller permitted himself a smile as he transmitted the answer—he was proud of it. Why not drive the train straight onto one of the night ferries equipped with rails to enable passengers, in times of peace, to travel between London and Paris without leaving their carriages?

The point of embarkation was obvious, the port already adapted for the transfer of a train from land to sea. Dunkirk.

SHE GAVE HIM a black leather blouse-style jacket, white shirt, and gray trousers, more money, papers identifying him as Hans Knoll, a shipping clerk employed at the docks, and—a masterly touch—a medical certificate asserting that he was deaf and

143

dumb and unfit for military service. At least his accent would not betray him.

The next day, confidence bolstered, he crossed the Elbe by bridge and found Bremer Quay. There, on a railway siding beneath the giant cranes, was the Rheingold, showing off its splendors in the May sunshine. It was the most dazzling train he had ever seen, almost decadent with its gold, cream, and purple livery.

Thoughtfully he left the quay, pointing to his lips when a dockyard policeman approached him and showing him the medical certificate. He followed the dockyard railway to its junction with the S-bahn.

Then he went to the main railway station. In the concourse of the elephantine building with its vaulted, glass roof he acquired a timetable. The Berlin express, the *Fliegender Hamburger,* took just over two and a quarter hours to get to the capital; with a full head of steam the driver of the Rheingold could probably make it in two. As Goering would expect the train to bear east at Wittenberge, half way to Berlin, they would have about an hour before he realized anything was wrong.

London had told Miller that morning that preparations were under way to parachute nine men into the Saxon Forest—apparently there was some difficulty in finding a qualified engine driver—so the hour's grace would give them time to establish themselves on the Rheingold.

He bought a copy of *Hamburger Abendblatt* and

read it over a cup of foul black coffee and a sugared doughnut at a refreshment stand. Germans, many of them in field gray or air force blue, rushed past with that special blend of determination and desperation that travelers reserve for railway stations. The station smelled of fish.

According to the newspaper, published complete with map, the Germans had reached the Channel at Abbeville. He ran his finger along the coast to Dunkirk. Supposing the Germans had taken it by the time the Rheingold reached France? There were still two days to wait before the bullion reached Hamburg.

He turned his mind to more local problems. When to take Becker? Answer: As near to zero hour—not yet determined—as possible. Where? The obvious place was the apartment overlooking the lake.

Should I drive him to the Saxon Forest? Miller sipped his disgusting coffee. Better, surely, to get him on the train in Hamburg; then both he and I will be on board in case anything goes wrong in the forest.

Picking up his newspaper and his timetable, Miller walked across the concourse to the entrance, then made his way down Spitalerstrasse toward the center of the city. Outside the Rathaus, the magnificent old town hall, he was approached by a madman in a dark green suit.

The man pointed at the newspaper under Miller's arm and spoke excitedly.

145

Miller pointed to his lips.

The man brushed flecks of foam from his own lips and began to use his fingers in deaf and dumb language.

Miller hurried out of the station.

WHEN HE GOT back to the house in Blankenese he found Gisella Hessen cooking an evening meal.

Whisky in hand, he watched her moving methodically and gracefully around the gleaming kitchen. There was a smudge of flour on her cheek and her blonde hair had lost some of its discipline; these two touches made her face softer.

He wanted to reach out and touch her.

There was still a coolness between them, however, that stemmed, in part, from his secrecy. He had learned in the past that it is always preferable to limit the participation of accomplices.

And she *was* a traitor and therefore flawed.

She dropped sausages into a saucepan of boiling water. As they spat back at her she said, "Tonight we are going to be very German. Wurst and sauerkraut and white wine from the Moselle."

"Do you still love Germany?" He sat down at the kitchen table.

"Of course." She stepped back from the gas stove. "That's why I'm doing what I'm doing."

He shrugged. "You're an idealist, there aren't too many of those left."

"I want to play a part in making Germany decent again. Most Germans are decent people."

"A lot of Jews wouldn't agree with you."

146

"Foreigners think that the German failing is arrogance. In fact, it's the opposite; it's meekness. Give a German an order and he'll obey it. Look at any street crossing, the pedestrians wait there till the lights change as if they were wearing leg irons. And that's why Germany is in this hideous mess, because the people have blindly obeyed the Nazis."

"And the persecution of the Jews, that was blind obedience?"

"You know something? It's the British who are arrogant, not the Germans. Do you really think anti-Semitism doesn't exist in Britain? Do you really think that there aren't people in your little islands who wouldn't joyfully go in for a bit of Jew-baiting given the right circumstances? If Britain had been brought to its knees like a starving beggar the way Germany was after the last war, then the people might have idolized Oswald Mosley the way the Germans idolized Hitler. At least," she said, laying two places at the table, "I do have ideals."

"And I don't?"

It was her turn to shrug.

"Difficult to have ideals when you discover that your lords and masters were willing to sacrifice you on the scaffold."

"And that was just as brutal as anything the Nazis could have devised. Put a few people like the man who ordered your execution into power and, if Britain had been in the same plight as Germany was in the early thirties, you could have had the same situation as we've got now."

She put three long sausages and a mound of

sauerkraut on his plate and fetched a bottle of wine from the refrigerator. He poured the wine; it tasted like cold dry sunshine.

She sat opposite him. "But there *is* a difference between you and me. I believe in what I'm doing. You're doing it to save your family's necks."

"And mine," he said. "Literally." He speared a sausage with his fork and the taut skin popped.

"So you don't have any right to moralize."

He supposed she was right. But *traitor*—it was a difficult word to swallow. He drank some more sunshine.

"Have you guessed what I'm planning?" he asked.

She nodded. "Take over the train, I think. It's the only answer. I was asking myself where you'll take it to. It has to be somewhere that you can ship it back to Britain from, because you can't arrange a rendezvous with a transport plane when the panzers are capturing the Allied airfields by the hour. So it's got to be a Channel port, hasn't it. And you're also running out of options there. Dunkirk or Calais would be my guess. But you'll have to be quick."

"First," Miller said, pushing his plate away, "we have to wait for the gold to arrive."

"Don't worry, I'm not interested in the details. Were you a successful thief?"

"Not bad. I didn't get caught. Well, only once, but that was different."

"Why steal in the first place?"

"Because . . ." That day at Southend, Vic's con-

148

sumption that needed treatment in Switzerland—not that he had ever kidded himself that he hadn't enjoyed the life. ". . . it was better than work."

Those gray eyes searched him. "You don't look like a thief."

"What do thieves look like?"

"Dishonest," she said.

"And I look honest?"

"Not exactly."

"I know, like a stockbroker. With my pinstripe on, that is."

"Not quite. You don't have that glow of good living. You look as if you ran to work every day."

"More often than not," Miller said, "I ran away from my work."

"You seem to have had a good education."

"At the most famous university of all, the university of life."

"You sound like an old roué. How old are you?"

"Twenty-three," he told her. "No chicken. There are nineteen-year-olds leading men into battle at this moment."

"What did you steal?" she asked.

"Gold mostly. You can be sure of gold. People hoard it. Not like diamonds. They put those in the bank and wear paste."

"Where did you find it, on old ladies' dressing tables?"

"In safes," he said. "To be precise, that's my profession. Safecracker. I suppose your safe is behind the painting of one of your ancestors in the living room? Sad." He clicked his tongue. "I could blow it with a packet of sherbert. And you Germans are supposed to be efficient."

"So you've looked at it?"

"Of course. Just as a plumber would look at a sink. Were you going to marry Otto?"

"Perhaps one day. We didn't talk about it. You wouldn't have liked him," she added.

"Because he was an idealist?"

"He was a preacher, really. Attacking persecution and corruption. He must have been making some headway or the Gestapo wouldn't have bothered to shoot him."

A clock chimed in the living room. Eight o'clock. London was due to call.

"Don't worry," she called after him, "I won't listen at the keyhole."

Everyone was on standby they said. Could he be more specific about timing?

The car pulled up at the end of the drive just as he finished transmitting. He looked through the attic window. The light was fading but he could see that it was a black Mercedes. Although the two men alighting from it wore plain clothes, he knew they were police of a sort, just as he had known when two men climbed from a black Wolsey outside his parents' terrace house, dispatching him through the cabbages and runner beans in the back garden and over the wall into the alley behind.

One was even wearing a brown leather overcoat, like Becker's. In May, he thought as he cut transmission and stowed the radio in a cheap suitcase he had asked Gisella to buy for just such an occasion. Policemen were obsessed by overcoats. In this case, he guessed, *Forschungsamt* agents recruited from the Kripo.

How had they traced him? Easy. Wessel had been interrogated and admitted that he had talked to Miller about the bullion. Bremer Quay had immediately been put under surveillance. And I walked right in front of their binoculars. Stupid. Then they trailed me to Blankenese, waited to get a fix on the radio, and picked up the last transmission.

But, thank God, no details of Operation Croesus had been given.

So why knock me off before I make contact again with London? Even easier. They don't want me to escape again and they know bloody well that with electrodes on his balls any hero will talk.

Gisella was waiting at the foot of the stairs.

"Police," he said. "We've got to go."

"We?"

"Of course. You've been harboring a spy. Even daddy can't help you now." He grabbed her arm as the first thunderous knock sounded on the front door. Had a policeman ever been known to ring a bell? "How the hell do we get out?"

She said, "I stay. Don't worry. Every time you go out I clean up every trace of you."

"But they saw me walk up the drive."

"Did they? Perhaps, perhaps not. In any case, you were only making your way to the tunnel."

"Tunnel? What tunnel?"

Another volley of knocks. They'd kick the door in next.

She pushed him toward the kitchen door. "It's an underground slipway really. It was dug years ago by the original owners when they found they couldn't build on the waterfront." She opened the kitchen door. "Over there by the summerhouse. That door to the right. Hurry."

"Where shall I meet you?"

"Tonight," she said. "In the Black Cat Club. At midnight."

"Where the hell's that?"

"It's where I work. And it's in the Reeperbahn."

He ran across the lawn in the dusk, gently closing the door leading to the slipway as the man in the leather overcoat rounded the house. It wasn't until he was standing on the soft river mud looking at the urgent fingers of light cast on the water by passing ships that the full import of her words occurred to him.

THE BLACK CAT wasn't, in fact, in the Reeperbahn, it was in an adjoining street, discreetly out of sight of the beckoning whores in the windows and the other ostentatious delights of Hamburg's red light district.

The front of the club was surmounted by a large black cat twitching neon whiskers. The rear entrance was less impressive—a battered, half-open door surrounded by dustbins full of cats, not all of which were black.

Miller pushed open the door. The doorkeeper, a bulky man with a badly stitched harelip, said, "Herr Knoll?" Miller nodded. "Follow me." Over his shoulder he said, "You're not really dressed for the Cat. That's why Fräulein Remer has put you in the back, out of sight."

"Fräulein who?"

"Your friend. A little more than a friend?" The doorkeeper looked back and smiled grotesquely.

"Sorry," Miller said. "I didn't quite catch what you said."

"You have a slight accent, Herr Knoll. You are from the south?"

"Trier," Miller told him. "The oldest city in Germany."

The club was in darkness except for a small round dance floor, designed for close contact, on which a girl who was wearing a shimmering, low-cut silver dress and holding a microphone, was singing in a husky voice.

Fräulein Remer—Gisella Hessen.

The doorkeeper led Miller to a table partially hidden by a pillar and then retired quickly, like a flushed-out gatecrasher. A waiter placed a half bottle of Krug on the table in an ice bucket. "On the house," he said.

He poured himself a glass of champagne and listened to Gisella singing. Her voice was competent enough, but if there was any copyright on style, then Marlene Dietrich had a case. She switched from love songs to parodies of national anthems. "God save our Gracious Führer . . ." The audience laughed uproariously and stamped on the floor—a few jackboots there by the sound of it. Victory was in the air and no one wanted to minimize it.

She left the floor to wild applause. She returned once, sang a number about the Germans marching down the Champs Élysées, and then, as the lights came on, joined a party of tipsy revelers sitting at a table beside the dance floor. The men were in civilian clothes, but they had a military swagger about them. She leaned against the chair of a heavy-shouldered man with cropped hair, and he touched her breast.

Well, long live idealism. What do you think about it, Otto, old chap, wherever you may be? From behind the pillar he scanned the other customers. Mostly top Nazis and the well-breeched parasites of war, he guessed. The massed personification of everything Gisella claimed to despise.

She left the crop-haired customer and moved to another table. There she kissed a thin-faced, wolfish looking man, with glossy hair and a slight resemblance to Goebbels, and sat beside him. He whispered in her ear, and, smiling, she nodded. At last, she came to Miller's table.

"You're very popular," he said in English, for no one was in earshot.

Her hair was combed pageboy style and the theatrical makeup was heavily applied; she looked a bit like Carole Lombard.

"Does that surprise you?" Sitting on the edge of his table, she said, "Give me a drink." She took the glass of champagne from his hand. "I know what you're thinking," she said, sipping from it.

"Oh."

"You think I'm a whore."

"There's a saying, I believe, to the effect that he who excuses himself accuses himself."

"I'm not excusing anything, I am one."

"Congratulations. Much easier to get on with than an idealist."

"I'm that too."

"The conflict must be agonizing."

"They're not . . ."

"I think the word's irreconcilable. I don't know what it is in German."

She lit a cigarette. "You sound very holy. For a thief, that is."

"I just wondered," he said, "how you find room in that dress for ideals."

The lights dimmed again, and two dancers ran onto the dance floor. They wore skimpy costumes, and, despite their breasts, Miller could see from where he was that they were transvestites.

"You don't understand," she said. She looked a little drunk.

He shrugged. "The only thing that matters is what we decide to do next."

"Not so long ago you didn't want to discuss your plans with me."

Which was true. The difference now was that he was on the run without a headquarters, and he had to trust her.

He said, "I've got to hide somewhere."

The two dancers had now flung off their spangled brassieres and their small, hard breasts bobbed energetically as they danced to the music of a piano-accordian.

"I'm afraid I'm a little tight," she said, staring into the champagne glass.

"Do you know of a place?"

She ignored his question and glanced back at the last table she had left. "I get drunk, you know, because it's the only way I can stomach these pigs. Maybe you can't understand, maybe everything is black and white to you, Herr Miller, but has it occurred to you that to get the information your people find so fascinating I have to be nice to these people? The man who was squeezing my breast is a colonel in the SS. The one with a face like a can opener is the head of the Gestapo in Hamburg."

The two transvestites had now stripped down to G-strings that left little doubt about their sex.

"Sophisticated isn't it," she said.

"It's getting late," he said. "Do you have a place?"

"How would a yacht suit you?"

"It would," he said, watching her warily.

"Good. A friend has lent me one, and it's moored

on the docks. Within sight of your train. I would join you except that I have other engagements."

"How will I find it?" he asked.

"I've drawn you a map." She took a used envelope from her rhinestone evening bag and handed it to him. "I've got you a car as well. A Volkswagen 60. It resembles a bug."

"Another friend?"

She handed him the keys. "The same one. He was a friend of Otto's as well."

As he took the keys their hands touched, and it felt as though a spark had passed between them. He asked, "How can I get into the docks at this time of night?"

"You still have your pass."

"Deaf and dumb mutes don't usually drive cars up to luxury yachts."

"It's not a luxury yacht." She lit a cigarette and blew a jet of smoke into the gray pall hanging over the tables. She seemed to have lost concentration. "Not luxurious at all," she said. "But comfortable." He knew that she had slept there with Otto. She looked at him, eyes not quite focused. "You have your pass, and you have this letter." She delved into her bag again.

The letter stated that Herr Hans Knoll was on official business, was staying on the motor yacht *Lorelei*, and was to be given every assistance. It was signed "Josef Hessen."

"Your father?"

"The open sesame. Forged, of course. By me."

He thanked her.

"And now I'll get back to my friends. Which do you suggest, SS or Gestapo?"

"Whichever's the most useful," he said.

"Well spoken." She stood up. "I'll come to the *Lorelei* at eight in the morning. *Guten nacht,* Herr Knoll."

"*Guten nacht.*"

He watched her make her way through the cigarette smoke to the table where the SS colonel was sitting. She resumed her position. The colonel put his hand back on her breast. The two dancers removed their G-strings. The lights went out. Miller left.

5

May 22

BEARD WAGGING AGITATEDLY, the Governor of
the Bank of England said, "Is there the
slightest chance that this man Miller can
pull this off?"

He looked at Logan, but it was Munnion who
answered him. "He's our only hope, sir."

"It's come to a pretty pass," the Governor said,
"when the fate of the Bank's gold rests in the hands
of a thief."

No one smiled. Soft rain touched the windows of
the Court Room.

Weaver lit a cigarette, making a performance of
tapping it on his cigarette case. Addressing Munnion, he said, "I must say it sticks in my craw a bit."

What sticks in your craw, Munnion thought, is
the bollocking you got when the head of Naval
Intelligence returned from New York where he had
been superintending the American end of the
aborted bullion transfer. He said, "Set a thief to
catch a thief."

"What's to stop Miller from doing a deal with Goering?"

Logan, wearing tweeds and looking as if he'd just returned from an unsuccessful grouse shoot, said, "Quite a lot."

Munnion looked at Logan with distaste. He was not proud of the part he'd played in this.

Grover spoke slowly, big shoulders hunched over the long table. "There's something else that should be concerning us, gentlemen." He took off his glasses and wiped the lenses with his tie. "How the hell did Goering get his information? How did he know the bullion was on the *Alaska*? How did he know the disposition of the escort ships? How did he get the timing so perfect?"

An aircraft droned overhead.

Logan spoke. "We must consider the possibility that the *Forschungsamt* has a very high-level source of information."

The Governor pulled at his beard. "I should have thought you would have begun to consider that a long time ago."

Logan didn't reply. Since Goering's coup every possible source was being investigated.

Weaver, combing at his smooth brown hair with his fingers, said, "At least the *Countess of Cork* has been sighted by naval reconnaissance aircraft and her position does verify what Miller has told us. She's been badly hit, and she's making slow but steady progress toward Hamburg. She should berth at about 1800 hours tomorrow."

"And is that all you can do?" the Governor demanded. "Watch her sail serenely into an enemy port with 500 million pounds worth of our gold on board?"

Weaver said, "We can't sink her and send your gold to the bottom of the sea, can we?" The Governor, his tone indicated, was displaying the sort of naivety that one expected outside the Senior Service. "Would it be possible to get a neutral power to intervene? America?" looking at Grover.

Grover said flatly, "No. In the first place, no one's supposed to know that the gold's destination is the United States. In the second, Roosevelt wouldn't get involved in anything like that before the presidential election."

Logan said, "I'm afraid we have to accept that, as Munnion says, Miller is our only hope. The nine *specialists* will be dropped tonight in the Saxon Forest. God willing it will be a dark night."

Logan could never resist recruiting the Deity.

GOERING COULD NO longer fly to Carinhall. With the British cut off, the French reeling, and the Belgians about to throw in their hand, it would have looked very odd if the commander in chief of the Luftwaffe had once again nipped off home.

So he had requisitioned a farmhouse three miles from his battle headquarters in the Eifel to use as his headquarters for Operation Argo.

As the *Countess of Cork* approached the mouth of the Elbe, he called Becker in his apartment in

Hamburg. Since Becker had arrived there, nothing but bad news had emanated from him. The Fifth Branch and *Forschungsamt* agent Miller was now exposed as a double agent. He was on the loose with information about the bullion snatch, and he knew that the *Forschungsamt* had a top-level source of information in London.

Surely, he thought as he waited for Becker to come to the phone, there couldn't be any more bad news.

Becker said, "Bad news, I'm afraid, Herr Feldmarschall. The *Countess of Cork* has started to take on water again."

Goering flicked a speck of dust from the sky-blue uniform he had designed himself. He attempted a sort of desperate joviality. "Are you trying to tell me, Becker, that she's sinking?"

Becker said he was.

"Will she make it to Hamburg?"

"We don't know, Herr Feldmarschall."

Always *we* when there was trouble. How he wished he was in Hamburg. If the advance through France and the Low Countries hadn't been so devastatingly successful, he could have taken time off to personally supervise Argo.

Could the gold end up on the sea bed? Surely such swashbuckling initiative couldn't be rewarded so miserably. Fortune favors the brave.

He said to Becker, "See to it, Fritz, that the *Countess of Cork* remains afloat."

He replaced the receiver.

162

A minute later it rang again. He picked it up. It was Hitler calling him back to the war.

HE SAID, "YOU'RE two different women."

She had arrived at 8:10 wearing light blue slacks and a navy sweater; she wore no makeup and, although her hair had once again been combed back severely, she looked vulnerable, like a woman just waking. The Black Cat was a bad dream: the day ahead hadn't yet assembled.

She said, "This woman is going to prepare breakfast," and, carrying a basket of food, went into the galley.

The smell of coffee reached him in the cabin. It was an intimate smell, as if they had spent the night together. Who had she spent the night with, SS or Gestapo?

He thrust aside the question and, standing on the steps leading to the deck, stared through a pair of binoculars. It was going to be another dreamy May day; beneath a pale blue sky, among the masts and funnels, he could just see the Rheingold. Two head-end coaches for the bullion, three passenger coaches for the escort, an armored car for protection. Well, they would need that.

He consulted his watch. The *Countess of Cork* was due in approximately thirty-four hours. And he still hadn't decided how to take Becker.

She came into the cabin bearing a tray. Coffee, slices of cheese and wurst, brown bread, and two apples. A healthy meal, incongruous when only seven or so hours ago they had been drinking champagne, enveloped in smoke.

She poured coffee and sat down. "So," she said, "Dr. Jekyll and Mrs. Hyde. Which do you prefer?"

"Dr. Jekyll," he said.

"Then you must only see me during the day. Before I take my potion."

"Where did you learn your English? It's better than mine."

"At the university. I learned French as well." She ate hungrily. "I listened to the news on the way." Through the porthole next to the Volkswagen 60 he could see a silver Mercedes picking up the sun's rays. "All bad. They claim the French Ninth Army has been annihilated."

"They being the Nazis, not the Germans."

"That's the way I prefer to think about it," she said. "More coffee?"

A ship hooted downriver somewhere; the yacht moved gently in the dock water.

He told her about the plan to capture the Rheingold.

"It sounds crazy." She bit into an apple. "Wonderfully crazy. Why are you telling me?"

"Because I need your help. And because . . ."

"Don't spoil it. You're telling me because I'm useful. Leave it like that. I like honesty, it's as scarce as good coffee." She lit a cigarette. "Did you believe me last night, about mixing with those pigs for a purpose?"

He nodded. "But that doesn't mean I like it."

"There's no reason why you should care," she said. "Absolutely none." She leaned back into a blade of sunshine and shaded her eyes. "Why do you?"

"I don't know," he said.

"Do me a favor," she said. "Go to my car and bring the rest of the provisions. If you don't show yourself occasionally it will begin to look suspicious."

When he returned she was naked.

Without speaking he took off his clothes. She was lying on a bunk and he saw how firm her breasts were, how big the nipples were, how thick was the furrowed, blonde hair between her legs.

He remembered other girls, not many, two or three, long ago, before he had looked at death, but he had never experienced a desire like this before.

She parted her legs and he lowered himself onto her, into her.

It was quick, hard, deep, and that, he sensed, was how she wanted it. A joining and a release without tenderness.

He didn't withdraw for a long time; instead they lay there being together.

The throb of a ship's engine reached them through the hull of the yacht.

"I thought I could never love anyone else," she said.

"You wouldn't have done," he told her, "if he had lived. But that doesn't take anything away from what we have. No one is meant to live in the past."

"I know, but when you've nearly drowned, its difficult to surface again. At least I thought it was," stroking his face.

"I know I shouldn't ask what I'm going to ask," he said. "That I don't have the right."

"Don't worry, never again, there are other ways of getting information."

Then he withdrew from her body and they made love with tenderness. Later, as the sun rose, throwing its blade on the floor of the cabin, they returned to what had brought them together.

"WE NOW HAVE thirty-three hours," he said.

He spread a map of Hamburg and its environs on the table in front of them. They had dressed but, sitting close together, shared each other's warmth.

He prodded Bremer Quay with a pencil. "As we know, that's where the loot will be transferred from the *Countess of Cork* to the Rheingold." He drew a line to the Saxon Forest. "That's where the assault force will be dropped, about fifteen miles away. Somehow I've got to get Becker onto that train here," prodding Bremer Quay again.

"Couldn't you drive him to the Saxon Forest and join the assault force there?"

Miller shook his head emphatically. "I've got to be in charge of this train all the way from Bremer Quay to Dunkirk. And being in charge means being in charge of Becker. If anything went wrong on this first stretch, the whole operation would be blown."

She said, "You can't show yourself by daylight. Every policeman in Hamburg will be looking for you. Becker will have seen to that. Nothing to do with the *Forschungsamt*, of course. Nothing to do with gold. You will be described as a dangerous fugitive to be shot on sight." She picked up the pencil and began to doodle on a pad of paper. "Describe Becker to me."

"Tall, stiff, very military, iron-gray hair."

"A deceptive appearance?"

Surprised, he said, "How do you know that?"

"I've met him."

"At the club?"

She nodded, moving fractionally away from him. "He's a sad man."

"Sad? I hadn't thought of it that way. Courage isn't his trump card if that's what you mean."

"Sad," she said. "He lost his pride a long time ago."

"And you help to restore it?"

She said, "That's how it is with a lot of men. All they want is their pride handed back to them for a short while."

He stood up and stared through a porthole, a slick of oil lit with dazzling colors floated on the smooth water of the dock.

"We need to get Becker onto that train," he said.

"It shouldn't be difficult."

He looked at her, knowing very well what she meant. She said, "We've got to be practical. I'll phone him to meet me at the club. I'll tell him my apartment in Hamburg is being redecorated, but I have the use of a yacht. Is that what you want?"

Miller nodded.

Gisella stood up, and walking over to the port-hole, looked out at the bright reflections on the water.

FOURTEEN HOURS LATER, an Armstrong Whitworth Whitley twin-engine bomber circled the Saxon Forest in pitch darkness. Whitley had been the first aircraft to bomb Germany—on March 19 that year—since the declaration of war; but tonight, instead of bombs, this one carried nine men.

When the German airborne troops played havoc behind the Allied lines in the Low Countries, Winston Churchill immediately ordered the formation of a parachute force. The first volunteers reported to Ringway Airport, Manchester.

They were to be called paratroopers—the word was already spreading among the volunteers—and these men in the Armstrong Whitworth Whitley were the first of them. They had received at the most a week's training, most of them less, one none at all.

They had been chosen because none of them had so far refused to jump from the platform at the tail of the bomber, pulling a ripcord and blossoming hopefully into the slipstream, and because each had possessed special qualifications in civilian life.

One had been a bouncer, one a getaway driver, one a marksman, one a thief, one a train driver. All of them had been given code names except the train driver, because he somehow didn't seem to merit one.

"Now," shouted the dispatcher. A parachute spread in the slipstream and a body disappeared into the darkness. "Now." And another. "Now."

"Any idea what that was all about?" the pilot asked, turning his head to address the dispatcher after the last of the nine had disappeared.

"Fuck knows," replied the dispatcher. "Better them than me though, poor sods."

The bomber banked and headed back toward England.

SHE BROUGHT BECKER back to him at midnight.

He came down the steps first, descending slowly and awkwardly.

When he reached the last rung Miller emerged from the galley, gun in hand.

"You!" For a moment Becker straightened up, then his shoulders sagged. He looked up the steps. "I thought . . ."

Miller heard Gisella's footfall on the deck.

It seemed ironic that Becker had come to the yacht to have his pride restored for a little while.

"I'm sorry," he said as he began to bind Becker's wrists with rope. And he was.

6

May 23 (1)

*T*HE FIRST SHOCK of the day came at dawn: the Rheingold had disappeared.

Of course, it was to be expected. The *Forschungsamt* knew Miller had located it so they had changed their plans.

He took the Luger from his belt and pointed it at Becker, who was lying on one of the four bunks. "Where is it?"

Becker turned his head and looked down the barrel of the gun. "I don't know. We were going to move it, that's all I can tell you. The docks people were looking for a suitable berth when I was . . ."

"Led astray? Come on Becker," Miller said in German, "you can do better than that."

A shiver ran through Becker's body. "If I knew I'd tell you. You know that." That's what I've become, his voice said.

"Then we shall have to get you to find out."

Gisella sat up in a bunk on the other side of the

cabin where she had slept alone. She was wearing the same blue sweater and her face was cleansed of makeup, but the early morning intimacy of the previous day had evaporated.

She said to Miller, "Don't worry, I can find out. I know the director of the docks."

"Is there anyone you don't know?"

"There's something else *you* should know." She swung bare legs out of the bunk. "I'm coming with you on the train."

He stared at her. The possibility had never occurred to him. "It's out of the question. No . . ."

"Place for a woman? Very British. Has it occurred to you that if I stay here I'll be picked up? I was seen leaving the club with Becker. Becker has disappeared. Sooner or later they'll realize what's happened, then," she spread her hands, "I'd rather stop a bullet than die slowly while they question me."

"All right," he said, "you'll be on the train." He realized that the prospect pleased him. "Make some coffee, then contact the director. What will you tell him?"

She pulled on her slacks. "I've got a friend whose kids are train mad. There's no secret that the Rheingold is here. I'll just tell him they want to see the pride of the German Railways before it leaves town. There shouldn't be any difficulties."

Miller tucked the gun back in his belt and said to Becker, "Later you will have to make contact with the *Forschungsamt* at your apartment. Give the

171

impression that you're still in charge, that you'll be on the dock when the Rheingold takes off."

Becker said, "I can't do anything until I've washed and shaved and drunk some coffee and smoked my first cigarette. Untie the rope, please." He held out his hands; it was almost an order.

While Gisella was making coffee and Becker was shaving, Miller switched on the radio. Boulogne had fallen. He consulted a map of France. The strip of coast in Allied hands was getting shorter by the hour and Dunkirk was in the middle of it.

Where was the assault team? Without them it didn't really matter where the Rheingold was: there wouldn't be an Operation Croesus.

Twice during the night, using a very high frequency that was unlikely to be monitored and a few key code words such as freight for bullion, Miller had tried to make radio contact, but there had been no response.

Now he tried again.

A voice answered in passable German. Everything had gone according to plan. One casualty, a broken leg. What time would the freight reach Friedrichsruh, focal point for the attack?

"Time unknown. Will call you back at 1600 hours."

When the voice began to swear in uncoded German, Miller cut the transmission.

They drank their coffee in silence. The shave had done wonders for Becker. He looked positively Prussian again and the wrinkles had fallen out of his pearl gray suit; that was good cloth for you.

Gisella was away for half an hour.

When she returned she told them that the Rheingold was ten kilometers downriver at Finkenwerder.

"And that's not all," she said. "The *Countess of Cork* has arrived."

Which meant that the Rheingold could be loaded with the bullion within an hour. Could leave Hamburg for Berlin before he had managed to reestablish contact with the assault force.

It was Miller's turn to swear.

HITLER SAID, "I'M considering committing only a few panzers to the pursuit of the British. I think the main thrust should be aimed at Paris."

"Masterly," Goering said. He had just returned from the farmhouse where he had telephoned the apartment in Hamburg. Becker wasn't available, but the *Countess of Cork* had apparently made it and prematurely at that—a repair crew based at Cuxhaven had boarded her and fixed both the leak and the damaged engine. "Masterly," he said again.

Hitler stared at him quizzically.

Goering, suddenly aware that he was overreacting to Hitler's tentative observation, added, "Don't worry, mein Führer, the Luftwaffe will finish off the Tommies."

Hitler nodded, apparently satisfied.

MILLER GOT BECKER to make his first call, under duress, ten minutes after Gisella had returned to the yacht.

Together they sauntered down Bremer Quay in the sunshine—summer had come early and intended to stay forever—Miller fractionally behind Becker, one hand inside his black leather jacket on the butt of the Luger.

The docks policeman, in a blue uniform at the end of the quay, looked at them without surprise; obviously Gisella and her father had many visitors.

"Show him your identification," Miller whispered to Becker, "just in case. You must have some pretty impressive signatures. Goering for instance?"

Becker showed the guard a pass and the man snapped to attention. Goering!

Miller told Becker to walk to the telephone kiosk a hundred yards away. "Now phone the station-master at the Hauptbahnhof and tell him you want the Rheingold to leave at six o'clock this evening—1800 hours, the time the *Countess of Cork* was originally intended to arrive."

That would be perfect timing. He would radio the assault force at 1600 hours and that would give them over two hours to set up their ambush.

Becker got through to the Hauptbahnhof, the main railway station. Standing next to him, Miller adjusted the receiver in Becker's hand so that he could hear the replies; the indifferent voices changed abruptly when Becker identified himself.

He got through to the stationmaster.

"Eighteen hundred hours? Of course, nothing simpler. The lines will be cleared straight through to Berlin."

174

Becker hung up. "Satisfied?"

Miller smiled at him. "As the man who jumped off the Empire State Building said as he passed the twentieth floor, so far so good." He then told Becker to call his apartment and reassert his authority.

RED SCARF KNOTTED rakishly, goggles high on his forehead, Hans Vogel stood on the footplate of 18 547 waiting to depart. If only Margarethe could see him now.

He might even get a medal. He who had started life lighting fires in the grates of locomotives and polishing their brass fittings. He grinned exultantly, one finger sawing at the cleft in his swarthy chin where smut tended to collect.

Smoke rose steadily from the chimney into the evening sky above the dock at Finkenwerder. The black body of 18 547 glistened, bronze eagle and swastika catching the rays of the evening sun. Every piston and valve was oiled, cups on the axles and connecting rods filled with oil. The tender was loaded with 32,000 liters of water and 8,500 kilos of the finest coal—no slate to block the tubes. The firebox was glowing fiercely, and inside the massive boiler, the engine's lungs, the steam that would drive the pistons that would turn the wheels was fermenting.

"Uncontrolled steam occupies 1,325 times as much space as the water that made it. Control the steam and you have thrust." How many times had Apprentice Vogel been told that? With James Watt thrown in, of course.

Vogel glanced indulgently at the squat figure of the fireman, face black with a fresh application of coal dust. What a lucky fellow the fireman had been to throw his lot in with him all those years ago.

"Everything all right?" he asked.

"Isn't it always?"

It always was. Water level and steam pressure gauges correct. Allow the water level in the boiler to drop below the top plate in the firebox or the steam pressure to rise above the red danger line, and you could have a disaster.

Both driver and fireman had awesome responsibilities. The difference between the two of them, Vogel reflected, was that the driver had flair as well. Which was why so many kids still wanted to become train drivers, those that didn't want to become Stuka pilots, that is.

He leaned out of the cab and peered down the quay. A group of dockers stood chatting and smoking, watched by bored steel-helmeted soldiers in field gray. No sign of Colonel Fritz Becker who was in charge of the operation—actually I'm in charge, Vogel thought, but there was another five minutes till six o'clock.

He consulted his schedule. It listed all the stations, curves, signals, gradients, level crossings, and railroad works between the docks and Berlin. He had made the trip twice to get it right and learned the schedule by heart; the only minor complication had been the sudden switch from one dock to another.

The line had been cleared for them, permission

given to exceed the speed limit of 120 kilometers an hour. According to the schedule they would reach Berlin in two hours.

Two minutes to go. Where the hell was Becker? Vogel wanted to keep to the schedule to the last second. If he displeased Goering the Feldmarschall might not listen to his request to allow Margarethe to live in Berlin.

A bug-shaped car entered the gates and pulled up beside the first coach behind the two head-end carriages attached to the tender. According to the latest rumor, the two head-enders had been loaded with parts of a secret weapon captured at sea from the British. Certainly the cargo from the *Countess of Cork* had been transferred in great secrecy.

But surely Colonel Fritz Becker, even if he was only a civilian retaining his military rank, wouldn't travel in a car like that.

Becker climbed out first. Behind him a man in a black leather jacket. Behind him a blonde girl, a looker. Vogel frowned: he hadn't been told anything about two extra passengers. Perhaps the man was the chauffeur, if such a car merited one. No, he was following Becker into the coach, keeping very close behind him, and the girl was following the two of them.

The stationmaster from Hamburg Hauptbahnhof, transferred to the docks for the evening, strode up to the coach, spoke in a manner that was plainly deferential, saluted, waved a flag, and flashed a green lamp at Vogel.

Vogel shrugged; stationmasters were stationmasters. He pulled the whistle cord, released the brakes, and, very gently so that the wheels didn't slip, eased open the regulator. With a great belch of smoke and a hiss of steam the Rheingold moved slowly forward.

APART FROM MILLER, Becker, and Gisella there was only one other passenger in the first-class coach. He was sitting in one of four red and gold armchairs grouped around a walnut-veneer table.

Miller prodded Becker in the back with the Luger. "Who's that?"

"Allow me to introduce you to Max von Ritter," Becker said.

7

May 23

THE MAN, WHO years later was to be brack-
eted with Miller as one of the two giants in
the bullion affair, was lean and hard with
slanting lines to his face. His hair was cropped, his
eyes greenish; he wore seaman's clothes, blue reefer
jacket, and black roll-top sweater, which contrasted
oddly with the carved ivory cigarette holder in his
fingers. A man of contradictions. A knight in tar-
nished armor. But dangerous just the same.

Von Ritter said, "And who the hell might you
be?"

"My name's Miller." He drew the Luger from
inside his jacket. "Please don't get up." And to
Becker, "Sit down. Over there. Beside him."

He surveyed the length of the coach. There were
eight more tables, four on either side, two chairs to
each of them—two extra had been pulled up to
Ritter's table. On each table stood a lamp. The
windows were framed with red and gold curtains

and the maroon carpet was patterned with cream diamonds that gave it a three-dimensional effect.

Gun in hand, he sat opposite Ritter and Becker.

Ritter turned to Becker. "Well, Herr Oberst, how did you get yourself into this mess?"

Antagonism there; it could prove to be an ally. It was probably connected with seniority. Ritter had been in charge of the original piracy at sea, Becker had been directing operations from Germany. Who was in charge now? Miller hoped Becker was.

Becker said, "The same way you have."

No rank, Miller noted. So presumably Becker was senior. Then why was Ritter so disrespectful? It was very un-Germanic.

Ships, canals, and docks sped past the curtained window. If there was no hitch, the assault force, which, as arranged, had made radio contact at 1600 hours, would make its move in ten minutes.

Ritter said to Gisella, "And who might you be?"

"A girl," Gisella said, standing beside Miller.

"I had noticed. May I ask you, or you," turning to Miller, "how you imagine you can pull this off? I am interested in impossibilities. I have always made them my specialty." His English was better than Becker's.

Miller said, "Where are the rest of the guards?"

"That's for you to find out. I'm surprised Becker hasn't told you already."

"In the armored car at the rear of the train," Gisella said. "And the coach next to it; I saw them as we drew up in the car. Including the bullion cars"—Ritter raised one slanting eyebrow—"and
180

the armored car, there are six coaches. One of them a diner."

"So we can all have a meal on the way," Ritter said. "Cozy." He pointed his cigarette holder at the Luger. "Are you a good shot? It doesn't look like one of the tools of your trade." He had switched to English now.

Miller tightened his grip on the butt. He said to Gisella, "Go and lock the door connecting us to the next passenger coach."

As she stood up, Ritter, smiling, said, "Supposing I tried to grab that cannon of yours. Would you shoot me?"

"Don't do anything stupid," Becker said to Ritter.

"Through the heart," Miller said.

"With the safety catch still on?"

As Miller glanced down Ritter made a grab for the Luger.

Miller pulled the trigger.

Ritter bounced back with the explosion.

Studying what was left of the cigarette in the holder, he said, "Jesus Christ, a marksman. Where did you learn that trick, in a music hall?"

Miller said, "Can't you read? This carriage is a nonsmoker."

Not bad, he thought, for his first shot fired in anger.

AN EVENING MIST had settled and the red signal glowed brightly in it.

Vogel saw it and couldn't believe it.

They'd promised him a through run. And there hadn't even been a distant signal to warn him about the red.

He grasped the brake handle and pulled it in an anticlockwise direction toward the fourth position, normal slowing and stopping.

The red light came at him like a tracer shell.

Shit!

Frantically he pulled the handle to three o'clock, the big-hole position where the air was released swiftly from the train pipe running the length of the train, forcing it into the brake cylinders. You only big-holed in an emergency because it could damage the wheels and other parts of the train.

The engine shuddered, sparks flew from the wheels into the dusk. The iron horse shrieked in agony.

But it stopped just the same, a hundred meters on the safe side of the red signal.

"Thank God," Vogel shouted to the fireman. "With a bit of luck there's no damage done."

Then the shooting started and Vogel knew that Goering would never make him his personal driver.

"TAKE THE ARMORED car first," the North Country leader of the assault force said. "Blast them before they go for their guns."

Three paratroopers, all wearing camouflaged combat dress and the new steel helmets adapted from motorcycle crash helmets and designed for aerial assaults, covered the armored car.

"They'll open up the turret to see why they've stopped," he said.

And they did.

Not wanting to cause visible damage to the armored car, they didn't lob grenades into the gaping mouth of its hatch just behind the antiaircraft gun. Instead they shot the first German soldier when his head and shoulders were clear of the opening. A paratrooper code-named the Marksman, armed with a Thompson submachine gun, climbed on top of the armored car. He shouted in German, "Come out, hands above your heads, or you'll get a grenade down your throats."

He was young and graceful with inky black hair just showing beneath his helmet, and, in a dispassionate sort of way, he found satisfaction in killing.

He waited. The reply came after a couple of seconds—a hail of bullets. Because the Germans couldn't sight him, their bullets passed harmlessly through the turret hatch, a couple hitting the rim and whining into the rising mist.

The Marksman shrugged. When the burst of shooting had spent itself, he moved closer to the hatch and keeping so low that he could not be seen by those within, knelt, rested his tommy gun on the edge and, rotating it methodically, fired a long burst into the bowels of the armored car. The noise of bullets hitting metal mingled with the screams of men.

The Marksman shouted down, "Okay, out you come."

One by one the Wehrmacht soldiers, three of them bleeding, climbed out of the turret.

The North Countryman, a big man with a scarred face who had an air of muscular authority about him, told the Marksman to go into the armored car and check it out.

Cautiously, he climbed through the opening. There was a single shot. "No trouble," he shouted from inside. "Not anymore." And when he re-emerged, "Three dead down there."

At that moment the shooting started from the passenger coach next to the armored car. Three rifle shots. The four paratroopers covering the train on either side shrank back into the bushes. Mist swirled in the light from the coaches. For a moment there was silence broken only by the hissing of steam from the engine.

Up at the front of the train, the Chauffeur, a sharp-faced seventeen-year-old from Newcastle who had driven getaway cars in peacetime and had falsified his age when war broke out, kept low as he approached the footplate, using the ground mist as cover.

"A one-man job," the North Countryman had assured them. "Just a driver and a fireman. They won't be armed. No trouble."

But one of them was.

As the Chauffeur jumped onto the footplate Vogel swung at him with the fireman's shovel. The Chauffeur parried the blow with the barrel of his tommy gun. "Christ, a bloody hero," he said and clubbed at Vogel with the submachine gun. Vogel ducked, swinging back with the shovel in a pendulum movement.

The fireman watched, momentarily paralyzed, as the two men fought. Then, as though he had been wound up, he grabbed a small hand shovel and scooped up a heap of glowing cinders.

Vogel's shovel missed the Chauffeur's head and struck the side of the cabin, spitting sparks. The fireman tossed the cinders at the Chauffeur just as he was squeezing the trigger of the tommy gun. Swinging his arm up to fend off the red-hot missiles, the Chauffeur loosed a burst out of the side of the cabin.

From the bushes came a cry, "Whose side are you on, you stupid sod?"

The cinders struck his combat jacket and his helmet and one scorched his cheek. The cabin smelled of sulfur. Vogel lunged at him again, forced low by the momentum of his previous attack, and the Chauffeur hit him on the back of the head with the barrel of the gun. Grunting, Vogel pitched forward onto the steel plate among the scattered cinders.

The fireman dropped his hand shovel and, lifting Vogel with one hand, kicked away the cinders.

The Chauffeur watched him, gun trained on his head.

He said, "I should kill you, you bastard. Do you speak English?"

The fireman said, *"Ich verstehe nicht."*

"You don't even look scared," the Chauffeur said. "Two bloody heroes." Shaking his head, he gestured to the fireman to lie on the plate and kicked away the rest of the cinders for him as he did so.

From the passenger coach next to the armored car, the Germans were still directing sporadic rifle fire at the British crouching in the bushes.

The North Countryman, who was kneeling behind a telegraph pole, beckoned the Marksman. "How many do you reckon?" pointing at the coach.

"How the hell should I know?" the Marksman said.

He drew a pistol and, as a steel helmet rose above the ledge of a window, loosed off a shot without apparently taking aim. A scream. The helmet disappeared. "Three at the most," the Marksman said.

"Okay. Fine. A long burst with your tommy gun about a foot below window level. That should get them in the guts. Then we'll rush them."

The Marksman, holding his tommy gun lovingly, sprayed the coach with bullets. One window, taking a high bullet, shattered, and from somewhere inside blood spurted, dripping from the shards of glass still spiking the frame.

The North Countryman stood up. "Let's go." He waved one hand forward.

The return fire from the coach was weak. But one bullet hit a young man code-named the Spotter in the chest. He had been a railway enthusiast and had claimed to know every mile of track in Europe. He died on the track beside the Rheingold.

As the others burst into the coach from both ends, the Germans threw down their arms. The Rheingold was in British hands.

They had been told to expect three civilians on board the train—a Brit named Miller who was supposed to be in charge of the operation and probably two Germans. But there were five, the two extras being girls. One of them, a blonde, was with Miller and the two German men; the other, a brunette with a lovely slut's face, was crouching, terrified, in the dining car separating the two passenger coaches.

The North Countryman and one of the team code-named the Mailman, a handsome young Welshman, took the brunette into the first coach.

Ritter smiled at her and said to Miller, "Ah, I forgot to tell you about her. After a long time at sea, one needs a few creature comforts. She's called Hanna. Unlikely name, isn't it?"

Miller gestured to the Mailman to cover Ritter, Becker, and the girl named Hanna with his tommy gun and stuck his Luger back in his belt under his leather jacket.

The Mailman pointed at Gisella. "And her?"

"She's on our side," Miller said.

The North Countryman fingered a scar running down his cheek. "Really? How nice for you. Anyway," turning to Miller, "I've been told that you're in charge, *sir,* so it must be all right."

Miller said, "Don't I know you? Woburn Abbey, 1937?"

"Oh Christ," said the North Countryman.

TWO A.M. IN Woburn Abbey, ancestral home of the dukes of Bedford. Moonlight. Explosives have been inserted in the lock of the wall safe lurking behind an oil painting of a morose duke from far back. The family is on holiday in the south of France, skeleton staff of two in a deep, tipsy sleep in another wing of the building. There are two men on this job, Miller and a burglar called Harvey, who three years later is to be code named the North Countryman. The safe, padded to contain the noise, blows. Silence. No movement. Miller takes the gold jewelry, Harvey the money, lovely white fivers and tenners. Carrying their bags, they run to the window Harvey has already forced. Light hits them, blinding them. Car headlights. They drop to the floor. Perhaps the occupants of the car haven't seen them. Harvey draws a gun. Miller whispers, "I said no guns." Crouching, they make their way to the back of the mansion. Harvey forces a kitchen window. They hear movement from the staff quarters, footsteps outside. They wait. The footsteps retreat, two sets of them. They climb through the window and make their way around the building in the direction of their car, a souped-up Vauxhall, parked behind bushes. In the driveway a Wolsey. Police. But probably only a routine check, two men. Keeping low they run for the Vauxhall. A voice: "Hey you, stop."

188

Harvey reaches the Vauxhall; Miller trips on the root of a tree, falls, pain knifing up his leg. One peak-capped policeman has almost reached the Vauxhall. Harvey revs the engine, but Miller, his leg on fire, can't make it. The Vauxhall takes off. So does the Wolsey, slowing to let the second policeman jump in, then accelerating. Miller realizes they think both of them are in the Vauxhall. A shot. The Wolsey plunges off the road into a tree. Swearing, the police return to the house. Miller gathers from their conversation that Harvey shot out a tire. While they telephone he limps away.

THE OCCUPANTS OF the coach looked from one man to the other.

The North Countryman said, "I meant . . . ," he took a grip on himself, "the prisoners. What are we going to do with them?" Whatever had passed between them had dispensed with any deference, spurious or otherwise.

"How many?"

"Four wounded, two badly. We killed three."

Miller said, "Put the two badly wounded onto the train. In the dining car. You," to the Medic, "go and patch them up. You," to the North Countryman, "look after the rest and get the dead out of the armored car. I'm going onto the footplate."

The driver was lying on the metal floor, groaning; the fireman lay quietly beside him. The Chauffeur stood over him, tommy gun steady in his

189

hands. Steam and smoke hung in tatters around them.

Miller prodded the driver with his foot. "He can't drive. Give me the gun and fetch our own man."

Their own man was in his mid-thirties, old for war. However, his face had an expression of inexperience. It was the look of a man who when he died would still be waiting for fulfillment. He had ginger hair and chipped teeth. His name was Pritchard, no code name.

Miller said, "Can you take over?"

Pritchard inspected the controls. He looked nervous. "A bit of a tall order," he said.

"Tall order? What in Christ's name are you talking about? You're an engine driver, aren't you? One engine is much the same as another, isn't it?"

Pritchard shook his head. "They're all different. But that's not the point. You want speed and I can't give it to you because I don't know where the gradients are and, more important, I don't know where the curves are. If I took a curve too fast we'd be derailed. In the daylight we'll be able to travel faster."

"A daytime driver. Jesus wept." Miller turned to the fireman. "Stand up," he said in German. "Can you drive this thing?"

The fireman nodded. "*Ja.*" Perhaps he had always wanted to be a driver.

Pritchard said, "Someone will have to stoke the firebox and check the water and steam."

"You will," Miller said.

He and Pritchard carried the driver to the dining car where the two badly wounded men were lying on cushions on the floor. The Medic was tearing up starched tablecloths to use as dressings; he had already made the coach smell like a hospital.

Miller went back to the footplate with Pritchard. "Okay," he said to the fireman, "move it." He told the Chauffeur not to let the fireman stop the engine for anything and, as the train began to move forward, ran back to review the troops.

THE NORTH COUNTRYMAN. Manchester. Age: 28. Occupation: scrap metal dealer (not an unusual trade for a thief). Married with two children. Pastimes: pigeon-racing and, Miller remembered, boozing when, that was, he wasn't stitching mail bags in one of His Majesty's prisons. Assessment: a flawed tough.

The Marksman. Mayfair. Age: 21, but looks younger. Occupation: unemployed. Query: contract killer? Single. Pastimes: shooting—anything and everything. Assessment: lethal. (Those dark eyes, flecked like bloodstones.)

The Prizefighter. Liverpool. Age: 32; Pritchard apart, the oldest. Occupation: bouncer. Married with five children. Pastimes: gardening and charity work. Assessment: a tank.

The Engineer. Birmingham. Age: 23. Occupation: garage mechanic. Married, no children. Pastimes: stripping and rebuilding engines. Assessment: Can repair anything from a pair of scissors to a Spitfire. (He was the one who had broken his leg.)

The Mailman. Wales. Age: 18. Occupation: radio operator. Single, and likely to stay that way; when you looked like a matinee idol, what was the point of getting married? Pastimes: music. Assessment: green but capable.

The Medic. Scotland. Age: 20. Occupation: male nurse. Married, just. Pastimes: football and football. Assessment: competent and one of those men who finds his true direction in wartime.

That left the Chauffeur and Pritchard, the two men on the engine now. The North Countryman, who had filled in the details about the others, told Miller about them as they walked the length of the train from the armored car.

The Chauffeur. Newcastle. Age: 17, promoted to 18. Occupation: getaway driver.

"A better one than you, I hope," Miller said.

"I want to talk to you about that."

"I don't," Miller said.

Single. Pastimes: auto racing. Assessment: a delinquent.

Pritchard. A southerner, Sussex or Surrey, the North Countryman thought. Occupation: engine driver ("Of a sort," Miller commented). Married with one boy. Pastimes: railways. Assessment: perhaps Miller had already formed one, the North Countryman suggested.

"Where the hell did they find him?" Miller asked as they walked through the blood-spattered, glass-strewn corridor of the first of the wagon-lits, passing the doors of each of the sleeping compartments as they went. This carriage was coupled to the armored car.

"Royal Engineers. You said you wanted an engine driver, you got one."

"Royal Engineers? When did he learn to parachute?"

"He didn't. Yesterday was his first drop."

"Christ! If only he knew as much about engines as he does about guts."

"None of us knows much about parachuting," the North Countryman said. "They asked for volunteers and the next thing we knew we were at Ringway."

"How did they pick you for this job?"

"A team, I reckon. You know, sparks, gunman, medic . . ."

"How many of you have done time?"

"Me, for one. The Prizefighter did a bit of bird, too, something to do with a brawl in a club in Birkenhead. And I think the Chauffeur's done a bit of Borstal. Drove a getaway car into a Woolworth's window."

"A fine body of men," Miller commented.

"We haven't all been as lucky as you." His accent was still as thick as treacle.

"It's not luck that matters," Miller said. "It's knowing what to do with it when you get it."

"I never got it," the North Countryman said. He lit a Woodbine. "And by the way, what the hell's all this about? They never told us. But they never do, do they?"

They. Those in authority. The upper class. The employers. Always on the other side of the barriers in the East End and the terrace where the North Countryman had been born. Miller could imagine the terrace now, a line of rain-wet slate roofs leading to the pit head or the mill or the factory.

Them. And I've become one of them. A stockbroker or an accountant. He grinned.

He said, "You weren't told because it's top secret."

"Well, it's about time we were told. You can't expect these lads to go on risking their necks without knowing why."

Miller thought about it. The story Goering had put around was as good as any. "The answer's in the two head-end cars."

"Go on."

"Parts of some sort of secret weapon. Even I don't know what except that it could win us the war. They were on their way to Canada for trials when the Germans captured them. Good enough?"

"It'll have to do," the North Countryman said.

As they entered the dining car a stream of sparks flew past the window. Beneath them the rhythm of wheels against rails, steel against steel, continued to accelerate.

The Medic looked up from one of his patients. "He's dead," he said. "I did what I could."

"And the other?" Miller asked.

"He'll live. He was bleeding to death from a wound in the groin, but I've managed to stop it." The German's face was chalk-white and his head lolled on the Rheingold's cushions.

The Engineer sat at a dining table, leg stuck into the aisle at an awkward angle. In front of him was a bottle of Courvoisier brandy. He took a swig from it. "Cheers," he said.

"Where did you get that?"

"The kitchen. It's a boozer's paradise in there. Enough grub to last Goering a week." The Engineer had what they called a homely face, his hair was thick with Brylcreem and his Midlands accent was raw.

Miller said, "Who said anything about Goering?"

"I just did."

Booze brave, Miller thought.

"It's his train, isn't it?" He moved his bad leg and winced. "His name's on the crate of brandy."

The Medic said, "Now it's your turn," knelt down and began to cut the camouflaged trouser leg away.

Ritter, Becker, and Ritter's girl were still sitting at the same table, at gunpoint, in the next coach. Gisella had moved away.

Miller took the radio from the suitcase and placed it on the table in front of Becker. "Now you have to help," he said.

Becker massaged the base of his spine. "What do you want?" he asked nervously.

"Contact Goering and tell him everything's going according to plan."

"I refuse."

"Well said," Ritter remarked. Even his voice seemed to have a slant to it. "I didn't know you had it in you." The girl named Hanna hung on to his arm, her pouting face still smudged with fear.

"I'm afraid you don't have any choice," Miller said to Becker.

"I still refuse."

"Then you're dead," Miller said. He nodded at the Mailman holding the tommy gun. His finger tightened on the trigger.

Becker said hastily, "I don't know Morse."

"I do. But in any case, you can speak personally to Goering."

"You can't shoot me here."

"Why not? You hardly feel a thing with a tommy gun at this range, it chops you to pieces. Didn't you see *Scarface*?"

The barrel of the Mailman's gun jerked.

Becker looked away from Ritter. "What do you want me to say?" he asked.

"Christ," Ritter said softly, "if only the men of Jagdstaffel 5 could hear you now."

"Just tell him," Miller said, "that we're heading toward Wittenberge. That everything's going fine but we may be late because we lost power coming out of Hamburg. Tell him you'll call again in two hours."

Miller picked up the radio and pointed to the first of the two head-end cars where the bullion was stashed. "We'll do it in there," he said, "in case of interference," smiling at Ritter.

He took the Luger out of his belt and marched Becker into the head-end van.

The wooden crates were piled the length, breadth, and height of the head-end car, which still retained traces of its days as a traveling post office— two cardboard notices lying on the floor bore the words *Per Eilbote* and *Eingeschrieben*. The coach, Miller thought, was a solid block of gold. And there were two of them.

At the entrance was a small space in the towering wall of bullion where two crates formed a platform. He put the radio on one of the two crates and activated it. "Okay," he said to Becker, "call your boss."

Becker hesitated, then put on the headset and began to transmit. Faintly, Miller could hear a tinny voice in the earphones; it sounded like a trapped insect trying to escape. Goering, the second most powerful man in Germany.

When Becker had finished, Miller made a note of the call signs. Becker was Rheingold, Goering, Edelweiss. Edelweiss, he remembered reading, had been the Rheingold's rival, an express that ran from Amsterdam to Basel on a different route, through Brussels and Strasbourg.

Miller turned to Becker, who was leaning against

the wall of crates. His Prussian features were crumpled. Miller said, "Now we're going to send a personal message to the director of German Railways ordering him to change the routing of the Rheingold and give us an uninterrupted journey." He took a page from an exercise book on which he had printed the route in capital letters. "Look. Instead of branching east at Wittenberge for Berlin we continue south as far as Stendal. From Stendal west to Hanover. Then through the Ruhr to the border with Belgium at Aachen."

Becker said wearily, "I don't know how to call the Deutsche Reichsbahn."

"Crap. You've been in touch with them for days. What's the Herr Director's call sign?"

"I don't know. Why don't you shoot me?"

Miller pressed the barrel of the Luger against Becker's fragile looking temple. "The call sign."

"Lorelei."

"Like the yacht. Is it another express?"

Becker nodded.

"All right, so we'll call Lorelei."

"They'll want confirmation from Goering himself."

"Oh no they won't," Miller said. "I'm going to transmit this message, and I'm going to do it in Morse."

"That won't be good enough," Becker said.

"It will if I identify myself as Edelweiss."

A slight twitching on one side of Becker's face

was the only sign that he had recognized yet another defeat.

THE NORTH COUNTRYMAN said, "Do you really believe we're carrying parts of a secret weapon?"

He and Miller were standing in the swaying connecting corridor between the second head-end car and the first coach.

"Why should I think otherwise?"

"Because you're a suspicious bastard like me."

Miller shrugged.

"Some secret weapon. All those crates stacked up to the roof."

"Who authorized you to go in there?"

"I authorized myself. I pried open one of the crates. And you know what I found, don't you."

Miller nodded.

"Makes Woburn Abbey seem like a twopenny bazaar, doesn't it."

"I wouldn't bring that up again. You used a gun, you ditched me." Miller had wanted to keep Woburn in the past but he couldn't help himself.

"I didn't have any choice. I was going to come back."

"But you didn't."

"The place was crawling with coppers. And you'd done a runner, anyway."

"I told you no guns."

"If it hadn't been for the shooter, I'd have been nicked. And you too, probably, when they realized you weren't in the car. They didn't get hurt, did they?"

"It was in the papers next day. Armed robbers. I didn't like that."

"So you didn't like it. So fucking what? The point is this time we're into the biggest heist of the century. We can't just sit back and do nothing about it, can we?"

"Can't we?" Miller wondered how Vic's cough was.

WHOOSH. A TRAIN traveling in the opposite direction rushed past in a blur of light and was gone.

Miller consulted the rough timetable he had drawn up. Any minute now they would know if the Rheingold had been diverted from the mainline to Berlin. If it crossed the Elbe then they were on their way to Standal.

Ritter said, "You'll never make it." Hanna was leaning against him and he was stroking her hair; she looked more relaxed, glancing occasionally at the handsome Mailman holding the tommy gun.

Becker stared through the window into the gathering darkness.

Ritter went on, "Goering is a wily old bird, you won't beat him in a game like this."

Suddenly Becker spoke up. "He was the bravest man I knew. One day he attacked a Handley Page bomber single-handed. He shot the two gunners, then the Sopwiths fell on him. He was wounded, his engine was hit, and his tank punctured. He hedge-hopped back to the German lines and crashed in a graveyard. The church was being used as a hospital. He was a lucky man too," Becker said. "They operated on a wound on his hip. There were sixty bullet holes in his plane, and before his convalescence was finished he was in the cockpit again, fighting. Yes, a brave man."

"What would you know about bravery?" Ritter said. He pinched the girl's cheek and she wriggled closer to him.

"Nothing any more. Once . . ." Becker let his long-ago courage slide away.

Miller stood up, grasped the handle at the top of the window, and pulled it down. Night air rushed into the coach.

"Nich hinauslehnen," Ritter said pointing at a printed notice. "Don't lean out of the window."

Miller leaned out. A broad ribbon of water. They were crossing the Elbe. He grinned into the darkness. He pushed the window back and the curtains stopped billowing. "We're on our way," he said to Ritter.

He drew the curtains—the Rhinegold hadn't been adapted for blackout—and sat down. Hanover was eighty miles away. If they kept up a good head of steam they would make it in an hour.

He considered the disposition of the paratroopers. Two on the footplate counting Pritchard. One here. So that was both ends of the two bullion coaches covered. Two in the dining car, one with an injured leg. One in the bullet-riddled coach. One in the armored car. The North Countryman patrolling. If they were attacked, their manpower was deployed to the best possible advantage.

When could they expect an attack? They had at best two more hours before Goering discovered what had happened. By that time they might just have reached the Ruhr. What would Goering do then? Certainly nothing that would destroy the two head-end cars and reveal his shining hoard.

No, he would have to be very careful. A blockage on the rail might have the same disastrous result. What would I do in his place? I would switch the points, that's what I would do, and send the Rheingold hurtling into a railroad cul-de-sac.

The girl said, "Max, I'm hungry."

"And I'm thirsty," Ritter said. "Miller, what about some sustenance? If I know anything about Goering this train will be a traveling Adlon."

Miller thought, I wouldn't mind a drink. And some sandwiches. "All right," he said. He called out to Gisella, asking her to get some Goering-style food and drink ready and to give the assault force sandwiches and beer, if there was any.

The girl, whose head was turned away from Ritter, smiled at the Mailman. She crossed her legs and her skirt slid back so that he could see the tops of her silk stockings and a little flesh above. Miller wondered if the Mailman appreciated such displays; if he wasn't just that bit too beautiful.

Gisella put a bottle of Krug champagne, smoked-salmon sandwiches, a glass bowl of caviar, and slices of brown bread on the table.

Ritter eased the cork from the champagne bottle; it hit the ceiling; Ritter caught it. He poured champagne, raised his glass. "To a golden opportunity. For you or me."

They all drank except Becker. Holding his gun in one hand, the Mailman tilted a bottle of pilsner into his mouth with the other.

"Champagne?" Ritter offered him the bottle.

The Mailman shook his head. He wiped froth from his lips, his eyes on other delights. Perhaps he wasn't too beautiful after all.

MILLER SAID, "MAYBE it was *my* pride you restored."

He and Gisella had moved to the far end of the coach and they were sitting opposite each other across one of the walnut-veneer tables.

"It never occurred to me it needed restoring."

"In fact, it needed rebuilding."

"I think I love you," she said.

"Never *think* it."

"Then I love you. Can *you* say it?"

"In German or English?"

"English. That way I know you mean it."

"I love you in English," he said in German. But he meant it just the same.

ON THE FOOTPLATE Pritchard shoveled coal into the hungry mouth of the firebox and observed carefully how the fireman handled the controls. At daybreak he would volunteer to take over. Really they weren't all that different from the controls he had become accustomed to; except, of course, that they were bigger and there were more of them.

He had kept his secret well enough so far, and he saw no reason to divulge it tomorrow. How would it benefit anyone to know that until now he had only worked on the footplate of a miniature train?

8

May 23 (3)

*I*N THE FARMHOUSE in the Eifel mountains, Feldmarschall Goering relaxed. Germany was winning the war, the gold was on its way to Berlin. If a snatch had been contemplated—a remote contingency—then it would surely have been attempted at the docks, before the Rheingold got under way with Becker in charge and troops on board the coaches and the armored car.

He undid the buttons on his powder-blue uniform and, hands clasped behind his back, strode up and down the timbered living room in deep and satisfying communication with himself.

Within a few hours he would be the richest man in the world. How had the second son (by his second marriage) of the consul general in Haiti achieved such stupefying success? The path to the gold heist was littered with *ifs*; all lives were; his were just that little bit bigger than other people's. Like myself, he reflected wryly.

If when he was five his father hadn't given him a Hussar's uniform he might not have developed his passion for martial dress and thus his passion for all things military.

If his godfather—and his mother's lover—hadn't lived like a feudal baron in his castle at Mauterndorf and snuffed out his father's personality, he might not have become so absorbed with power.

Goering poured himself a glass of chilled Moselle wine. White wine, he had been told, was not as fattening as red.

If Manfred von Richtofen hadn't been killed, he wouldn't have taken over his Flying Circus in 1917 and might not have moved in the same circles as the Swedish beauty Carin von Kantzow.

Ah, Carin. If only she had lived to share his glory. He might even have shared the gold with her. But she had died in 1931 after only nine years of marriage.

But never forgotten. Not many wives had a Carinhall to be remembered by.

If, and this was the most important *if* of all, he hadn't met a mustached ex-corporal in the Army named Adolf Hitler in 1922 and fallen under his spell—and been shot in the abortive putsch of 1923.

Goering winced, holding his thigh where the bullet had entered.

That had been when drugs had taken him over. Morphine to kill the pain from the wound and banish the nightmares that came with it. Only one experience had been worse: the treatment to cure the drug addiction. He still took the occasional shot, but only to provide an illicit spasm of pleasure.

If he hadn't married Emmy, the Aryan blonde actress, who had given him strength when he needed it.

If he hadn't fallen victim to the glandular disease that had made his body gross. Then I would have been in the skies leading my squadrons into battle, after all I'm not fifty yet.

If.

Goering sighed.

The *ifs* had been the footsteps to surrogate fulfillments.

Power. Possessions.

Gold.

The phone rang.

Emmy.

"Hermann," she said, "I'm worried about you."

He held the telephone away from him and smiled at it fondly. "Why's that, *liebling*?"

"The strain must be terrible."

"Nothing to worry about," he told her, sipping the wine. "We're winning. The British are trapped."

"Your health is not good," she said firmly. "Are you sleeping well?" *Better,* she meant, he never slept well. "You're not . . ."

"No," he said, "no drugs."

No need for them. He had sufficient stimulus as it was.

"Are you sure?"

"Quite sure."

"You see I dealt the cards today and they were ominous."

Goering raised his eyes to the ceiling. "Deal them again, my love," he said, "and now I must go. There are decisions to be made."

He hung up the receiver. Such superstitions. At least they were wrong today.

NEITHER LOGAN NOR Munnion was superstitious.

They dealt only in facts, although it was Logan's habit to adapt them.

Sitting in a room in Blenheim Palace, seat of the dukes of Marlborough, a wing of which was now housing part of Britain's burgeoning intelligence service, they had been waiting a long time for facts.

Logan reached for the bottle of Johnny Walker Black Label on the desk between them, poured himself a measure, and passed the bottle to Munnion.

"So what do you think?" Munnion asked, as much to break the thickening silence as anything else.

"We can only wait." The silence reassembled.

Two hours earlier Logan had once again been given a hard time by Churchill at Number 10. Ironic, Munnion mused, that they were sitting in Churchill's birthplace.

Munnion stuffed Airman navy cut into his pipe, lit it, and picked up a newspaper. A comedian named Alec Pleon had been fined £20 for making a reference to Hitler in the revue *We'll Be There*. Apparently the script hadn't been passed by the Lord Chamberlain. Funny people the British.

He scanned the columns of disaster and stopped at an advertisement for Horlicks: WHY DOES ANXIETY HIT SOME PEOPLE SO MUCH HARDER THAN OTHERS?

Finally Logan spoke. "Five minutes to twelve. We should have heard from Miller by now. I'll have to phone Winston at midnight and tell him it's gone cold on us. If anything goes wrong it was probably engineered at this end."

Munnion stood up and walked to the window. He peeled back a corner of the blackout and peered into the darkness. He didn't know what he expected to see. A single searchlight was switching the sky. Backward and forward, just like we've been searching for the traitor.

"It could be anyone," Munnion said returning to his chair. "A clerk at the Bank who got wind of the shipment, a docker . . ."

"A policeman," Logan said. He pulled at the knot in his Guards tie; for once he was wearing a pinstripe instead of tweeds—Churchill wasn't a tweedy man although he did wear some odd outfits. "Winston wants to know what to tell Roosevelt."

"Tell him the rescue operation is under way."

"He'll want more than that. His whole political future's at stake. And the future of the United States."

"Then all we can do is wait. As you just said."

"Winston isn't a patient man. Nor is Roosevelt."

Logan sipped some Scotch. On his desk was a photograph of an elegantly remote woman with a small mouth and shingled hair lit by studio lights. She would have to be remote, Munnion reflected, married to Logan. He thought of his own wife, Madge, and their two boys, too young yet to be conscripted—but how long would the war last?—in their small detached house in Sidcup. Really, the head of security at the Bank should have a more prepossessing home. As head of the City's Fraud Squad he had often had the opportunity to feather his nest, but he had always held the view that the one person you had to respect was yourself.

"Why did you say a policeman just now?"

"Not you, of course," Logan replied irritably. "But someone in security. As you said, it could be anyone."

One minute to midnight.

Logan said, "I suppose I'll have to call Winston."

His hand reached for the phone. It was stopped by a knock on the door.

"Come in," Logan said.

A middle-aged man in a shiny suit handed him a printout. When the man had gone Logan said, "It's from Miller." He reached for his one-time code pad. Frowning, he studied it for a few moments. Then he said, "The gold is in our hands and the train has reached Hanover." He almost smiled.

ANOTHER TRAIN. ANOTHER COUNTRY.

In a coach once called Ferdinand Magellan,
210

renamed U.S. Railway Car Number 1, Franklin D. Roosevelt, President of the United States, on his way from New York to Washington, tried to relax.

But, although the car was luxuriously appointed —four bedrooms, diner, kitchen, lounge, whistle-stop platform—the President, a polio cripple for nineteen years, was finding it difficult this evening.

Just when he had virtually decided to stand for an unprecedented third term as president, Churchill had thrown a gold brick into his calculations.

In his first message to Roosevelt as Prime Minister, Churchill had asked for a fleet of mothballed destroyers, an armada of aircraft, and an arsenal of weapons. On loan. And as security—"a gold seal of trust," he had written in a secret message—he had dispatched the Bank of England's bullion to the United States.

Loan! Roosevelt hadn't the slightest doubt that when the war was over Churchill would ask for the gold back. He could almost hear him. "Without the gold in our vaults the foundations of democracy will collapse."

Nor had Roosevelt the slightest doubt that Churchill's reasons for shipping the gold across the Atlantic had been twofold: not only had he wanted to establish trust, he had wanted to keep his loot from the Germans if they conquered Britain.

And what had happened? The Germans, Goering to be precise, had got the gold before the Germans had even begun to plan an invasion of the British Isles.

What capital the Republicans would make of

211

that if it ever leaked out, just when some of the isolationists were beginning to accept that neutrality was unacceptable. *FDR trades arms for gold and loses it*; they wouldn't be slow to point out that the *Alaska* was an American ship. What a field day cartoonists like Talburt and Roche would have with that.

Roosevelt removed his pince-nez, sipped his Old Fashioned, and addressed himself to the blunt, bullet-headed man sitting opposite him. "Let me have another look at that message from Grover," he said.

J. Edgar Hoover, head of the FBI, took the print-out from his briefcase and gave it to the President. Roosevelt didn't normally summon Hoover to his presence for personal consultations, but this was a special case.

Roosevelt scanned the terse decoded words from his informant installed in the U.S. Embassy in London, in the absence of any coordinated overseas intelligence network (Roosevelt didn't place much faith in the views of his jaundiced ambassador, Joe Kennedy).

BRITISH CLAIM BULLION RECAPTURED STOP ENTRAINED FOR CONVEYANCE CHANNELWARDS STOP LAST REFERENCE HANOVER STOP GROVER

Roosevelt handed the message back to Hoover. "So there we have it," he said. "The gold's in the hands of a bunch of gangsters led by a thief. What do you rate their chances of recovering it?"

"Zero," Hoover said. He had never been re-nowned for diplomatic niceties. "Would you put Al Capone in command of Fort Knox?"

"I should never have let myself be bamboozled by Churchill. It's the story of his life, inspired manipulation followed by catastrophic foul-ups." Roosevelt finished his Old Fashioned. "Have you got a newspaper?"

Hoover handed him *The New York Times* and Roosevelt spread out its map of the European battlefronts on the table between them. He found Hanover and, prodding it with one finger, said, "So where would you take that train?"

Hoover studied the arrows rampaging across northern France and Belgium. "Through the Ruhr, I guess. Then into Belgium somewhere near Liege. Then?" He shrugged. "Brussels, Gent, it doesn't matter a goddam, it's doomed."

Roosevelt pored over the map. "Personally," he said, "I would head for where the fighting's fiercest. In occupied territory Goering can take more measured steps to recapture the train. So, as Belgium's about to throw in the towel, I would turn south, then strike west through France. Then I would fall in with the British retreat."

"They can only retreat to the sea," Hoover said. "What then?"

"Ingenious people, the British. *Perfidious Albion*. Don't forget the Channel is *their* moat. The point is where will they try to cross it?" Roosevelt's finger searched the pocket, barely sixty square

213

miles, in which the British were trapped. "It would have to be here, wouldn't it?" finger stopping. "So that's where the golden express will be heading for, Dunkirk."

"It stands as much chance of getting to Miami," Hoover said.

9

May 24

SOMETIME, MILLER KNEW, von Ritter would try and make a break for it.

When?

As the crow flies, the distance from Hanover to Dunkirk is 330 miles. You would probably have to add on another hundred or so because of the diversions, say 450 miles. If they kept up this speed, about 80 mph, that would mean another five and a half or six hours. Add on a couple more hours for inevitable delays and you could get there in a supremely optimistic eight hours.

So Ritter had between now, 2 A.M., and 10. Miller didn't think they would make it in that time but that was the sort of period Ritter had to consider.

He contemplated Ritter across the remnants of the sandwiches and the empty glasses. The stale wake of the meal reminded him that he was tired. Hanna was already asleep, nestled against Ritter. Becker was staring stiffly ahead of him, and Gisella was at a table at the end of the coach, writing in an exercise book.

What I want more than anything at this moment, Miller decided, is to go to bed between freshly laundered sheets and make love to her, feeling her warmth against the coolness of the sheets, then sleep and, on waking, find her still there.

Ritter said, "What were you thinking about just then?"

"Gold," Miller said.

How many people knew about the gold on the train? Ritter, Becker, Gisella, myself, the North Countryman. The girl beside Ritter? He doubted it. I wouldn't tell her if I were Ritter. Hanna gave a little snore, a baby's snore.

"Gold? Just possible. Some men feel that way about gold. But I would have guessed that you were thinking about a woman." Ritter looked past Miller at Gisella. He smiled at Miller.

"I think about gold the same way."

"How frustrating for you." Ritter slotted a cigarette into his holder and lit it. "Myself, I like diamonds. On a woman. Did you ever steal diamonds, Mr. Miller?"

"What makes you think I was a thief?"

"You forget that we had the same employer. In Germany, that is." He glanced at Hanna. Her mouth had fallen open. "Can you deposit her somewhere? Over there perhaps?" He nodded down the aisle. "Pull up a couple of chairs."

Miller arranged three chairs and laid the girl on

them. The Mailman licked his lips. Miller covered her thighs with her skirt.

He said to the North Countryman, who was walking past, "Get something to bind her wrists."

The North Countryman returned with some wire. "Cheese wire," he explained, "for cutting throats."

The girl, who had woken up, began to tremble.

"Don't worry," said the Mailman, "he won't hurt you."

The North Countryman bound her wrists, and after a while she lay back and closed her eyes again.

"That's better," Ritter said. He stretched.

Becker said, "Do you mind if I lie down?"

Ritter said, "And dream you're a hero?"

Becker stared at him levelly. "Dream about a stranger," he said. "A young man I once knew." And to Miller, "I am very tired."

Miller told the Mailman to escort Becker to the dining car and bind his wrists. He took the Luger from his belt.

Ritter looked at the cigarette smoking in his holder. "I don't want another one ruined," he said in English. "So you were primarily a gold thief?"

"I preferred gold, yes. There was something secure about it."

"But not diamonds?"

"Too many fakes around. What did you do before you became one of Goering's personal crooks?"

Ritter seemed to be taking his time answering.

The Mailman returned but Miller waved him away to the end of the coach.

"A thief?" he asked. "Pimp, pickpocket?"

Ritter said at last, "I was in the SS."

That was, Miller realized, why Ritter could treat Becker like something he had found on the sole of his shoe.

"I noticed your expression change when I said that," Ritter observed. "A trace of contempt perhaps?"

"Did you expect admiration?"

"The SS are the toughest troops in the world. And the best."

"They're bloody good at shooting women and children, if that's what you mean."

Ritter's complexion was pale, and his greenish eyes glittered.

"Only the minority," he said. "The majority are good soldiers, fine soldiers. A few have given us a bad name." He leaned forward. "You don't understand."

"Don't tell me," Miller said. "Germany's full of idealists."

Ritter ignored him. "I joined when I was seventeen. It was wonderful. You had to be as fit and healthy as hell to get in. You know, we *were* the elite. And we looked like it and acted like it. Those black and silver uniforms, the marching, the training. And it wasn't all just swagger. We were the personification . . . is that right? Sometimes my English is not too good . . ."

"It's fine," Miller said.

218

". . . of the new Germany. The Fatherland rising from the ashes. And, yes, we gloried in it. Why not?" He looked anxiously at Miller. "And all of us would have given our lives for the little man with the mustache who had shown us the way to be strong again and, yes, we also admired Goering even if he was a little ridiculous because at least he had panache . . . Is that right?" He paused. "Anyway, he had balls. Guts. Okay, so he was fat. But we Germans don't mock everything like the British. You laugh at everything. It is a defensive mechanism, I think."

"As it is with you?"

"Perhaps."

"So what went wrong?" Miller asked.

Ritter removed the cigarette end from the holder and squashed it in the cut-glass ashtray. "The butchers and the bullies started kicking people."

"Well, of course, I suppose they would. What did *you* do about them?"

"Nothing. Not when it mattered. Did you do anything about the British fascist leader, Mosley?"

"Mosley never took over England," Miller said. "Besides, I was just a thief. What did you expect me to do?"

"The British, did *they* do anything?" Ritter held up one hand. "I can tell you, nothing. Until they were forced to declare war. They're so self-righteous. They talk about all these so-called crimes against humanity—Czechoslovakia, Sudetenland, Austria, all that—and what did they do?"

"Nothing," Miller said. "But we're talking about

you in that glorious black and silver uniform. You weren't in Gilbert and Sullivan, you could have done something."

"I did do something finally," Ritter said. "Not much, but I stopped thinking about the glory that was Germany and started thinking about the glory that could be Max von Ritter." An angle returned to his face. "I became a pirate of sorts."

"Robbing the rich to help the poor?"

"Robbing the rich to help Ritter. So you see we're two of a kind. Except that I was a pirate, not a drainpipe thief."

"I don't like heights," Miller said. "I always go in through the French windows. And I crack safes, not heads. Who did you rob, Jews?"

Ritter leaned farther forward and there was venom in his tone. "I thought we'd get round to that sooner or later," he said.

Miller prodded the Luger toward him. "Sit back, that's it, relax, that's the way, and answer the question."

"As a matter of fact, I robbed the gangsters who robbed the Jews."

"Very commendable," said Miller.

"You don't believe me?"

"I neither believe nor disbelieve—my philosophy."

"And smug with it."

Miller supposed he was right.

"So what happened to the *Alaska*?" he asked suddenly.

"The *Alaska*?" Ritter looked nonplussed. "We sunk her, why?"

"And the crew?"

"Ah, I see, you think I ordered them to be machine-gunned in the sea? Sorry to disappoint you, Herr Miller. I took them on board the *Countess of Cork*. They were taken off at Cuxhaven and will remain prisoners until the end of the war, which shouldn't be very long."

Miller, annoyed that Ritter hadn't given him reason to despise him, asked, "How did you get transferred from the SS to the *Forschungsamt*?"

"Simple. I was going to be disciplined for appropriating a rich gangster's property. I may well have been shot. Anyway Goering intervened and saved me. Apparently I was just the sort of man he was looking for."

Nothing to condemn him for there. Miller looked down the coach. Gisella had finished writing and was putting the exercise book away in a shopping bag she had found in the kitchen.

Ritter caught his glance. "Look," he said, "why don't you go and try your hand at seduction. You know, 'Tomorrow we might all be dead.' That sort of stuff, it never fails. And leave me alone for a while with Hanna."

Miller beckoned to the Mailman. "Tie up his wrists with wire," he said, "and don't let him move."

He stood up and made his way toward Gisella Hessen. It was a little late for seduction, he thought.

THE DINING CAR was a set piece from the Crimean War, and Gisella, walking its length, talking to a couple of casualties, was Florence Nightingale.

Vogel had recovered sufficiently to talk to her excitedly in German. He was sitting at one of the dining tables drinking beer from a brown bottle.

As he talked Gisella shook her head frequently.

"What was he saying?" Miller asked.

"He says he knows this part of the track—he guessed where we diverted. He says there are some dangerous curves and we're going too fast. He wants to go back to the footplate."

Miller addressed Vogel. "The fireman is driving."

Vogel said, "Firemen are firemen, drivers are drivers." Miller understood. The difference between lookouts and cracksmen. "In any case," Vogel went on, stabbing the air with the beer bottle, "you'll have to stop soon to take on water and coal. I'll take over then."

"All right. If you think you're fit enough. When will we have to stop?"

"When we get to the Ruhr. If you don't take on water then the engine will blow up."

Miller studied Vogel. Despite the dressing on the back of his head and his pallor, he looked like a dangerous man. A braggart, perhaps, but dangerous just the same. Cleft chin the devil's within, something like that. He and Ritter would be a formidable partnership.

He tested Vogel. "You know, of course, what's on this train."

Vogel said, "Of course," and Miller knew that he was a man who had never learned how to say, "I don't know."

"Then you realize it could blow up if the train was derailed."

Vogel poured the last dregs of the beer down his throat. "Anything could happen."

Well, he was right there. Miller parted the curtains and stared into the fleeing darkness. A line of dark sentinels, pines by the look of them, flashed past. A light glimmered weakly in the distance. A farm, he decided. Cozy and smelling faintly of hay. The good farmer and his wife tucked up in bed. The farmer was himself and his wife was Gisella.

He shook his head. He felt tired. Yes, anything could happen. Particularly when they reached the Ruhr, because by that time Goering would have realized that the Rheingold had been diverted. They could do without that stop for water and fuel. But if they did, and Vogel was right, then the engine would blow up and £500 million worth of gold would be left sitting on the track waiting for Goering to scoop it up.

He joined Florence Nightingale on her rounds, the Medic hovering behind them like a house surgeon escorting important doctors around his ward. Except that with his flinty features and big hands he looked more like a truck driver than a medical man.

They stepped over Becker, who was lying on cushions, eyes closed. Beyond him lay the wounded German soldier. His eyes were also closed, his breathing shallow.

The Engineer looked happy enough, despite his broken leg, which the Medic had splinted. He smelled of brandy and the bottle in front of him was half empty.

"Medicinal purposes only," he said and grinned foolishly.

Miller took the bottle from him and led Gisella to a table at the end of the coach.

"Whisky?"

She nodded. He went to the stainless steel kitchen and took a bottle of Chivas Regal from a cupboard. He added water and ice from the fridge.

There was a lamp on the table. The tablecloth, the only one the Medic had left unscathed, was starched and incongruously clean. Dark red curtains were drawn across the window, and on the walnut-paneled wall was a rack for two bottles of wine. As he sat down Miller felt something sharp protruding from the side of the cushion. He pulled out an old breakfast menu and a brochure about the running of the Rheingold.

The breakfast seemed to have been reasonably priced.

1 Frühstuck: 1 Portion Kaffee,
Tea, oder Kakao mit Sahne und Zucker, Brötchen,
Zwieback und Butter
RM. 1, 40.

The pamphlet contained details of the route of the Rheingold and how the railways were run in the early days of steam. It included sketches of the hand signals used beside the track—one arm extended *all clear*, one arm raised above the head *caution*, two arms *danger*.

He showed the menu and pamphlet to Gisella and surveyed the dining car. The Rheingold was the sort of train he would have liked to travel on in peacetime, with businessmen and film stars and statesmen—and spies.

They touched glasses. Her gray eyes looked into his. He could smell her perfume. He fancied for a moment that they were on their honeymoon. Except that she was still wearing the navy sweater and blue slacks.

She said, "You've changed. You're not a thief any more, but still you're different from what I imagined."

"Imagined?"

"For my lover. I thought his eyes would blaze with fervor. I thought he might have a beard."

"I can grow one."

"No," she said, "it wouldn't suit you."

He coughed and she said, "That chest of yours, is it very bad?"

"Not too bad. Not as bad as Vic's, my brother's. They thought I had tuberculosis but I didn't. Just creaking bellows. But they're getting better."

"You need someone to look after you," she said softly, and she was right, he did.

"I'm going to have an hour's sleep," he said. "You should, too."

He laid some cushions in the aisle between the dining tables. He lay down and drew her down beside him. He put his arm around her waist.

"Good night, Charlie," she said.

She closed her eyes, and Miller noticed with surprise that tears were trickling from her closed eyelids.

"Hey," he whispered. "What's the matter?"

"Nothing." She brushed ineffectually at her eyes.

"The future?"

"Something like that. The present. This war."

"We wouldn't have met if it hadn't been for the war."

She snuggled closer. "That's right, we wouldn't have had this, you and me here."

He kissed her forehead. The tears dried up. Her breathing steadied. He closed his eyes.

The engine hooted, leaving the sound behind in the night.

He slept. And dreamed that he was standing on a platform awaiting execution. But this time the instrument of death was the guillotine. The blade slammed down, severing him from Gisella so that they stared at each other across an abyss.

He cried out to her and in his sleep whimpered, and this time it was she who soothed him.

GOERING COULDN'T BELIEVE it.

A simple telephone call from the farmhouse to

Berlin to confirm that the Rheingold had arrived—the crates were to be transferred to Luftwaffe headquarters and then in trucks to Carinhall—and the glittering future had fallen apart.

"No, Herr Feldmarschall, the Rheingold has not arrived."

Stunned, Goering stared at the receiver in his hand. Then, "Get me the director."

It took a couple of minutes. The voice of the stationmaster at Berlin was a confusion of drowsiness and fear. No, the Rheingold had not arrived. A call had come earlier from the headquarters of the Deutsche Reichsbahn that it had been diverted.

Diverted. That was when he knew.

With one finger he cut the connection with the babbling voice in Berlin.

Who? Where? How?

He remembered Miller.

He waited for his fury to subside. Then he called the director of Deutsche Reichsbahn.

The director's tone was smug, the voice of a servant who believes he has served his master well. Swiftly, Goering cut it to ribbons.

Where was the Rheingold now?

Somewhere between Hanover and Hamm.

"It's got to be stopped," Goering snapped.

"*Ja*, Herr Feldmarschall, but . . ."

"But what, Herr Direktor?"

"I have given instructions for its free passage to Aachen."

"Why the hell would I want the Rheingold to go to the Belgian border?"

The now flaky voice of the director gained a little strength. "The order was transmitted with your call sign, Edelweiss."

So Becker had broken. Curiously Goering felt no anger about him. Whenever he thought about Fritz Becker he remembered him in the cockpit of an Albatross alongside Udet and Boelike and the brothers Lothar and Manfred von Richtofen. Becker had rescued him when a Camel had come in from the sun. He had registered fourteen kills before the bullet had smashed his spine.

He said, "Herr Direktor, there is a very simple way to stop the Rheingold . . ."

When he had finished with the director he went to a first-aid box in the bathroom, and from it he took a hypodermic syringe and an ampule of colorless liquid.

He wiped alcohol on the inside of his arm and half filled the syringe. He paused as he was about to sink the needle into his flesh.

This isn't the way, he thought. I have a battle on my hands. After all these years I have a battle. He threw the syringe and the ampule into the wastebasket, and his hand grew tense as it had once just before he pressed the firing button of a Spandau machine gun.

IT WAS THE Chauffeur, not Pritchard, who noticed that 18 457 was slowing down.

The Chauffeur, although only a teenager, with a schoolboy's face and a deceptive air of innocence about him, was sensitive to speed. You had to be when you were a getaway driver.

Pritchard was too busy shoveling coal into the firebox to notice that the fireman was braking. His shoulders ached, his eyes burned. It had never been as hard as this on the Romney, Hythe, and Dymchurch Miniature Railway, even though on its small footplates he had to be driver *and* fireman.

"Hey," shouted the Chauffeur above the roar and hiss of the engine, "why are we stopping?" He put his hand on the brake. "Why?"

The fireman pointed ahead. He mimed a signal falling into the horizontal position.

Pritchard said, "That's the German position for stop. But he can't have seen a signal, he's seen a red light."

The Chauffeur leaned out of the engine. The red lamp burned a hole in the darkness.

The Chauffeur snapped his head back into the cabin. He stuck the barrel of the gun in the fireman's back. *"Nein,"* he said. "Keep right on." He waved his free hand forward.

Pritchard shook his head agitatedly. "He can't," he yelled. "There must be an obstruction. Another train, a cliff fall . . ."

The Chauffeur shouted, "We'll have to risk it. You heard what Miller said, don't stop for anything." He possessed, Pritchard realized, a reckless authority far beyond his years.

"Miller? What does Miller know about trains?"

The Chauffeur pushed the gun barrel hard into

the fireman's back. "Keep going," he shouted. He waved his hand more urgently.

The fireman shook his head vigorously.

The Rheingold's gallop slowed to a canter.

The Chauffeur grabbed the collar of the fireman's blue and coal-black jacket and pulled him away from the controls. He pointed the tommy gun at Pritchard. "Let's see what you know about trains. Get this bastard's steam up again."

"You don't understand . . ." Pritchard rubbed his hands on his vest beneath his combat jacket.

The engine, riderless, shuddered.

"*You* don't understand. If you don't get this fucking train going again *tout suite* then I'll kill you."

Pritchard grabbed the regulator and brake lever and, as he did so, became intoxicated. Staring exultantly into the darkness, watching the red light accelerating toward him, he thought, At least I'll die on the footplate of a charger, the ride I always wanted.

The 18 547 picked up speed.

Maybe the line had subsided, perhaps another train had broken down ahead, maybe a bridge or a tunnel had collapsed. Whatever the peril ahead, the end result at this speed—100 . . . 110 . . . 120 kilometers an hour—would be catastrophic.

The fireman braced himself against the side of the engine. The Chauffeur's hands on his gun were white knuckled.

The first bullets hit the steel flanks of the engine. At first Pritchard didn't realize what they were. The

Chauffeur did. He shouted, "Get down," dropping into a crouching position. The fireman followed; Pritchard stayed at the controls.

A bullet smashed the boiler water-level gauge and whined around the cabin. The fireman cried out. On his blackened hand was a white furrow turning red.

Then they were past the ambush.

THE BULLETS RAKED the coaches, splintering wood paneling and breaking more windows in the carriage already blasted by the assault force. No one was hurt.

Miller, holding Gisella tightly in his arms, said, "No one shoots as badly as that. They didn't expect a moving target. We should have stopped, according to their reckoning." He kissed Gisella. "The game's only just beginning," he said.

10

May 24

DAWN.

A Wagnerian sunrise lit Germany's confidence trick, the Ruhr.

Here in this congestion of industry on the Fatherland's western limits, a mighty armory had been clandestinely assembled in defiance of the provisions of the Treaty of Versailles, designed to keep Germany's teeth drawn.

Guns, tanks, ammunition. Off the assembly lines in Dortmund, Duisburg, Essen, they had rolled in many artful disguises. For agricultural tractor read tank.

By 1935 Germany's conquerors in the Great War had awoken to the fact that the vanquished were girding their loins again. By which time it was too late to stop them. On March 17, Heroes' Day, the rebirth of the German war machine was openly celebrated.

As the Rheingold approached it, the Ruhr looked

awesome. The sky was deep red and full of portent, and banners of black and white smoke flew from the tall chimneys. You could sense the molten turmoil of the place.

Gazing at it from a window of the dining car, Miller thought, That is where Goering has got to try and stop us. The heart of the Ruhr was only sixty miles from the Belgian frontier. After that they were outside the control of the German Railways.

But first, before they got into the heavily staffed rail heads of the Ruhr, they had to take on coal and water.

SITTING IN THE back of his Maybach taking him from his headquarters to the farmhouse, Goering seethed with mixed emotions.

He was, of course, overjoyed at the runaway victories of the German war machine spearheaded by the Luftwaffe, but Operation Argo had suffered another unbelievable setback. The Rheingold had swept contemptuously past the red signal, and the fire from the machine gunners had apparently been as effective as gravel thrown against a window.

What now?

His headquarters staff was aware that the Rheingold with the secret weapon on board had to be stopped, but obviously this was to them of minimal importance compared with the conquest of Europe. So the farmhouse still had to be used to direct Argo, otherwise word would get around that the Reichsmarschall had cracked up, worrying more about a train than the fleeing Tommies.

Goering rubbed the diamond-studded rings on his fingers. There was one major obstacle to any attack on the Rheingold: if it was too violent—using, say, antitank guns—the golden hoard might be exposed.

Goring closed his eyes at that terrible thought.

A rail block, another locomotive perhaps? If the Rheingold smashed into it then once again the ingots might be spilled all over the track. Anything frailer and it would charge straight through.

The Maybach drew up outside the farmhouse.

Goering strode into the living room and poured himself a glass of wine.

So what was the answer?

At the Military Training College at Lichterfelde, before being commissioned with honors to Prinz Wilhelm Infantry Regiment 112 at the age of nineteen, he had amazed his instructors with his precocious instinct for military strategy.

"First draw the enemy." He heard his young voice as, with chalk in hand, he drew a swashbuckling arrow on the blackboard. So I must draw the Rheingold. The inspiration presented itself and took a bow.

Goering grinned and rubbed his hands together. Despite everything, he was enjoying himself. He picked up the phone and called the director of Deutsche Reichsbahn.

THEY TOOK ON water and coal at a maintenance halt

southwest of Hamm. The halt was staffed by two railwaymen; the North Countryman locked them in their restroom and ripped out the telephones.

While the fireman supervised the loading of the coal into the tender through a chute and the water through a hose, Miller consulted Pritchard.

"What," he asked, "would you expect to see if there were a diversion ahead?"

"In Britain, a yellow distant warning signal," Pritchard told him. "But in Germany it's different. Here they use a top signal giving the go-ahead—the arm raised at 45 degrees, that is—and below it another signal at the same angle. That's a distant warning and it could mean the points ahead have been switched."

"They would *have* to do that, would they?"

"Of course, the train would have to slow down. If it took a point switch too fast it could be derailed."

Miller pondered, then he turned to the Chauffeur. "Okay," he said, "it's my guess that they will try and divert us. Sidetrack us. It's the obvious thing to do. So let the fireman slow down when he sees the distant warning signal. And you," to Pritchard, "keep a lookout down the line. When you see points ahead, make sure he," nodding at the fireman, "stops the train."

Pritchard said, "I don't think the fireman should drive any more. The Medic has dressed his hand but it's still pretty bad. And he lost his nerve when we got shot up."

Miller called out to the Medic, "How's Vogel shaping up?"

235

"He's all right. Got a nasty headache, that's all."

Miller said, "Bring him out." And when Vogel appeared: "Now's your chance, but you do whatever these two tell you," pointing at Pritchard and the Chauffeur.

"Supposing I refuse to take orders from laymen?"

"Bang," Miller said, two fingers to his temple.

Pritchard said to Miller, "I can take over, that's why I'm here."

"Vogel knows the route, you don't. Just keep shoveling until Vogel slows down, then look out for the points."

Despondently Pritchard, followed by Vogel and the Chauffeur, climbed onto the footplate. With great gasps of steam and smoke escaping into the early morning sky, the Rheingold began to move toward the center of the Ruhr.

IN HIS HALTING English, Vogel shouted to Pritchard, "You were a fireman in England?"

"Fireman *and* driver," Pritchard yelled back and wished he hadn't.

Vogel stared at him. "You joke?"

"No joke."

"It is impossible."

Not on the Romney, Hythe, and Dymchurch it wasn't. Pritchard hoped that Vogel wouldn't ask him to elaborate: he needed his wits about him and he tended to wax passionate on the subject of miniature railways. So many people ridiculed them, little realizing that their drivers had to acquire the same skills as the footplatemen on full-size locomotives, especially when the trains, like those on the RH and D, were performing a public passenger service. How many main-line drivers would appreciate the difficulties of taking a scaled-down Pacific up the incline outside Dymchurch over Fehr's crossing to Hoorne's Bridge? How many would believe that, on the descent from Star Dyke, Captain John Howey, the RH and D's mentor, had coaxed Hurricane up to 35 mph?

Vogel adjusted the regulator. Pritchard calculated that they were traveling at about 80 mph. Vogel was a fine driver. A bond undaunted by language difficulties linked them.

Vogel asked, "What train did you drive?"

"The Blue Train." He regretted that, too. The Blue Train he had driven wasn't the famous express.

Vogel looked impressed.

"In Kent," Pritchard said miserably. "In England." And then to avoid prolonging the agony, "Fifteen-inch gauge—381 millimeters." The Blue Train, introduced in 1938, had been the line's *express*—engine, tender, and ten Hythe coaches painted blue.

Vogel was silent. Then he uttered a phrase that, coming from him, was one of the most beautiful Pritchard had heard, "That must be very difficult."

"You have to know a few tricks," he admitted.

And so you did. Especially when you were driving old Hercules, brought out of mothballs in 1936-37 to haul hoppers loaded with ballast. It was the rumors that Hercules and other engines and coaches were to be converted into armored troop trains to protect that part of the Kent coast that had made him volunteer for the assault force. If more drivers were needed on the RH and D it was a safe bet that reliable old Tom Pritchard would be recalled from the Royal Engineers camp near Liss in Hampshire.

And that would be the end of the dream—to drive an adult train—nursed since he had driven the first Saturday Special in 1927 from New Romney to the duke of York's camp at Jesson. He hated himself for belittling the RH and D but there it was. He had been stuck with it for thirteen years because he had failed medicals for the Southern, Great Western, LMS, and LNER.

When war was declared he immediately volunteered for the Royal Engineers as a qualified locomotive driver, omitting to tell the recruiting officer that his qualifications didn't extend above the waistline of a normal-sized engine. Then the call for a driver for a dangerous mission came and here he was hurtling at 80 mph into unknown perils.

And reveling in it. It was stirring enough to be on the footplate of a giant Bavarian beauty, but to be recapturing a secret weapon for Britain. The dream had been fulfilled with a fanfare of trumpets.

He shoveled in more coal, making sure it was evenly spread.

Vogel, hand cupped to his mouth, shouted, "You wonder why I allow this to happen?"

Pritchard thought, Because you've got a gun in your back, and shrugged.

"Because no harm must come to this engine." Pritchard understood that. "And I know that you British will never get away with this."

Pritchard leaned out of the engine. Ahead he saw the two semaphore signals raised at 45 degrees. He shouted to Vogel.

Vogel was already braking. They were traveling fast but Vogel managed it smoothly enough. Vogel was good.

The Chauffeur gave Vogel a prod with his gun. "Not down the siding. *Comprendez?*"

Vogel nodded.

With luck, Pritchard thought, there wouldn't be any shooting at the points. The Germans assumed that all they had to do was wait down the siding for the Rheingold to steam into their hands. With luck there would be manual controls on the points.

There were.

With a shudder and a hissing sigh the Rheingold drew up before it reached the points. Pritchard leaped out.

It was a V junction, the main line continuing into the Ruhr, the siding slanting away toward a steel works 500 yards away. Pritchard could see furnaces burning below the chimneys.

He grasped the chest-high lever and pulled. Nothing. Figures were emerging from the smoke billowing around the steelworks.

He pulled again. A slight movement. His arms had lost their power from all that shoveling. *Come on Tom.* Another slight movement.

The figures running from the smoke wore field gray.

Miller joined Pritchard. Together they pulled.

The soldiers were 300 yards away. Two were kneeling down, leveling rifles.

The Marksman was lying on top of the armored car peering down a Number 4 Lee Enfield fitted with a telescopic sight.

"Once again," Miller said.

Another fractional movement.

Two sharp cracks. One bullet hit the line, the other the engine.

The Marksman fired. Pritchard saw one of the kneeling soldiers rear up and fall, clutching his chest.

His partner remained kneeling. The others were running toward the points.

They pulled again and suddenly the lever slipped back so easily that they stumbled back; then they were running for the train. Already 18 547 was inching forward as Vogel, gun in his back, manipulated regulator and brakes.

Miller jumped into the first coach, Pritchard onto the footplate. Ponderously the engine got up steam.

One soldier reached the locomotive.

He began to climb up to the footplate. The Chauffeur grasped the barrel of the tommy gun and clubbed him away with the butt.

On the top of the armored car the Marksman discarded his Lee Enfield and picked up a Schmeisser submachine pistol abandoned by the German soldiers when the train was ambushed in the Saxon Forest.

The Schmeisser gave a rasping cough and there were no more pursuing soldiers.

Staring at the bodies beside the track, Pritchard thought, I've come a long way since the RH and D.

AS THE RHEINGOLD stormed out of the Ruhr toward the Belgian frontier, Miller permitted himself a luxury. He went to the first of the two head-end cars to catch a glimpse of the gold.

He had intended prying open a slat on one of the crates, perhaps the same one that the North Countryman had levered. But the German soldiers had done the job for him. A bullet had punctured a hole in one of the crates at eye level.

Miller peered through the hole. A golden eye stared back.

"WHY WERE YOU never caught?" she asked.

"Because I made a point of studying why and how villains get caught. The main reason is that they commit the same sort of crimes in one area. I spread myself around. North and south, county by county. The ideal robbery, of course, is the one-off. Enough funds to keep you in luxury for the rest of your life."

They were sitting in the dining car drinking coffee and he was thinking: *Almost at the border. Goering will make a real effort there, and what the hell can I do this time?*

A one-off," she mused. "Like robbing the Bank of England?"

"Exactly. But even that wouldn't be a one-off for Goering. He's a kleptomaniac on the grand scale. The thieving is a substitute for something. Those brave old flying days, perhaps."

He will be desperate and take risks..

"I didn't know you were such an admirer of the Feldmarschall."

"When I was recruited into the Fifth Branch and then his own intelligence setup, I studied him. In every fat man there's a thin man trying to get out. In his case a thin hero."

Maybe he will blast the train with antitank guns hoping that the shells don't hit the head-end cars.

"You know," he said, sipping his coffee, "Goering and I have a lot in common. I tried to become a flyer in '38 when the writing was on the wall, but they wouldn't have me. So here we are, two frustrated pilots who have become thieves."

"Except that you were a thief first."

"True, but don't forget that after war broke out I was stealing for king and country."

He told her how he had been recruited by the Germans.

"Why did you always steal gold?"

"Because it's pure—22-carat gold, that is—and beautiful and indestructible. And it's always a better deal than cash. If you grow up in hard times then you appreciate something that's forever. I dreamed that I would pull the biggest gold heist ever. Do you know who holds the record?"

She shook her head.

"Stalin. During the Spanish Civil War. In November 1938, with the help of some fellow travelers among the Republicans, the Russians shipped 16 million fine ounces of gold out of Spain. It's never been seen since."

"Is there more than that on this train?"

"Bet your life. And I'm taking it back!"

I've got to pull the greatest escape trick since Houdini.

"Do you think," she asked carefully, "that you'll . . ."

"Go back to my bad old ways?" He smiled at her. "Not now." *We're almost there. Think.* "Do you know the easiest way to spot a gold smuggler?"

Again she shook her head.

"Look for a drunk. The gold's so heavy that when they've got it tucked in a smuggler's jacket they stagger all over the place."

Think!

"What was the biggest robbery you ever did?"

"I don't know about the biggest. The one I'm most proud of was a robbery from a gold hoarder's cellar in Skipton, Yorkshire. I went disguised as an architect . . ."

Disguise!

"Excuse me," he said and ran down the coach.

THE RHEINGOLD APPROACHED the border at a stately pace, thus puzzling the young Wermacht captain in charge of the ambush who had been told to expect an express hurtling toward him at least 150 kilometers an hour.

He frowned. Everything was confused in this wooded countryside at the crossroads to Germany, Belgium, and Holland, at the foot of the Eifel mountains. There really wasn't a border any more since the Germans had overrun the Low Countries, and a lot of the orders from OKH headquarters in the Eifel where Hitler was ensconced didn't make too much sense.

This one was even more perplexing because it hadn't come from the OKH, it had emanated from the Luftwaffe's mobile headquarters. And such was the chaos reigning in and around Aachen that no one had questioned it. Did you query a command from Goering?

Could there be something terribly wrong?

The captain focused his field glasses on the Rheingold. It looked more like a vehicle for a state visit than a runaway train manned by desperadoes.

He lowered the glasses and contemplated his de-

tachment, armed with Panzerbüc—
guns, MG 34 machine guns, and s—
his frown deepened. The Rheingold
begging to be devastated, the cabin
tive a receptacle waiting to receive s—

He thought about the dynamite s—
track a kilometer down the line and uttered a sigh
that was halfway to being a moan.

The Rheingold was two kilometers away, approaching a sweeping curve in the track. It looked very grand with the midday sun gleaming on its purple, cream, and gold paintwork. And what an engine. The captain loved trains; he had been trained to blow up tanks, not trains.

As the Rheingold went into the curve he panned the field glasses along its length—engine, tender, two head-end coaches, three passenger carriages, and at the tail, an armored car with an antiaircraft gun pointing at the sky.

But who was that standing on the platform of the gun? Whoever it was he had the posture of someone expecting plaudits, not bullets. There was an infantry unit camped down the line waiting to be sent into Belgium and . . . my God, he was returning a salute from them!

The captain adjusted the fine focus on the field glasses. The man was wearing field gray . . . lock of hair falling across his forehead . . . postage-stamp mustache . . . and the train was coming from the direction of OKH headquarters!

The soldiers serving under the captain that day

. got the note of raw terror in his voice as he
.ed them to lay down their arms and raced for
.e field telephone to tell the crew along the track to
defuse the dynamite.

MILLER RAISED HIS head above the rim of the turret
on the armored car and shouted to the Mailman,
"Are we in Belgium yet, Adolf?"

The Mailman, who had been wearing the
wounded German's tunic, said, "About three miles
across the frontier."

"Then you'd better take that mustache off and
come down. The Belgians aren't quite so keen on
the Führer as the Germans."

"Heil Hitler," said the Mailman, and came down
very quickly.

11

May 24

*T*HE ORDER THAT was to make possible the miracle of Dunkirk, the evacuation of 338,226 Allied troops, two-thirds of them British, was made by Hitler at 1231 hours. After conferring with Field Marshal Karl von Rundstedt, commander of Army Group A, he decided to halt the panzer groups attacking the retreating British Expeditionary Force, French, and Belgians from the west.

Various reasons have been given for the order. Hitler wanted to keep the panzers for Operation Red, the second phase of the French campaign; he didn't want to totally humiliate the British because he wanted them to be amenable to negotiation; he believed Goering's boast that the Luftwaffe would pound the British into surrender.

What is more likely is that it was a combination of all three motives that prompted him to call a halt. It was his first mistake of the war.

MEANS THERE's still hope," Logan said when
old about Hitler's order. Earlier he had heard from
Miller that the Rheingold had crossed the German-
Belgian frontier.

He prodded a map on his desk in his office in
Blenheim Palace. A schoolmaster's finger; it should
have been ingrained with chalk.

Then he traced a pocket stretching from the English Channel into France and Belgium. "It looks
like an army boot," he said. "If the Rheingold can
reach a point somewhere near the top then it could
reach the heel; that is, the Channel."

"Did Miller give you his route?"

Logan shook his head. "He didn't have time. But
if I were him I would head for Lille. The position
there is chaotic—all to the good—and it's on the
main rail line."

"Then," Munnion said, peering over his shoulder, "he'll become part of the retreat. From Lille it's
about forty miles to the coast. But we don't know
what he'll run into. Hitler might have called off his
panzers to the west but Army Group B will plunge
in from the east."

"He's done well so far," Logan remarked,
straightening up from the map.

"Isn't that an understatement? How are his family, by the way?"

"Family?" Logan looked vague. "Oh, they're all
right."

"Have you told them what's happened to
Miller?"

"Not yet," Logan said. "It wouldn't ⟋ ᵔ ⟍
it?"

Munnion sat opposite Logan and lit ⟍
Why wouldn't it do, he wondered.

"They wouldn't be able to resist telling ev⟍ ryone
that their son wasn't a traitor. Before we knew
where we were the cat would be out of the bag.
German agents who will be sniffing around the
home will realize that Miller's working for us."
*Rubbish, because the Germans knew by now that
Miller was on the Rheingold.* "And, of course, we
don't want to risk it leaking out that we were shipping the gold to North America, do we?"

Finally Munnion understood. It wasn't a question of holding back *now*: Miller's family was *never*
going to be told that he was a hero. The debacle
must never be revealed. And with a terrible certainty
he knew that it wasn't beyond Logan's calculations
to return Miller to the condemned cell. Or have him
executed in some other way.

Logan said, "You're a very capable man."

"So I've been told."

"But you sometimes forget this is total war.
What's one sacrifice compared with saving the British people? If this ever got out, then morale would
collapse like . . ." He pointed out of the window at a
silver monster pulling at its moorings, ". . . like a
punctured barrage balloon."

"I sometimes wonder," Munnion said, "if anything's worthwhile if we're going to lower our
morals to the level of the Gestapo."

'reedom's worth saving," Logan said. "By the way, I've got a lead on Goering's contact in London. I'm waiting for confirmation."

Munnion waited for him to elaborate. Instead he said, "Now let's get down to some planning. As you know, on May 20 Churchill took the precautionary step of ordering Admiral Ramsay to get together a fleet of small rescue ships 'in readiness to proceed to ports and inlets on the French coast.' I think it's time we got our own ship on the move, don't you?"

WHEN HE HEARD that the Rheingold had crossed the German-Belgian border, Goering took a modicum of comfort from the fact that Hitler had confirmed the order, confided to him earlier, that he had halted the panzers west of the trapped Allied armies.

That meant that the Führer had faith in the Luftwaffe's ability to annihilate the fleeing Tommies before they tried to escape across the Channel. So he could use any means at his disposal to get among them—and get near the Rheingold.

Standing beside Hitler in OKH headquarters, Goering grinned fiercely. Really, this man Miller and his desperadoes were proving to be worthy opponents. Even at this distance he could smell the scent of battle and, when he closed his eyes, see the glint of gold.

VON RITTER MADE his move at nightfall.

All afternoon the Rheingold had been picking its way through Belgium north of the Ardennes, the

would hardly be carrying tommy guns—toward the toilet on the other side of the wood-paneled wall between the passenger coach and the first head-end coach.

Ritter held up his hands. "Can you untie these, please?"

"Is it necessary?"

"Without going into details, yes."

The Mailman turned to Becker. "You undo the wire for him."

"Very commendable," Ritter said, grinning. And to Becker as he untwisted the wire, "Not so commendable."

"All right," the Mailman said in his sing-song Welsh accent. "Less chat, in you go."

Becker appraised him. "You know something? You should have been a film star. Shouldn't he Hanna."

The girl smiled at the Mailman and ran her tongue around her pouting lips.

The Mailman jerked the Schmeisser. "Do what you've got to do and do it as quickly as possible." It was impossible to climb out of the toilet, he had already checked that.

When Ritter was inside, the girl raised her skirt and rubbed the inside of her thigh with her bound hands and said in halting English, "He's right, you are very handsome." She stood up and came closer to the Mailman, raising her skirt again. "Perhaps when we get to wherever we are going you will see that I am treated well . . . I will be good to you . . ."

She was just outside the toilet now, and, drawing the edge of her black French panties with one finger, she said softly, "Here, feel how good I would be."

She screamed as the Mailman stretched out his hand.

The door of the toilet swung open, slamming the Mailman against the frame of the passenger coach door. As he tried to regain his balance, Ritter grabbed the Schmeisser and clubbed him on the jaw with the butt.

Ritter blew the girl a kiss, opened the exit door of the coach, and, lowering himself onto the foot-ledge, slammed it behind him. At the same time the girl stepped over the Mailman's body and pulled the brass handle of the alarm beside the luggage rack over Becker's head.

Becker watched her, brushing at a tick that had sprung to life beneath one eye.

The wheels shrieked against the rails, the coaches bucked.

Miller reached Hanna before the train stopped. "What the hell . . . Where's Ritter?"

The Mailman groaned.

Hanna said, "He jumped. That way," pointing to the door on the wrong side of the train.

Miller wrenched open the door. The train stopped. Miller jumped onto the track. Ritter lowered himself onto the shoulder of the embankment on the other side.

Pritchard shouted, "What's wrong?"

Miller, peering down the track, shouted back, "You tell me."

"Someone pulled the communication cord."

He must have jumped clear as the train slowed down, Miller thought. He might be half a mile back by now. But what can he do except raise the alarm, and by that time the Rheingold will be in Allied-held territory. Just then, Ritter started shooting.

Ritter had reached the steel step leading to the footplate; as he raised himself over the edge of the cabin, the Chauffeur didn't stand a chance. Machine-pistol bullets tore into his chest, slamming him against the controls of the engine. A ricochet hit Vogel in the eye and he fell backward, clawing at his face; his falling body saved Pritchard, who dived out of the cabin on the opposite side to Ritter, taking a bullet in his arm.

Ritter let him go: killing wasn't the object of the exercise. He fired a long burst into the gleaming, blood-spattered pipes and gauges. Steam hissed, scalding water spurted. The 18 547 sighed.

Still holding the Schmeisser, Ritter jumped from the footplate. And into the arms of the Prizefighter.

Wrenching himself free, Ritter tried to aim the gun, but the Prizefighter was too close to him.

"I've bounced better than thee, lad," the Prizefighter said, thrusting aside the barrel of the gun with his right arm and hitting Ritter in the belly with a fist like a rock.

Ritter bent forward as air rushed from his lungs and fell to one side. As the Prizefighter came in with his boots, Ritter grasped one of them. The Prize-fighter fell.

Gravel flints shifted beneath them. Another fist hit Ritter but he was already turning away from the blow, his body accelerating as he rolled down the embankment.

A ditch half filled with water lay below. Ritter splashed into it, face submerging. He tried to breathe too quickly and took water into his lungs. Choking, he surfaced. He felt as if he had been hit by the locomotive.

A landslide of flints announced the Prizefighter's arrival. He hit the water beside Ritter. Seeing the white blur that was his face surfacing, Ritter chopped with the blade of his hand, hoping to find the neck.

A grunt. But the blur was still there. Ritter suspected that, although he was built like a tank, he didn't possess much stamina. He could hear him breathing heavily. Too much beer.

He picked up a heavy flint and swung it at the blur. Another grunt. A pause in the breathing. Water swirling closer. More stamina than I thought. . . .

Arms encircled him, so powerful that he could feel the push of biceps against his chest. He did the only thing possible in the circumstances and brought his knee up as sharply as the water would allow into the Prizefighter's crotch.

The arms went slack long enough for Ritter to

tear himself free. Where to? He stretched out an arm to the far side of the ditch. Ahead and behind lay water; the only way was up again, crabwise, to avoid being spotted by the figures silhouetted against the lights of the train.

It was the Medic who brought him down in a rugby tackle as he reached the top of the embankment and started to run, and the Prizefighter, laboring up behind him, who pulled him to his feet and hit him on the jaw. The Marksman would have shot him between the eyes if Miller hadn't stopped him.

Ritter asked Miller later why he had saved him. Miller said, "Because we're going to need a fireman," but he wasn't sure if that was the whole reason.

IN THE CABIN of the locomotive, Miller surveyed the damage. In death Vogel had snarled; the Chauffeur had shed a couple of years.

To Pritchard, who had a field dressing tied to the wound on his arm, he said, "How bad?" pointing to the damaged controls.

Pritchard said, "Pretty bad. Regulator crocked. Boiler water level and steam pressure gauges smashed . . . valves, compressors damaged . . . cylinder cock—if that's left shut the cylinder could burst."

"Can you get up enough steam to limp to a siding?"

"Me?"

"Who else? Vogel's dead."

It was then that Pritchard confessed.

SHOVELING COAL INTO the firebox, Miller shouted, "Couldn't you have told us, for Christ's sake?"

Pritchard, hearing the shout above the wounded roar of the engine, turned. "It wouldn't have done any good, would it?"

"Is it much different, driving a full-size engine or a bloody little toy?"

Not a toy! "Yes," he yelled over his shoulder. He leaned out of the engine and peered into the darkness. Perversely, he was once again enjoying himself.

The Rheingold was traveling at about 15 mph; even Hercules had gone faster than that. But he daren't try and push 18 547 faster.

The principal danger was that, before he spotted a siding, a train coming up behind them would smash into them. With luck, all night traffic would have been canceled because there would be no schedules for signalmen in this war-torn pocket of Europe.

A cloud passed over the moon, the darkness thickened. Another danger, of course, was the obstacles ahead—there had been enough of them during the day.

The moon reappeared from the cloud. Ahead he spotted them, two shining ribbons veering to the right. Gently he stopped 18 547.

"What's up?" Miller shouted.

"We've got to do our double act all over again," Pritchard shouted back. And after they had man-handled their second set of points that day, "Do you know something?"

"You're a Spitfire pilot as well?"

"I've never been out of England before."

"I should have known," Miller said.

As the armored car at the rear of the Rheingold turned into the siding another train roared past, missing it by inches. Off to the war, wherever that was.

12

May 25

O NE A.M. THE Rheingold was at rest in the moonlight at the end of the siding leading from the main line to a coal mine abandoned by the Belgians during the German advance. From the engine came the ring of metal upon metal, as the Engineer patched up its sounds, a daunting task, Miller suspected, although the Birmingham mechanic with the Brylcreem-bright hair and scarred hands, his own leg patched up by the Medic, would never admit it. With him, examining 18 547's ruptured vitals, was Pritchard.

The dining car, where Ritter, Becker, Hanna, the wounded German soldier, and the fireman were confined under guard, was quiet. The Marksman was a motionless silhouette on the platform of the antiaircraft gun. He never seemed to get tired.

Miller, standing beside the tender with Gisella, said, "If the engine isn't fixed by dawn we're in trouble. Time's running out." He paused and stared at the hills of mined coal around them, peaks of fragmented silver light reaching for the stars. He picked up a nugget. "Carbon, like diamonds. But more beautiful in the moonlight than rough diamonds, which only look like dirty glass." He handed her the nugget.

"How many carats?"

"Twenty perhaps. I'll have it set for you."

"In gold, of course."

He said, "If we don't make Dunkirk, you'll have to make a run for it. Join up with the Allies. If you fall into German hands you'll be shot."

"And you?"

"I'm an old hand at escaping execution." He began to walk toward the looming skeleton of the pit head. "Let's reconnoiter."

When they were past the hills of coal they came to a village. It appeared to be deserted save for a couple of cats prowling its main street and a dog howling somewhere.

In the moonlight the village had a certain haunted beauty, but by day it would be a squat and forlorn place. What sort of lives did the inhabitants lead? The men burrowing, hewing, drilling in twilight depths; the women cooking and scrubbing and waiting. Perhaps they had fled in relief, escaped their bleak birthright.

Miller peered through a window of a cottage. No, they'd been happy here. There was a rocking horse in one corner of the living room and two chairs in front of a small black fireplace and, opposite the rocking horse, a clock that surely chimed. Unhappiness couldn't have survived in such a room, it would have been suffocated. So many people thought contentment couldn't exist in humble circumstances. Why, there was more contentment in his family's terrace in the East End of London than on any block in Mayfair. A radio playing Sandy MacPherson on the BBC theater organ, a blackened kettle on the hob, bread and dripping and a Lyon's individual pie and a game of cards—that was contentment.

The door of the cottage swung in a gentle breeze fanning down the street. He went in and Gisella followed. He smelled the familiar residue of smoke from a coal fire and other homely breaths from abandoned lives. On closer inspection there were signs of hurried departure—documents scattered over the table, cupboard door wide open, a cracker tin emptied amid a small heap of crumbs. He touched the coal ashes in the fire; they were still warm. This family, this whole village swept up by communal instinct, must have fled just ahead of the German tanks, like animals before a forest fire. And by now probably overtaken by them and perhaps swallowed up.

Miller sat in one of the chairs in front of the fire. It was a rocking chair, and he began to rock gently as she sat opposite him. They might have been there for years.

She asked him how he had become what he was

and, surprised, he replied that he thought he had told her.

"No," she said. "But please tell me now. In this place."

SOUTHEND IN THE '20s. Sea and gray mud, one indistinguishable from the other. Dinghies and sailing shops resting crookedly in this lovely, gurgling grayness and sea gulls diving from blue rents in the sky. The smell of salt on the air, and cotton candy, and, as you passed the guzzling mouth of a pub, beer. He loved it all. The longest pier in the world; the endless promenade, which, according to his mother, who liked to mix pleasure with education, was one of the banks of the mouth of the Thames; the amusement arcades; paddling in the little waves; a picnic with cold beef sandwiches and Pan-Yan pickle and Tizer; a stick of candy with SOUTHEND entering one end of the peppermint tunnel and emerging intact the other. They couldn't afford it, what with his father being on the dole and Vic's cough costing more by the day, so his parents kept telling each other, but it was happiness, something to look forward to twice a year, even if they could only manage daytrips. And they were together. Family.

A promenade shop spilling its wares onto the pavement. Painted cardboard birds on string at the end of sticks, which chirruped and fluttered their wings when you ran with them; celluloid wind-

mills that spun their arms frantically when you held them above you in a breeze; comics and masks and buckets and spades and shrimping nets. But it was one of the cardboard birds, with a sparrow's face and bright green wings, that he was after. He glanced up and down the promenade. His father was going for a pint, so he had said, and his mother for an orange drink outside the pub with Vic and himself. Rehearsing his lines, "Can I have it, please, please, and I won't ask for anything at Christmas," he had snatched the stick and, with the bird fluttering in his wake trilling, run to the pub to ask for the money to pay for it. And hadn't heard the cry from the shopkeeper, "Hey stop, you little bugger," but had felt the policeman's hand like a talon on his shoulder. Still felt it.

The magistrate, a woman with short graying hair cut like a man's, who seemed to be very concerned with society, whatever that was, had placed him on probation and said something privately to his father that had caused his face to crumple and, remembering how sun-bright his face had been under a handkerchief on the day it had happened, he had cried for the first time since the cardboard bird had been snatched from him. Outside the court his father had said, "Don't worry me old mate, them what's got nothing always take it out on them what's got everything." But although he knew what his father meant, they certainly hadn't got everything. He decided that one day he would do something about that.

He was just ten at the time.

ROCKING HIS CHAIR gently, he told her that, apart from the money for Vic's treatment, his family had never accepted financial aid from him. Eventually they understood he was earning it dishonestly. By the time his father began to suspect, however, it was too late: he was an established thief.

Miller had still found ways to help them. They had bought the terrace house they rented, for instance, for £300; the real price had been £500, but Miller had paid the owner the £200 balance without their knowledge. He had faked a win on the football pools and taken them on vacation, and he had bribed the publisher of a local newspaper to give his father a job.

There had been bad moments, of course. Once when the police came for him, but he produced a watertight alibi; once when the alibi was leaky and he had fled, returning when the leaks had been stopped.

As for the rest of the money he had accumulated, that had been spent on his education, his accent, the whole grand deception of his existence. What balance there was had been banked.

Loving him, she said, "Not the Bank of England, I hope."

"Piggy bank," he said.

"We could have been happy here," she said, gesturing in the moonlight.

"Anywhere. Perhaps when this is all over I'll buy a jewelry store. Be on the other end of the game. At least I should be able to make the place burglar-proof. Would you like that, you and me partners?"

She nodded, not sure how her voice would emerge. She got up and closed the door and kissed him and held his face to her breasts. She knew then that there had to be one last time for them, and pushing him away, she stood in the moonlight in front of the still-warm ashes of the fire and began to undress.

Then, when he, too, was naked, she pulled him down beside her on the rug with a desperation that, thank God, he could not yet understand.

Her passion matched her desperation. She wanted all of him. "There . . . there . . . there . . ." And he must want all of her. "Here . . . here . . . yes . . . ah . . ." Her wildness had reached him as he kissed her mouth and her breasts.

At last he was inside her, where he belonged.

Then they were fighting each other, possessing each other, and sharing each other. They cried out together in that abandoned room where others had shared, and she knew that the echoes would follow her down her life.

"Stay there," she whispered. "Stay inside me."

"We're one," he said. "Always will be."

And because she knew how forlorn such a hope was, she began to sob. When the tears had spent themselves, she forced herself to return to her torment: how to betray him.

WHY HIM?

Walking back to the pithead, past the empty cottages and the small, crouching church, she glanced at his profile, at its self-taught assurance that sometimes even he wasn't aware that he possessed.

Why you?

She had expected a spy, a man of furtive habits, someone paid to deceive. Instead she had met a secret patriot who had suffered the ultimate injustice.

He had walked, damn him, into her life as if their meeting had been preordained. He had thrust doubt into the crusade that she and Otto had forged.

Lying in a pine forest during the long vacation from the university, after making love for the first time among the thin shafts of dusty sunlight, she and Otto, his face so earnest, had planned the salvation of the Fatherland. Small beginnings in Hamburg that would multiply and reach out across the country.

They were very young and they were naive, but it wouldn't be the first time that a thorough reformation of society had been conceived by youth. Gazing at the mosaic of blue sky high in the cathedral dome of the forest, they had sworn to excise the cancer from Germany; to refurbish the hopes that ordinary decent Germans had cherished at the beginning of the decade.

Then Otto had been betrayed and shot. The Nazis acknowledged no shade of patriotism other than their own depraved creed. She had been prepared to follow him in death until she realized that their crusade had been left in her hands.

Miller said, "There's a light in that cottage." He turned down a lane, and she tucked her hand under his arm and held onto it tightly.

The British had heard about Otto and her through their agents, and when war was declared they approached her, confusing her ideals with a propensity for treason. As a high-class whore, she had seduced secrets from her clients and passed onto the British what she thought fit.

But treason? Oh, no. Working as a double agent, she became the link between the British and Hitler's enemies within the Third Reich, among them Admiral Wilhelm Canaris, head of the German military intelligence, the *Abwehr*. Both wanted to cut off the grotesque head of Nazism.

With Hitler and his henchmen gone—a British agent had once suggested removing the Gs and Hs from the English alphabet, Goering, Goebbels, Hitler, Himmler, Heydrich, and Hess—there could be a negotiated peace. And a new Germany.

"Wait a minute," Miller said. "It could be booby-trapped."

You would have thought he had been a professional soldier all his life. She smiled despite everything and gripped his arm tighter.

In addition to her radio outlet with British Intelligence, Canaris had given her access to one of his own agents in London, code named Eros, because it was easier to contact him by radio then to risk internal transmissions that were tapped by the *For-*

schungsamt, the Gestapo, and indeed his own *Abwehr*.

Ostensibly Eros worked for the Fifth Branch of the Luftwaffe, but, according to Canaris, he was as zealously dedicated to exterminating the madmen leading Germany as Gisella herself. "He's one of us," he had confided. "With access to many secrets in London." At the time she had noted that the clever, prematurely gray admiral hadn't been exactly outgoing.

Everything had gone smoothly enough until Goering had grabbed the gold and Miller had arrived in Hamburg.

With an incalculable fortune destined for the private coffers of Goering, the personification of everything she and Otto had detested, what could she do?

Most of her acquaintances would have said that an oath taken by two young lovers in a pine forest was nothing more than an indiscretion. Not so. The dreams of youth were the ones that counted, and if you peered through the years there they were, bright and agonizing.

She had in her power the means to honor that oath, to thwart the second most powerful Nazi in Germany—Goering! how they had loathed him— to avenge Otto's death, and, more practically, to fund the new Fatherland with gold.

Could she confide in Miller? Impossible. Like her, he loved his country despite what they had done to him. What's more *they* were holding his family hostage.

No, she would have to deceive him. But ever since the moment when she had known this she had prayed that the final decision would be taken from her. That the bullion would sink before it reached Hamburg. That Wehrmacht troops commanded by one of the honorable generals would intecept the Rheingold.

No longer. They were in Belgium, dangerously close to Allied-held territory. She would have to act tonight. Tell Canaris through Eros where the Rheingold was hidden.

She tried to comfort herself. In a way honoring my oath to Otto is honoring my feeling for Miller. He is my second love, my true love, and he will understand that I have to keep my promises, otherwise everything is meaningless.

Stupid bitch! He's been betrayed once. Would *you* understand?

Miller, who had been investigating the inside of the cottage, returned and said, "It's all right. No booby traps. Come in and meet Louise."

Louise was about eighteen, plain but attractive enough with brown hair and an olive skin. She spoke French with a slight accent, Flemish probably.

She was sitting in front of a broken-toothed gas fire sipping a glass of red wine.

Miller asked her why everyone had gone, leaving only her.

It had been the priest's doing, she said in a sullen voice. The village had been very religious, a full church every Sunday, and when he had heard that the Germans were coming he had commandeered every car, bicycle, and baby carriage and led his flock away from the Stukas.

"And you?" Miller asked in French. "Why didn't you go with them?"

"They wouldn't have wanted me," she said. "They never did. I was always a stranger. In a way it was my opportunity to escape."

Miller spread his hands. "Why?"

The girl said, "I came here because I fell in love with a man from the village. He never married me, and the villagers decided I was a whore." She drank some more wine.

"Did the Germans come here?" Miller asked.

"They came through. They hardly stopped. They will come back." She shrugged.

"And you?"

"It can't be any worse. Perhaps better."

Gisella asked, "Where are you from?"

"Malmedy," the girl answered.

"Can we do anything?" Miller asked.

The girl shook her head and poured herself some more wine.

As they walked back to the pithead Miller said, "An outcast. I suppose it happens in many villages."

Gisella didn't reply. She knew the real reason why the girl hadn't joined the other villagers as they fled. Malmedy was the German-speaking area of Belgium; her accent had been German, not Flemish. She was a traitor, a member of Hitler's Fifth Column, which was causing disruption ahead of his tanks.

But it wasn't the fact that the girl came from Malmedy that had made Gisella suspicious about her. She had sensed her dishonesty. It seemed to her she had recognized herself in a different guise.

As they reached the metal framework of the pit-head and saw the Rheingold nestling among hills of shining coal, Miller delivered into her hands the means to betray him.

He said, "I've got to radio London." Then, rubbing his face with his hands, added, "God, I feel so tired."

She heard herself say, "You get some sleep, I'll send the message." And the Delilah in her added, "Don't forget I've had more experience radioing London than you."

Say no.

"All right," he said. "I'll have to have my wits about me tomorrow. God knows what lies ahead of us."

"There," she heard herself say. She pointed at a watchman's hut beside the pit-shaft. "There'll be a bed of sorts in there."

There was. A camp bed covered with a coarse blanket. "Like the blankets in Wandsworth," Miller said.

While she waited he fetched the radio and some

maps from the Rheingold. In the hut he found a child's drawing book; it was filled with crayoned pictures of structurally unsound houses; there was even a train there with hopper wagons instead of carriages; jolly suns with yellow fingers beamed above all the drawings.

He turned over one of the houses. "Before it falls down," he said, smiling, and with a stub of pencil and the help of a map wrote the message to be transmitted to London.

"Our position now," he said. "Our proposed route. Our estimated time of arrival—if such a thing is possible—at Dunkirk. And tell them," writing rapidly and glancing at Gisella at the same time, "to make sure the ferry's on its way." He paused. "At the end—love to Vic and my parents." He handed her the sheet of paper; she turned it over and the sun beamed at her.

He lay down on the camp bed, hands behind his head. She bent and kissed him. "I'd love a jewelry shop," she said. "If . . ."

But he was asleep.

She picked up the suitcase containing the radio and took it to a moonlit spot beside the pit-shaft.

She got quickly through to London but the call sign she tapped out in Morse code wasn't Miller's.

She gave Eros the current position of the Rheingold, its intended route, and arrival time at Dunkirk.

She wished she could have sent the message to Miller's family. How she wished it.

When the message had been acknowledged she closed the suitcase.

On the way back to the hut she put her hand in the pocket of her slacks. Her fingers touched the nugget of coal. Twenty carat. She wanted to cry but there is a despair beyond tears that is arid ground.

She let herself into the hut. Miller was breathing rhythmically. She bent and kissed him lightly on the lips. "Good night, Charlie," she whispered.

13

May 25

MILLER SAID, "I thought you told me you could repair anything."

"Almost anything." The Engineer winced as he turned his splinted leg awkwardly.

"Except railway engines?"

"This is tricky," the Engineer admitted. "I could do it if I had the right gear. I need brass, copper, solder, and a blowtorch."

Miller turned to Pritchard. "Would it move with the work he's already done?"

Pritchard scratched his ginger hair. "Not a chance. It would blow up."

"Then we'll have to get the gear," Miller said. He rasped his hand on his unshaven chin. Dawn was breaking, the rim of pale green on the horizon transformed into the northern lights by tracer shells and Very lights. Coal, slag heaps, and the skeleton of the pit-head tower loomed around them. "I'll have to steal it. Another crime against society." He grinned.

He was still wondering what to do when he saw the convoy approaching in the distance along the track beside the main railway. A convoy, possible breakdowns, tools. He ran to the dining car and roused Becker.

"Put your jackboots on," he said, "there's work to be done." And to the men in the SS uniform: "Smarten yourselves up. You're supposed to be crack SS troops, not Fred Karno's Army."

Von Ritter said: "Jump to it, Fritz, or you'll get your wrist slapped."

Miller said to Becker, "This is what I want you to do."

With the North Countryman wearing an SS corporal's combat jacket and helmet and carrying a machine pistol, Becker walked toward the main line a mile away. As he did so Miller fired a red Very light from the armored car.

The convoy halted. A Wermacht captain climbed out of a mud-spattered staff car. Accompanied by a sergeant, he walked briskly up to Becker and gave the Nazi salute.

Watching from the dining car, Miller wondered what he would do if he were in Becker's shoes. Obey the menace of the North Countryman's gun or try a double-cross. The latter was easy enough: the North Countryman didn't speak German. On the other hand, as soon as the captain barked an order and soldiers started leaping from the convoy he would pull the trigger.

Ritter said, "It would be so easy . . ." His expression was wistful. "All Becker has to do is explain the position to the captain and tell him to take it easy. Walk calmly back to the convoy and tell a sniper to pick off Becker's guard."

"Then I'd shoot Becker, and if I missed, someone else would get him."

"By that time you would have lost because the troops in the convoy would have opened up. But don't worry, Becker won't let you down. And the captain will obey him because he's in SS uniform. I should know." Ritter smiled tightly. "What have you told Becker to do? Get tools?"

"And materials." Becker, Miller thought, looked so rigidly honorable, the personification of the Prussian officers you read about in books about the Great War; only the monocle was missing. Could a spark of courage be ignited in his soul?

The captain turned and spoke to his sergeant, who walked briskly back to the convoy.

Becker stood quite still.

Gunfire rumbled in the distance.

A thrush began to sing on a starved poplar tree growing from a slag heap.

The sergeant reached the convoy. He went to the canvas-roofed truck. The tailgate of the truck came down.

When the sergeant turned he was holding a tool box, blowtorch, and sheet metal.

"Asshole," said Ritter looking at Becker.

LUNCH WAS BIZARRE.

More smoked salmon and caviar washed down with champagne —the beer had run out—in the dining car of a luxury express parked in a coal mine a few miles from a battleground.

Miller never wanted to drink champagne again; he thirsted for a pint of bitter.

"What I wouldn't give for a bowl of stew," the Prize-fighter remarked.

"Or fish and chips," the Medic said. "Wrapped up in a copy of the *Glasgow Herald*. After Celtic whacked Clyde. The last football match I saw," he explained to the Prizefighter. "We won, one nothing."

They were eating their lunch at one end of the dining car, guns beside them, still wearing their SS combat uniforms. Ritter, bound hand *and* foot since his escape bid, sat with Hanna at a table opposite Becker in the middle of the coach. Miller and Gisella sat on the other side of the aisle. The fireman, whose wounded hand had gone septic, and the wounded German soldier lay on cushions at the far end of the car, watched by the Mailman.

The Marksman still sat on the platform of the antiaircraft gun while the North Countryman patrolled outside.

From the engine came the sound of repair work as the Engineer and Pritchard worked on its wounds.

From time to time Wehrmacht units on their way to the front stopped to ask what had happened. Becker always obliged.

"Who do you support?" the Medic asked. "Liverpool?"

"Everton," the Prizefighter said. "The Toffees. They drew two all with Blackburn, September second. Same day you saw Celtic I'll wager. They all had to stop playing after that."

"And I backed Gordon Richards in every race at Manchester that day."

"Win?" The Prizefighter grimaced as he tasted some caviar. "Who put salt in the blackberry jam?"

"Did I buggery. He didn't win a single bloody race." A scowl crossed the Medic's freckled features. "I wonder who Hedy Lamarr supports," pointing his fork at the Mailman.

"I wouldn't take the piss too much, lad. He's not as soft as he looks."

"He's got an eye for the crumpet, I'll say that for him," the Medic said looking at Hanna. "What I couldn't do to that on a dark night in the Gorbals."

The Prizefighter fingered his flattened nose. "You talk about handsome up there. What about you, lad? You look as much like a quack as Joe Louis."

"I became a male nurse because it sounded cushy. Worst thing I ever did. Best thing that happened to me was the war." He took a swig from a bottle of Krug. "Well, no one can say *you* don't look what you are. What do you do in your spare time, duff up Liverpool supporters?"

"As a matter of fact," the Prizefighter said, "I breed pigeons."

"Pull the other leg," the Medic said, "it's got bells on it."

He stood up and, gun in hand, walked to Miller's table. He cleared his throat; he wasn't sure how to address Miller; no one was. "I think it's about time we did something about the wounded," he announced.

Miller looked up from his smoked salmon. "Plural?"

"The fireman's pretty bad. His hand looks like a football and he's got a fever. As for the other Kraut, he's lost a lot of blood. He'll have to have a transfusion soon or he'll snuff it."

"How long?"

The Medic shrugged. "Impossible to tell."

"Twelve hours?"

"Maybe."

"Then do your best for him," Miller said. In his profession he had rarely had to exercise authority, and his use of it surprised him. "We can't hand either of them over to the Germans—they'd blow it. So they'll have to wait until we catch up with the French or the British."

Ritter spoke from across the aisle. "You know something, Miller? You astonish me. So far you've managed to pull this thing off, and I didn't think you had it in you. You looked competent enough and yet . . ." Ritter sipped some champagne.

"And yet?"

"Contradictions. A man wearing a disguise. I knew the outer skin, not the inner one. A tough shell and a soft center? I wasn't sure. Until now. But I'll tell you something else: put you in the British army and you wouldn't make second lieutenant. It wouldn't matter if you could speak ten languages and read Homer backward, they'd still sniff out your background. That's what's wrong with the British, they're snobs. Poona and all that."

Becker stood up. He said to Miller, "I wish you'd known me a long time ago. In another war." He pushed his way past the girl and walked down the aisle.

"Hey," Miller shouted, "where the hell do you think you're going?"

Becker walked on. The Medic and the Prizefighter barred his way. He pushed the Medic aside, showing surprising strength.

The Prizefighter aimed his machine pistol at Becker's erect back. He looked to Miller for guidance. Miller held up his hand.

Becker left the coach and walked toward the armored car. Miller jumped to the ground.

Becker was fifty yards away. The Marksman peered at him through the telescopic sights of his Lee Enfield.

Miller shouted to Becker to come back. Becker ignored him. He had passed the armored car and was near the edge of the mine shaft.

The Marksman shouted, "Now?"

Again Miller raised his hand. He shouted once more. Becker walked on.

"Now?"

Still Miller kept his hand raised. He called out, "Not in the back, Becker."

Becker turned.

Miller dropped his hand.

The Marksman shot him in the chest.

He staggered back into the mine shaft.

As he disappeared, Miller saw a monocle drop from his eye. But that was only his imagination.

ALL MORNING GOERING had been waiting for a precise map reference for the Rheingold so that as soon as it entered Allied-held territory, he could send in his Stukas.

By lunchtime, nothing.

He ate and drank ravenously in the farmhouse. Three kinds of wurst, cheesecake, and Rhine wine.

What the hell had happened to his source in London? Fraulein Hessen should have contacted him by now, and he should have contacted me.

The train seemed to have steamed off the map of Belgium.

Other intelligence sources were functioning well enough. The Belgians were on the point of conceding defeat; Gort had honed down his objectives to a mass escape bid from Dunkirk with a last-ditch defensive position on the Aa, Scarpe, and Yser.

Why couldn't the source for Operation Argo be as efficient? Had he been blown?

God forbid. Goering downed a quarter liter of wine. Not that it mattered in the long run. The British had as much chance of shipping the bullion out of France as Gort had of getting his weary Tommies across the Channel.

But where was the Rheingold? In a tunnel?

The teleprinter in the kitchen began to chatter.

Goering finished his wine in a gulp and strode over to it.

When it stopped he tore off the message and compared it with his code pad.

In a coal mine?

He consulted a map of Belgium and checked out the reference. Well, there *were* coal mines in that vicinity. If the Rheingold was heading for France, in the direction, as he anticipated, of Lille, then it would have to pass through that area.

Trapped in a coal mine. At the end, presumably, of a siding. A sitting target. And he wouldn't have to use Stukas and risk smashing open the crates.

Fräulein Gisella Hessen you have done well. A pity, for you that is, that you don't realize that although Eros—God of love, of all things—works for the Fifth Branch of the Luftwaffe and, more pertinently as far as you are concerned, Admiral Canaris and his holier-than-thou cronies, his real employer is the *Forschungsamt*. My brains, my collectors.

Swaggering, he left the farmhouse and told his driver to take him back to his mobile headquarters.

When he got there he gave his orders. It had worked before, it would work again. One final strike and no more skepticism from his own staff or the Wehrmacht generals.

The Midas touch, and a singularly ingenious one.

THE CAUSE OF the delay in the message from Eros to Goering was a summer storm that crackled across Europe, disrupting radio communications. So garbled was the Morse that reached Berlin from London for private transmission to the farmhouse in the Eifel, that no one dared relay it—something resembling a *coal mine* had materialized in the middle of a message about a train. Send such ludicrous intelligence to the Feldmarschall at your peril.

By the time Eros had unscrambled the frantic queries in London from Berlin, there was only time to retransmit the guts of the message, because he was due to attend a vital meeting—vital in its way to all the warring factions—and his absence would be viewed with extreme suspicion. But the fact that the Rheingold was delayed in a coal mine, together with the all-important map reference, was surely all that mattered. If the Rheingold managed to evade whatever Goering threw at it—a doubtful proposition—then the rest of the message, the train's route and its estimated time of arrival would reach the Feldmarschall through the normal backup channel.

With this channel in mind, Eros, wearing a fawn raincoat and carrying a copy of *The Times* under one arm, made his way to the meeting in the City by way of the Central Line Subway, joining it at Bond Street, not far from his apartment in Mount Street.

The two Special Branch officers, Wilson and Macdonald, detailed to follow him but not to make any approach until he had passed material to a second party, followed at what has always been described, but never defined, as "a discreet distance." Behind them, at a still more discreet distance, walked two more SB men with instructions to detain the second party after material had changed hands.

Eros bought a ticket and ran down an immobilized escalator to the eastbound line, thrusting his way through the waiting passengers to the far end of the platform, which was deserted save for a balding man wearing a brown sports coat with leather patches on the elbows.

"I bet it's in *The Times*," Macdonald said.

"Par for the course," Wilson said. "Like the two briefcases."

"He's got one of those too," Macdonald pointed out.

"Want to bet?"

Macdonald shook his head. "Sign of weakness. Don't you read Edgar Wallace?"

"I only ever read one book," Wilson said. "By a fellow called Woodbine Willie. He said playing with yourself made you go blind."

"And did it?"

"Where are we?" Wilson asked.

Looking everywhere except at Eros, they continued to wait on the fringe of the crowd, two City-sleek men in gray hats and dark suits disguising the rugby toughness of their physiques. Opposite them on the far side of the electrified line a poster warned, CARELESS TALK COSTS LIVES. The station smelled of trapped electricity; a train rumbled along the line somewhere down the black hole of the tunnel.

The man in the sports coat tapped Eros on the shoulder.

"Can I have a look at the sports page?" Wilson mimicked.

"Come on, here we go," Macdonald said.

They passed the man in the sports coat heading for the exit, who would be stopped by the two other SB officers, and came up beside Eros.

Wilson said, "Mr. Bernard Riley Grover?"

Grover swung around. "That's me. What can I do for you?"

Wilson said, "We have a warrant for your arrest."

The American took off his spectacles. Without them his face was bare and dangerous. "Really? On what charge?" voice slow and careful.

"You're charged under the Treachery Act of 1940. It became law two days ago in case you're interested."

"I'm interested but I shall, of course, claim diplomatic immunity."

Down the platform the man in the sports jacket was making a fight of it as they hoped he would, diverting attention from what they were going to do.

The roar of the approaching train grew louder.

"We thought you would," Wilson said.

"But there's a war on," Macdonald said.

"Not in the United States there isn't."

"You'll have to come with us, sir."

"I don't think so." Grover hunched his shoulders beneath his raincoat.

The train roared into the station and Wilson and Macdonald released their grip on Grover's arms and abruptly pushed him backward.

He tottered on the edge of the platform for a moment before falling in front of the train.

"Stand back," Macdonald shouted, "there's been an accident."

HOW DID YOU get onto him?" Munnion asked.

"Routine," Logan replied. "Procedural stuff. Goering's information was so precise that it had to be someone at the top with access to all the details. Someone in the Court Room. Even you." He gazed steadily at Munnion across the desk in his office at Blenheim Palace.

"You checked me out?"

"Of course. You had me worried for a while: you were just too predictable. Do you always inspect the roses in your front garden when you get home?"

"Not any more," Munnion said. "I dug them up yesterday and planted cabbages."

"So by a process of elimination it came down to Grover."

"I wonder why he did it," Munnion said.

"Hoover and Roosevelt had been fooled by him. He was a Kennedy man, even more anti-British than Joe. And we also discovered that he had German antecedents. Very pro-Hitler was Mr. Grover."

"But why work for Goering?"

"Because, I suspect, he was also in for a pot of gold."

"Do Hoover and Roosevelt know about all this?" Logan frowned. "Is there any reason why they should? Grover had an accident, that's all anyone needs to know."

"And the agent he was passing Fräulein Hessen's information to . . . Is he willing to be turned?"

"Not willing, indecently eager. He can't do anything about the intelligence Grover's already transmitted—the current position of the Rheingold —but he can bend the rest of the Hessen girl's message and anything else she sends to Eros."

"It's a pity," Munnion remarked, sucking at his pipe," that he was allowed to send the map reference."

"A pity? Of course it's a pity, damn it. Save your truisms. We only got airtight confirmation that Grover was our man this morning, and Macdonald and Wilson must have picked him up just after he'd contacted Berlin. In Intelligence everything seems to be just that little bit late. *If only*—those are the passwords of our profession."

"Your profession," Munnion said. He sucked harder at his pipe but it had gone out.

"We should thank our lucky stars we got onto him at all. From now on, everything relayed to Goering from London will be misleading."

"If it matters anymore."

"If anyone can save the day it's Miller."

"Thank God you weren't a little bit late there. In saving him from the gallows," Munnion added in case Logan's memory was playing tricks on him.

When Logan didn't reply, brooding on *ifs* no doubt, Munnion said, "There are a couple of things that puzzle me."

"Oh?" Logan stared at the photograph of the iceberg with the shingled hair; she stared back unsympathetically. She looked, Munnion decided, as though she had just discovered that her husband wasn't in *Who's Who*.

"One, why didn't Fräulein Hessen warn Grover that Miller was actually staying at her house?"

"Oh, she must have done that all right." Logan leaned forward and brushed a speck of dust from his wife's cheek; women like that weren't supposed to have dirty faces. "That was why the *Forschungsamt* heavies turned up there. And now I'll give you some inspired guesswork; she recognized them for what they were, Goering's private army."

"So?"

"Apparently Gisella Hessen doesn't want the Feldmarschall to get his sticky little fingers on the gold. That was why she helped Miller to escape."

"Then why," Munnion asked patiently, "has she been passing information to a *Forschungsamt* agent in London?"

"Elementary, my dear Munnion. She thought he worked for the Luftwaffe's Fifth Branch and a group of idealists within Germany who want to see the rebirth of a noble and unsullied Fatherland. Don't we all?"

"Devilish clever, Holmes," Munnion said. "But surely she must have realized she was being double-crossed when the *Forschungsamt* agents turned up at her house."

"Not really. She probably thought there had been a slipup in Hamburg; after all, the Fifth Branch and the *Forschungsamt* are pretty close to each other. She warned Grover to confine his intelligence in the future to their man in Berlin."

"How the hell do you know that?" Munnion asked.

"Because we found a note in Grover's apartment." Logan picked up a sheet of creased Basildon Bond notepaper from his desk and read from it. *"Confirm with Hessen that all future contacts in Germany will be confined to admiral. Underneath he's scribbled, Some hope."*

"Admiral?"

"Canaris. Head of the Abwehr. An honorable man, or as honorable as any intelligence chief can be." He held up one hand. "Don't say it." He lit a Rhodian; his tobacconist must have run out of Churchman's. "The intriguing thing is that Canaris is now working for us. But of course he doesn't know that Grover's been blown."

"That's one way of putting it." Munnion said. "Tell me, why didn't the Hessen girl tell Grover about Operation Croesus when she first got the details from Miller? Why didn't the Germans know we were going to hit the Rheingold in the Saxon Forest?"

"You would make an admirable interrogator," Logan said.

"It has been known."

"One good reason. Grover knew everything there was to know about the hit in the Saxon Forest. Why jeopardize her position by sending a superfluous message?"

"And did Grover tip off the *Forschungsamt* in Hamburg?"

"Indeed he did, according to the evidence we found in his apartment."

"Search warrant?"

Logan didn't laugh. "But by the time the message reached Hamburg, Becker had been kidnapped by Miller with the help of the girl. As he and Becker used one-time pads, there was no way anyone else could decode the message."

Munnion relit his pipe; it gurgled unpleasantly but these days you had to utilize every strand of soggy tobacco. "So the poor bitch who wanted to keep the gold out of Goering's hands for the Fatherland's sake has been helping him all along. Are you going to tell Miller that he's got a traitor, traitress rather, on the Rheingold?"

Logan shook his head. "No point. We'll intercept any messages she sends from now on. Who knows, Miller may have got emotionally entangled with her."

What, Munnion wondered, would you know about emotional entanglement? His pipe had gone out again and he stuffed the bowl with Airman. "Was it absolutely necessary to kill Grover?"

"Absolutely. He would have claimed diplomatic immunity. Who knows who he would have gone blabbing to then."

Munnion waited for him to add, "It was God's will," but this time he kept God out of it.

SITTING ON A garden seat beside the polio-crippled President's wheelchair in the Rose Garden of the White House, where even he hadn't been able to install a wiretap, Hoover tried everything he knew to pry the secret from Roosevelt.

But the President, looking, as always, deceptively benign with his sparse graying hair and pince-nez, fielded the questions with accomplishment.

Hoover: "Have you heard from Churchill today, Mr. President?"

Roosevelt: "He's in constant touch over this gold thing."

Gold thing! What a way to dismiss the greatest threat to his political future since his fight to reform the Supreme Court.

Even the weather seemed to be aiding and abetting the President's deception. A perfect May day with scents of burgeoning blossom on the air and an aircraft chalking a tranquil line across the morning sky.

"Anything new?" Hoover asked.

"As I told you, the train was damaged. But they're working on it."

"Nothing more?"

"Churchill seems to have the utmost confidence in this man Miller."

"And you?"

"I have to be guided by what Churchill thinks."

"He must be going crazy with worry."

"It's difficult to tell, this side of the Atlantic."

Suddenly Hoover, who had arrived uninvited, came out with it. "Mr. President, are you leveling with me?"

A pause. A laugh, godammit.

"Have I ever done anything else?"

There was no decisive answer to that: they weren't very close. Hoover only knew, knew in his bones, that he wasn't being told the whole truth.

"Not that I know of," Hoover said.

"Then relax. Enjoy the sunshine."

He's reveling in it, Hoover seethed.

"By the way," Roosevelt said, smiling at him, "Eleanor saw you arrive and wants you to stay to lunch. She's cooked it herself."

What, Hoover wondered, have I done to deserve that?

IN THE CABIN of the engine, the Engineer worked methodically, despite his broken leg.

As he worked he whistled, taking frequent swigs from a water bottle. Miller, becoming thirsty, picked up the bottle and drank from it. It contained brandy.

The Engineer smoothed his hair, still as oily bright as when he jumped from the bomber. "When you work in the inspection pits all day you need a few bevvies."

Miller considered bawling him out, but it didn't look as if it was affecting his work. He wondered what the man would do when the war was over. Could he be expected to settle in the pits once more?

What will any of us do?

The work was finished two hours later. By the time the Rheingold steamed away from the mine, the Engineer was quite drunk.

14

May 25

T HE TWO GLIDERS appeared before the Rheingold had reached the main line.

At first no one on the train realized what they were. Some thought they were stricken aircraft, confusing them with the towing aircraft that had swooped in with the afternoon sun behind them before veering away in the direction of the German frontier.

The Marksman was one of the first to realize what they were but even he, trying one-handed to operate the 40 mm antiaircraft gun, didn't comprehend how lethal were these silent, big-winged aircraft sailing toward the ground like gulls floating on a breeze. They looked so innocent, so vulnerable.

The defenders of Fort Eben Emael, pivot of the Belgian defenses at the junction of the River Meuse and the Albert Canal, had also been deceived. Seven hundred and fifty of them snugly deployed beneath the casemates and turrets of their *impenetrable* fortress.

Impenetrable until Hitler's secret force, glider-borne assault commandos armed with demolition charges, landed on top of it and unceremoniously drew its teeth with explosives.

During the assault on Fort Eben Emael, two of the gliders had become detached from their tow planes; these were the two that Goering had mustered for the attack on the Rheingold. There were eight assault troops in one, seven in the other, all members of the Koch Detachment, so named because their commander was Captain Walter Koch.

Koch was not there today, and they were led by Kurt Stehr, a nineteen-year-old lieutenant, a blond, blue-eyed physical fitness fanatic. His instructions were to do whatever the hell he liked, provided the two head-end coaches on the train were left intact.

From the air the target looked easy as it backed laboriously along the siding leading from the coal mine to the main line. Stehr knew, however, that now, as the gliders floated helplessly on the last lap of their flight, was the most dangerous time. And that looked suspiciously like an antiaircraft gun on the last coach.

Stehr, dressed in heavy combat uniform and helmet, and weighted with guns and stick bombs, looked anxiously at the glider beneath him. The antiaircraft gun seemed to be snouting in its direction.

Calmly, the Marksman, still clad in his SS combat uniform, manipulated the elevating mechanism of the gun. He had always done everything calmly, dispassionately; even the three killings he had undertaken—two in Paris, one in London—after leaving college in Switzerland. He couldn't say that he actually enjoyed killing: he merely derived satisfaction from the clean finality of execution. He sometimes wished that, like others, he could experience excitement, fear even, but he had never been touched by either; as for the call of patriotism, that was a total mystery to him, not merely because he was only a naturalized Englishman, but because he couldn't understand why anyone should have any feeling for a country. In his book you were born an individual and that was where your allegiance lay. At twenty-one he was a lonely young man and in his detached fashion he enjoyed his loneliness. He knew he would die young, and he regarded that prospect with a similar detachment—just so long as the death was violent and clean.

The barrel of the gun sank, seeking the low altitude of the two gliders. Really, the gun was a two- or three-man job. It reminded him of a Bofors. He knew almost everything there was to know about almost every gun, but AA weapons weren't his strong point.

The first glider was almost on the ground now, the second, closer to the Rheingold, almost too low for the gun. If only there were two or three of them manning it; but at least he had loaded it with one shell in case of an emergency.

As he fired the gun he had no idea whether trajectory and elevation were correct. He was following a gunman's instinct.

The recoil was spirited. The mayhem in the air terrible if you had feelings about such things.

The big silent bird just disintegrated. Bodies fell from the sky. The tail of the plane went that way, the nose the other. He thought he could hear the screams of the dying men, but, with the sound of the train's wheels on the rails, he couldn't be sure.

He abandoned the AA gun and went below. There was a lot of work to be done. The first glider had landed, spilling out men into the fields beyond the main line and they would be seeking revenge.

Stehr was the first out. Appalled by the human debris that had fallen around him, he waited tensely behind a hedge, Schmeisser machine pistol in his hands, while one of his men assembled an MG 34 light machine gun and another put together a PZB 38 antitank gun.

Ahead of him the train stopped. So they were going to stay and make a fight of it. Good strategy from their point of view. It would have taken time to reverse down the main line, stop, and change into forward gear: they could be blown off the track while they did that. This way, the only target they presented from this angle was the rear of the armored car and, above it, the antiaircraft gun. Well, they'd get that bastard if it was the last thing they did. Where was the gunner? He's mine, Stehr thought.

He peered through the hedge, which was threaded with white convulvulus. There was no movement from the train. They were waiting until the commandos came at them from the side. Stehr wondered what weapons they had. He gripped the machine pistol tightly as though it were a piece of exercising equipment. In the distance he could hear gunfire; rifles crackling, machine guns coughing, and the intermittent crump of cannon or mortar. And yet the sky was so tranquil; for some reason its color, pale blue, made him think of the skies over his home in the countryside near Munich.

Where was the gunner?

Ten feet to his right a heap of combat uniform and flesh whimpered. He took a pistol from its holster and put a bullet into the heap. The whimpering stopped.

Such a tranquil, early summer sky.

His sergeant said hoarsely, "The antitank gun's fixed, lieutenant."

And, farther away another voice, "The MG 34's ready."

So here we go.

Covered by the machine gun and the antitank gun, six of them moved forward, pressed close to the grass. A bullet zipped into the ground beside him.

Kneeling, he raised the Schmeisser and loosed off a burst at the armored car. He heard the bullets hit it with metallic impotence. Stupid. He hit the grass again and, smelling clover, tried to work out his strategy. *Ideot*. He should have done that before.

The attack on Fort Eben Emael had been rehearsed half a dozen times before, but not the attack on the pride of the German Railways.

Obviously the first priority was the armored car. If that was immobilized then the train was theirs. There was one snag: there were some Germans on board, among them a former SS officer named von Ritter and one of Goering's old cronies from the last war named Becker. It wouldn't do to kill either of them.

He gestured to the men who had crept forward with him. Three around one side of the train; two—three including him—around the other.

In the armored car the Marksman, helped by the Mailman, was assembling a light machine gun, an MG 34 like the one trained on the Rheingold from the fields across the track.

They were joined through the rear exit of the last coach by Miller, Luger in hand.

He said, "Can you get that thing," pointing at the MG 34, "on top of the car before they get you?"

"I think so." The Marksman's hands, strong but well cared for, worked deftly with the parts of the MG 34. "I thought the Schmeissers would see us through, but here we need the range. You know, open ground all around us. This is accurate at 2,000 meters, more on a tripod."

The Mailman said, "You'd better hurry up. A couple of stick bombs and we're done for."

"Perhaps," the Marksman said reaching for a

spare barrel, "you'd better get back to the ladies. They'll be worried sick without you."

The Mailman said, "Knock it off. It was me who went up there before," pointing above him. "Remember? Heil Hitler."

The Marksman tested the tripod. "Okay, now you can get up there again. After me—I speak German. We've got the SS uniforms, right? So I'm going to shout to them that we've taken the armored car. Killed the shit who shot down the glider. They'll be so overcome with joy that they won't see you coming up behind with the gun."

"I'll go first," Miller said. "I speak German."

"With an accent. They'd shoot you as soon as you opened your mouth."

"And your German is perfect?"

"Of course." He handed the gun to the Mailman. "Now I'm going up slowly. I'll call out to them as soon as my head's above the opening." He put on his steel helmet bearing the SS runes. "With luck they won't open up and I will be able to get past the antiaircraft gun onto the top of the car. There's a flat surface there, a gun mounting. But you won't have time to do any mounting. Just slam the tripod down and roll out of the way."

Miller said, "They must have spread out on either side of the train."

"Correct." The Marksman's dark, flecked eyes appraised Miller. "Five or six of them, by my reckoning. Two in reserve. The MG 34 should be able to

301

pick them off. I'll swing around in a complete arc. You," to the Mailman, "drop back down here as soon as you've rolled clear. Don't hang around so that the ladies can see you being a hero, they wouldn't want anything to happen to that handsome face of yours, would they."

The Mailman said, "When this is over I'll make sure something happens to that face of yours." The Welsh lilt gave his voice a peculiar menace.

But the Marksman was halfway up the steel ladder. There was an explosion nearby; it sounded like mud and turf pounding the sides of the armored car.

Miller said, "Stick bomb. Thrown too early."

"It means they're getting close," the Mailman said. Carrying the machine gun, he climbed two rungs of the ladder behind the Marksman.

Miller listened while the Marksman shouted to the Germans. "Hold your fire. We're SS. We've taken the armored car and killed the dirty pig who shot your glider."

Silence.

Then a voice not too far away. "Identify yourself."

The Marksman went onto the roof. The Mailman went up behind him and waited, head just above the surface.

The Marksman shouted, "Rottenführer Adolf Reinicke."

"Unit?"

"Verfugungsdivision."

How does he know about these things? Miller wondered.

The Mailman was emerging from the hatch behind the Marksman.

Stehr spotted him. "How many of you?" he called out to Rottenführer Reinicke.

"Just the two of us. But there are more Germans in the train. Two of them. Both Luftwaffe. Von Ritter and Becker."

That tallied. But still Stehr worried. In the gymnasiums of his youth there had never been any need for decisions. Unconsciously he tensed his trim stomach muscles.

From behind the cover of a small mound of grass—that was just about all the cover there was within shooting range of the train—Stehr shouted, "You two come down." His voice, against the breeze, sounded puny; he hoped it reached.

But they were coming down. Or lying down— one of them disappeared.

A window in one of the purple, gold, and cream carriages shattered. There was a man standing there. And through the broken window a voice carrying strongly on the breeze, "I'm von Ritter. Watch out, it's a trick."

The first burst from the machine gun on the roof of the armored car caught Stehr in his finely muscled torso. The bullets felt like boulders hitting him. He didn't believe it. To one side of him another commando reared up. The arc of bullets widened, sending up gouts of turf and dried mud and, as it reached the edge of the mine, coal dust.

But there was still the backup, Stehr remembered, the MG 34 and the antitank gun. He was doing pushups in the gym and there was a terrible pain in his chest.

The Marksman swung the MG 34 around and fired a long burst, taking in all obvious cover. Three hits. Silence. He kept low behind the machine gun on its tripod. From his left there came a short burst from a machine pistol. He swiveled the machine gun again and blasted the area from which the firing had come. He heard a scream.

Behind him a carriage door slammed. The Marksman cried out, "Keep down for Christ's sake." If the officer in charge of the glider-troops remembered any of his training—although he didn't seem to have retained too much—he would have arranged covering fire.

The antitank gun opened up at that moment, good meaty whacks as the bullets tore through the armored plating below him. The Marksman aimed the MG 34 across the main line track toward the hedge skirting a field there. He was about to shoot when he noticed Miller running toward the field on the other side of the train, using the coaches as cover.

The Marksman shrugged. Heroes he had no time for. There was probably another gun there in addition to the antitank gun. He fired a burst from the

MG 34 to divert the gunners' attention. He was right. A machine gun opened up from beside the hedge.

Miller ran to the left of the shooting, keeping low. A beautiful target just the same. What did he want, a decoration? The Marksman fired again but the gun was overheating; he picked up the spare barrel.

Miller hit the ground; as he did so he threw a stick bomb. Up it soared, then down. The Marksman watched with detached interest. An explosion. Debris and dust and unidentified objects flying over the hedge.

Silence again save for the sound of distant gunfire and, high above, a Dornier droning toward the German border.

The Marksman waited for Miller to get up. Miller stood up cautiously. Nothing. The Marksman watched him approach the hedge. Stop. Wriggle forward on his belly. Nothing. Miller peered over the top of the hedge, then stood up and, turning to face the Marksman, slit his throat with the blade of his hand: they were dead.

The Mailman, very important, emerged from the armored car and walked down the length of the train, slowing down as he passed the coach where the two girls were. Look at me, brave and handsome with it.

The burst from the machine pistol just reached him; he fell back as though he were catching the bullets.

Stehr, squeezing the trigger of the Schmeisser, thought, That last pushup, they said I couldn't make it. But I fooled them. And he died.

AT NIGHTFALL THEY steamed into No Man's Land. Behind them the Germans, ahead the French First Army. Exactly where was debatable. All they knew was that they had crossed the Belgian border and were in France near Valenciennes.

Shells burst around them. French or German? That was also debatable.

Pritchard, after initial hesitancy, handled the controls of the engine with panache. He might have been driving crack expresses all his life. He was wearing the fireman's goggles, and his lips were drawn back from his chipped teeth in a fierce grin as, leaning from the cabin, he peered down the track.

Beside him the Prizefighter shoveled coal into the firebox. Miller had ordered Ritter to do the job. A mistake. Ritter had refused and Miller should have guessed he would. Miller had threatened to shoot him and Ritter had said, "Between the eyes if you would," and Miller hadn't pulled the trigger and had lost face.

A flare burst above the train flooding the countryside with stark white light. Seeing figures on the track ahead, Pritchard braked. Their uniforms were unmistakably French, steel helmets much neater than the German coal skuttles or the British soup plates. The train stopped.

From the dining car came the strains of a very

scratched *Marseillaise*. The German uniforms had been thrown out of the windows. Gisella's Tricolor was draped from a window.

A French officer holding a pistol called out. From the platform of the antiaircraft gun came a flow of immaculate French. Miller jumped to the ground and stared at the Marksman in amazement.

The French officer bowed and lowered his pistol. The Marksman joined them. "You heard what I said?"

"What astonished me was the way you said it."

The Marksman had invited the French to break open a few bottles of champagne and eat what was left of the smoked salmon and caviar. He had told them that the train had been captured from the Germans together with the components of a new missile of some sort, but the officer had seemed more interested in the champagne.

"Then let's crack a few bottles," Miller said.

The champagne fizzed in the dining car. The Marksman and the French officer talked animatedly. Miller regarded him with renewed interest. Why should a killer speak fluent French? Then again, why shouldn't he?

The Marksman turned to Miller; his eyes still reminded Miller of bloodstones; his pale face was expressionless. "He says the French intend to make a stand at Lille."

"And the British?"

"He says they're running away as fast as their legs will carry them."

Running away? Miller had never thought of it

like that. But that's exactly what they were doing. They had no alternative. The politicians and the blinkered generals had seen to that.

"Aren't any of the French running with them?"

"Some. But it's the French who are holding the Germans back to let the British escape. Or so he says. He also says that as soon as the Belgians surrender they're done for."

"Just out of interest," Miller said, "how do you come to speak French like a Frenchman?"

"Because I *am* one," the Marksman said.

"HALF FRENCH," HE explained as the Rheingold headed for Lille, leaving the Frenchmen, the wounded German soldier, and the fireman behind.

The North Countryman was manning his guns while he took a break in the dining car.

"Which half?" Miller had found a bottle of Vichy water, and he was sharing it with the Marksman. Suddenly he had realized that, Pritchard and the North Countryman apart, he didn't know any of their names.

"My father's."

"Your mother was English?"

"Irish. Dublin."

Half French, half Irish; room for conjecture there. "But you don't have any accents."

"I went to school in Switzerland," the Marksman said. "We lived in London, in Mayfair."

"So what are you doing in the British Army?"

"I'm naturalized British." He didn't elaborate. His dark eyes looked steadily into Miller's.

"So what did, does, your mother do in Ireland . . . England?" he asked, confused.

"She's a musician."

"And your father?"

"He's dead. He came from Marseille. He was a gangster."

At last Miller understood. A little.

PROGRESS AT NIGHT was desperately slow.

The British had commandeered trains and were coaxing them amateurishly toward the coast; the line had been blown in a couple of places and it took the Engineer an hour to carry out makeshift repairs; obstacles loomed as dangerous as icebergs at sea. Once Pritchard had to drive an abandoned engine onto a siding.

In the fields on either side of the line stretched a phantom cavalcade of refugees. Occasionally shells fell among them. The ranks parted, then closed again, the progress as remorseless as it was hopeless.

Did they know they were being abandoned? Miller wondered. Their acceptance of their plight annoyed him. As he saw their silhouette flickering past a line of poplar trees like a shot from a silent movie, he was reminded of the great mass of mankind that passively submits to the follies of the few.

As they passed through Lille, churches and factory chimneys stark in the moonlight, they saw a town burning ahead. Miller consulted his map. Armentieres probably. *"Mademoiselle from Armentieres, parlez-vous?"* They were among the battlefields of the last war—Ypres (Wipers), Passchendale, Vimy Ridge, Mons—when men had died by the millions with guns in their hands, but passively just the same. The war to end all wars . . . *"Inky pinky parlez-vous."*

The wheels of the coach locked. The train stopped. He heard an English voice, "Get down from there whoever the hell you are." He drew his Luger and ran to the door of the dining car.

IN THE ENGLISH Channel an extraordinary fleet of ships was heading for Dunkirk. Forty destroyers, ferry boats, drifters, coasters. Among them the *Twickenham Ferry*, which before the war had shipped London and Paris-bound trains between Dover and Dunkirk. The passengers had mostly been wealthy but none had possessed the sort of riches the *Twickenham Ferry* was on its way to collect this trip.

GOERING HAD HIS greatest inspiration for Operation Argo at about the same time a Territorial captain in the 91st Field Regiment, Royal Artillery, was holding up the Rheingold at gunpoint.

15

May 26

SUNDAY AND A day of national prayer in Britain.

The order to begin Operation Dynamo, the evacuation of Allied troops from Dunkirk, wasn't to be given until 6:57 that evening, but troops were embarking in the makeshift fleet long before that.

In packed churches all over the land, worshipers prayed for their deliverance. Among them Oliver Logan, chief of Britain's Secret Service; he added an additional prayer of his own.

Thirty-five miles southeast of Dunkirk the day dawned gently. The sunshine was fragile and mist lay in pools in the low-lying countryside. If it hadn't been for the sound of men at war, the dawn would have presaged a Christian Sabbath of blessed tranquility.

The sunlight made a ceremony of the exit of a locomotive from the servicing sheds north of Lille.

Like the engine of the Rheingold, it was a beautiful black brute, another cone-nosed Bavarian S 3/6 Pacific; a little long in the tooth but revered by its drivers.

On the footplate of the engine, which had once pulled the Edelweiss express, were two Frenchmen, employees of SNCF, the nationalized French railway company formed three years earlier. The engine was owned by the Dutch and Swiss railway companies, but at times like this such niceties were meaningless.

Neither driver nor fireman was disturbed that he was driving for the Germans: both were members of the Fifth Column. Coupled to the engine was an unpainted coach from the railway sheds containing two dozen Waffen-SS.

The members of the SS detachment were all crack Leibstandarte Regiment, originally formed as Hitler's bodyguard. But they had grown up since then and were currently storming around France under the leadership of a swashbuckling ex-butcher named Sepp Dietrich.

It was Dietrich's policy to take no prisoners and to pay scant attention to orders from Wehrmacht generals. He obeyed Hitler—sometimes giving the orders his own interpretation—and occasionally listened to Goering. He had accorded the commander in chief of the Luftwaffe more respect than usual when a reward "beyond your wildest dreams" had been promised if he could spare some men.

Goering's plan was simple and effective as far as Dietrich, an exponent of brutal simplicity, could make out. With only one carriage the Edelweiss could get up a good head of steam and catch the Rheingold, which Goering had now located in disputed territory northwest of Lille.

Near Hazebrouck and the branch line to Abeele, there was a fork to the south for slow trains to pick up passengers at minor stations. But there would be nothing slow about the Edelweiss's progress along the fork; by the time it rejoined the main line it would be well ahead of the Rheingold—and blocking the line. With stick bombs, antitank and machine guns the Leibstandarte task force would make short work of the British.

"But don't let any of your gangsters interfere with the contents of the first two head-end cars," Goering had said on the phone.

A pause. "Why? Is that where my reward beyond my wildest dreams is located?"

"Just tell them to leave them alone. Don't worry, you'll get your reward. Will you go with them?"

"No chance," Dietrich said. "I'm up with Guderian on the Aa Canal *interpreting* the Führer's order to stop attacking the Tommies from the west."

"Don't worry," Goering said, "the Luftwaffe will finish them off."

Dietrich said, "So it's true what I've read. You do know a hell of a lot about railways."

"It's always been my hobby," Goering said.

313

Dietrich wished Goering had allowed himself more time to study Spitfires and Hurricanes.

THE TERRITORIAL CAPTAIN was a sandy-haired man in his mid-thirties who wore his small, sharp-bristled mustache like a medal. It was the early hours of the twenty-sixth, and Miller was observing him in the moonlight. The captain appeared to be uncertain how to handle his authority. Miller knew the feeling.

The captain had shouted at Pritchard on the footplate, "Who's in charge here?"

Pritchard, intoxicated with 18 547, jerked his head backward. "Miller," he replied.

Nonplussed, the captain stabbed his Enfield .38 in Pritchard's direction. "And who the hell might you be?" voice snapping with uncertainty.

"Tom Pritchard." He wiped his hands on a rag.

"Name, rank, and number!"

Miller, wondering what the captain had done in civilian life, came to their rescue. "I'm in charge," he said. "What can we do for you?"

"Are you a commissioned officer?"

"I'm not even a noncommissioned one," Miller said. "Not even a soldier. What do you want?"

The captain digested this. Miller became aware of other figures materializing in the poplar trees behind him. The captain became enraged with his own uncertainty. "Explain yourself, man."

Miller explained, up to a point.

The captain pounced. "I'm relieving you of your authority. Taking over the train," he explained.

"Sorry," Miller said.

"I'm warning you . . ." The captain took a hesitant step forward.

"And I'm warning you that you've just stepped into the line of fire of a machine gun."

The captain glanced at the menacing silhouette of the Marksman lying behind the MG 34 that he had now bolted to the roof of the armored car.

The captain said, "I'll have you court-martialed."

"You can't. I'm a civilian." And then, taking pity on the man, "Why do you want the train?"

The captain hesitated. "We've got wounded," he said. "We've got to get them to Dunkirk."

Miller peered into the poplar trees. He saw men lying on the ground. He heard one of them sigh. There was no despair in the sigh, just disbelief. Miller knew the man had died.

"How many?" he asked.

"Fifteen stretcher cases. Half a dozen walking wounded. We drove into a minefield. One of ours," the captain added, aggression seeping from him.

"Of course we'll take them," Miller said.

He noticed Ritter staring at him from a window. Ritter smiled and tapped the side of his head with one finger. But Miller suspected that he would have made the same decision.

BY 10 A.M. THE Rheingold was close to Hazebrouck. The three carriages were now hospital wards, and the Medic was doing his best to treat the casualties.

Two stretcher cases had died and Miller had been

surprised at the docility of their deaths. In their eyes he saw the same submissive acceptance that he had noticed in the refugees.

Two other soldiers were dying; one had lost an arm, the other a leg; they made little fuss. Anticipating death, they fished wallets from the pockets of their crumpled uniforms and gazed at photographs of women and girls and children.

Those who glorified war should see these men, Miller thought. Even at school children were taught to applaud battle.

And yet war was the making of some men. The Engineer, Pritchard, the Medic . . . me?

He glanced at the captain, who was now content to be divested of his authority. He had ordered his men to nail Red Cross flags to the roofs of the coaches but Miller had countermanded the order. You don't transport loot under the protection of the Geneva Convention—and troops manning a hospital train weren't allowed to carry arms.

"A Red Cross flag isn't going to stop a Stuka," he had pointed out, and with a shrug of his shoulders the captain had relinquished leadership.

It was the Marksman who reported that a train was following them.

Stepping around the casualties, he came into the first passenger coach and told Miller, "It just stays behind us, about half a mile back. The engine looks the same as ours. Classy."

Miller said, "It can't get past I suppose."

"There's more to it than that. It's loaded with

troops and they've got lightning flashes on their helmets. I saw them through the telescopic sights of the Lee Enfield."

Ritter looked up interested. "SS. I wonder which regiment. Did you notice any other emblems?"

The Marksman looked at Miller. Miller nodded at him and he said, "I saw what looked like a skeleton key."

Ritter was silent for a moment. Then he said, "You've got yourself a fight. The *crème de la crème*. The Leibstandarte. Their commander's called Dietrich. His name means skeleton key in German."

Intuitively Miller said, "Your old regiment?"

"We took an oath. 'I swear to you, Adolf Hitler, as Führer and Reich Chancellor, loyalty and bravery. I vow to you, and to those you have named to command me, obedience unto death, so help me God.' Do you know that when we were training we had to dig ourselves in and let our own tanks drive over us?"

"But you turned against them."

"'. . . so help me God.' God wouldn't have liked some of the things they did in Poland." Ritter looked down at his bound wrists.

Miller spread his map on a table. Watched by a soldier with a bloodstained bandage around his head, he examined the last stretch of their journey, the twenty miles of track from Hazebrouck to Dunkirk. He found what he was looking for: the point where the Leibstandarte train would overtake them and block the track in front.

He grabbed the Marksman's arms. "What explosives have you got in the armored car?"

"Plenty of ammunition, a few sticks of dynamite."

"The tools of my trade . . ." And he was running through the coaches, leaping over the wounded, followed by the Marksman.

He pointed at an olive-green, domed canister strapped to the armor-plated wall of the armored car beside a rack of rifles. "That's a mine." He undid the strap. "A Tellermine, 1A 7B. There are four layers of TNT in that."

"So what are you going to do, blow us up?"

Miller talked as he worked. "Ever heard of sympathetic detonation?"

"If one explosive blows then everything around it explodes?"

Miller nodded. "Take a look at the Leibstandarte."

From the turret the Marksman shouted down, "About a mile behind." He came back down the steel ladder.

Miller went on talking to the Marksman—and himself. "There's a loopline about five miles ahead. They're going to accelerate down it, rejoin the main line, and block our escape route. If they succeed we don't stand a chance. So what I'm going to do . . ."

"I know what you're going to do," the Marksman said.

"And you know what I want you to do?"

But he had already gone to do it.

Miller examined the Tellermine. It had a brass setting screw with two arrows on it, one marked *scharf* and the other *sicher*, which meant "safe."

He placed the mine in one corner of the car, wedging it with a rifle. Around it he stacked sticks of dynamite, stick bombs, and ammunition.

He worked deftly, the familiar excitement building up inside him. He saw moonlight silvering gracious lawns, smelled the marzipan odor of gelignite, heard a footfall on a gravel drive.

He turned the arrow on the mine to *scharf*.

He climbed up the steel ladder. The pursuing train had closed. Only half a mile between them now.

THE MARKSMAN, STRUGGLING with the coupling joining the armored car to the rest of the Rheingold, glanced behind him. The German girl named Gisella was leaning out of a window. She seemed to be waving to the train behind them. Waving? No, signaling, two arms held above her head. Odd. He would have to tell Miller about it.

WHEN MILLER JOINED him, they crouched at the rear exit of the passenger coach struggling with the coupling cock and hose coupling. There had to be an easier way but Miller didn't know it. Beneath them sleepers raced past like the ammunition belt of a machine gun.

The Marksman aimed his tommy gun at the hose coupling and fired a burst. The coupling disintegrated but still the armored car stayed with the rest of the train. One telling jolt and the Tellermine would blow. And the dynamite. And the grenades. Goodbye gold. Goodbye us.

Instead of the footfall on the gravel drive, Miller heard Vic's cough in the passage outside their bedroom when they were very young and saw the frost patterns on the *inside* of the window. What a way to bring up a boy with TB.

The Marksman pointed at three steel cables that had reinforced the hose. He fired again. The cables parted.

Miller pulled him into the passenger coach. "There it goes," he yelled as the armored car lost momentum and started to slip away from them.

SO THEY WERE Leibstandarte in the train following the Rheingold. As Miller and the Marksman ran down the carriage, von Ritter strained against the wire binding his wrists and ankles. To make matters worse, since he had managed to struggle to his feet and smash the window to warn the glider-borne troops, he had been bound to one of the tables bolted to the floor.

As he strained, wire cutting into his flesh, his mind zigzagged, as it frequently did these days, to his own years of glory.

March 7, 1936. With the Leibstandarte, aloof from the Wehrmacht troops in their gray battle dress, on the east bank of the Rhine, poised to march into the Rhineland, to reoccupy what was rightfully Germany's. What exaltation as, dressed in their black coats braided with silver, they swaggered into Saarbrücken, the warriors returned after the humiliations of 1918.

Children throwing garlands ... pretty girls blowing kisses ... *"Deutschland über Alles"* sprouting from the bugles and trumpets of the Saarbrücken town band ... and on the Leibstandarte armbands, the words *Adolf Hitler*, the heroic genius who was leading Germany back to the greatness it deserved.

Ah, such intoxicated righteousness. Not that he was any saint. To be SS, in particular to be Leibstandarte, you had to be a bit of a buccaneer. True, their swashbuckling style came in for criticism from hidebound generals, but jealousy was to be expected. And as for morals, if you were Leibstandarte you had to fight off the girls, and he had never used violence against women.

After Austria and the Czech Sudentenland—the Leibstandarte was the guard of honor for Hitler at Carlsbad—and Czechoslovakia proper, came Poland. And dishonor. It had never been part of his code to slaughter civilians—old men, women, children.

Looking up, Ritter saw that Gisella Hessen had come up almost beside him. "I've brought you a glass of water," she said. And then leaning toward him, whispered, "Hold out your hands. The Englishmen won't be able to see what I'm doing." And when he did, she brought out a pair of wire cutters from the shawl that was wrapped around her arms and began to cut the wire.

"Thank you Fräulein. I always wondered about you."

"I've warned the SS in the train following us. If the train driver was an old-timer, he'll have understood."

"Why are you doing this?" Ritter asked.

"Because I'm a German and for many other reasons that I don't expect you to understand."

"Perhaps," Ritter said, "I understand more than you think."

The wire was cut, and standing in front of him so that she blocked the view of the Medic, she handed him the cutters so he could work at the wire on his ankles.

He hesitated for a moment, eyes on the tommy gun lying beside the Medic. He jerked his head to the girl to tell her to move to one side. As he did so, the train plunged into a tunnel and into darkness.

He leapt to his left, brushing against the girl, and grabbed the tommy gun with one hand, clubbing blindly at the Medic with the other. His fist connected with something, the man's face by the feel of it; the Medic grunted and fell. He kicked, connected again.

He had intended to climb outside and crawl across the tops of the coaches and the tender to the footplate; like they do in the movies, he had thought at the time. But the tunnel had changed everything. The Rheingold was slowing down.

Whoever was driving would have to do that. All he would be able to see in front of him was a circle of light, and with the signaling system immobilized there could be blockages ahead.

The train was stopping.

Donnerwetter! If Miller had done what he would have done in his place, he had released the armored car primed to blow up on impact with the pursuing train. Miller would have been able to accomplish that easily enough; he was an explosives expert.

So the Rheingold was half plugging one entrance to the tunnel, the armored car probably doing the same at the other end. One horrendous explosion and the blast would charge through the tunnel, blasting the Rheingold out of the orifice like a shell out of a cannon.

Ritter opened the side door and jumped into the darkness.

The circle of light looked a long way away. He smelled the steamy, rusty odor of railways. *All I need now is a train coming in the opposite direction.*

He reached the footplate. In the bright orange light from the firebox he could make out the figures of Pritchard and the Prizefighter.

He leaped on the footplate, swiveling the tommy gun from one to another. He said, "You'd better get her out of here," and told them about the bomb that was the armored car at the other end of the tunnel.

Pritchard said, "We can't, there's water ahead. They must have blown a dike or a canal."

Ritter peered into the darkness. He heard the water rather than saw it, a deep fluid gurgle.

"Don't you have headlights?"

"They were shot out."

"Then forget my gun." Ritter lowered the barrel. "Forget everything except shifting this engine. If you don't . . ."

Pritchard grasped regulator and brake, the dressing on his wounded arm slipping. They heard the wheels moving, felt them slipping in the first rush of water.

The engine inched forward. The pursuing train wouldn't be inching: it would be charging. Any second now, Ritter thought, flinching instinctively. The Leibstandarte troops will be killed. And me with them. Ironic, like life. Obedience unto death, so help me God.

The wheels gripped.

Steam made billowing protests around them, roaring and barking. Peering down, Ritter saw wings of water flying from the wheels.

The water was climbing higher, reaching the surging pistons.

Pritchard shouted to the Prizefighter, "In the old RH and D days we would have been submerged."

Daylight filled the cabin. The water was over the pistons and it was all around them turning the tall cornfields into marshes.

"It's hopeless," Pritchard shouted as the engine lost momentum outside the tunnel. "We need a backup engine."

The explosion was louder than anything Ritter had ever heard. And yet the results were curiously languid, masonry and metal rising and falling against the blue sky with measured grace.

Except in the tunnel. There the blast stormed the darkness like an express. And, like a backup engine, it hit the last coach of the Rheingold, propelling the whole train through the water onto the dry, sun-burnished track ahead.

RITTER RECOVERED FIRST.

He shouted to Pritchard, "Okay, now stop."

Pritchard called out to the Prizefighter, "Keep shoveling. We need all the steam we can get."

"In that case . . ." Ritter said, aiming the tommy gun at the controls, just as he had done before.

"Oh no you don't."

With one hand Pritchard pulled the emergency whistle cord. The Rheingold's cry of alarm shrilled across the cornfields. Distracted, Ritter swung the barrel of the tommy gun to one side and Pritchard fell on it.

The Prizefighter hit Ritter behind the ear. As he fell Ritter tore the gun clear of Pritchard and squeezed the trigger.

Pritchard felt the bullet tear into his chest. He leaned over the side of the cabin. There were cornfields all around him. And red poppies growing in them.

THE OTHER CASUALTY was the Marksman. A sheet of

325

razored steel plating from the armored car tore through the door at the end of the last coach slicing through his skull.

His flecked eyes looked steadily into Miller's. The way a Marseille gangster's son should die, the eyes said.

He tried to speak. "The girl . . . a signal."

"Don't try to speak," Miller said.

"Must . . . the girl . . . signaled to the Germans."

Then he did an extraordinary thing. He managed to raise both his arms. "Like that," he said as he died.

So Hanna had tried to warn the SS; good for her. Two hands? A memory spread its wings and fluttered; frowning, Miller tried to capture it but it escaped. And it was only much later that he remembered that Hanna couldn't have signaled anyone with two hands raised independently because they were bound together with wire.

GOERING THOUGHT, THIS man Miller, he's a genius and a hero and nothing would give me greater pleasure than to stand him blindfolded in front of a firing squad.

So now that the train carrying the SS had been blown up, there was only one weapon left: Stukas.

Worthy adversary that he was, Miller wouldn't be able to do much about Stukas. No one could. Or against a firing squad. He suspected though that when Miller's time came he would reject the blindfold. He was that sort of man.

16

May 26

HALFWAY ACROSS THE English Channel the *Twickenham* Ferry was making slow but steady progress through the crowded shipping lanes leading to and from Dunkirk.

The 2,996 -ton vessel was one of three night ferries launched in 1934 to enable railway coaches to travel direct from Victoria Station in London to the Gare du Nord in Paris, and vice versa. The service, which began on October 14, 1936, was the first and only through passenger train connection between the two cities.

Each vessel had five rail tracks on its main deck, which could accommodate a total of twelve sleeping cars. This meant that you could bed down in a wagon-lit blue coach in London or Paris and wake up in one or other of the two capitals without noticing that you had crossed the Channel—unless the sea was rough and you were a bad sailor.

To enable the coaches to be shunted smoothly on

and off the handsome, two-funneled ferries, special locks had to be built at Dover and Dunkirk to cope with the tides and keep the level between ship and quayside level.

Standing on the bridge of the *Twickenham Ferry,* the skipper, a bearded ex-Royal Navy mariner who was not amused when he was described as a glorified train driver, peered across the Channel.

"It's like trying to drive a bus through Epsom High Street on Derby Day," he informed his first officer.

"Aye, aye, sir," replied the first officer, who tended to be monosyllabic in the powerful presence of the captain.

"And while everyone else is taking off Tommies we're supposed to pick up some Jerry train."

This time the first officer was less than monosyllabic. He didn't reply because he couldn't understand it either.

"Well I'll tell you this, I'll take the train all right but I'll also take as many poor troops as I can get on board without sinking."

"Aye, aye, sir."

"And another thing."

"Sir?"

"Do you think these stupid buggers in Whitehall who gave this order know that the dimensions of European trains are different from ours? That the French rolling stock for the night ferry had to be smaller to comply with the British loading gauge?

In other words, that if this Jerry train is too big it will crash into our ship like a very large member entering a very small orifice?"

"I doubt it, sir," said the first officer.

THEY WERE ON the last hazardous stretch, about five miles from Dunkirk harbor, according to Miller's calculations.

After they had been blown out of the tunnel, the Rheingold had stopped briefly. Now Pritchard, badly wounded but insisting he could still drive, was on the footplate, combat jacket over the bandages around his chest. The Prizefighter, who had overpowered Ritter, was acting as his fireman.

Ritter was bound to a chair next to Hanna in the dining car, trussed like a chicken by the Medic, whose left eye had closed to a slit where Ritter had hit him. Around them were grouped the wounded British troops and their captain.

Miller and Gisella stood together in the first passenger coach, gazing at the defeat all around them.

Shells were bursting, some very close to them. Geysers of floodwater shot up, and old, shuttered houses from which white flags fluttered were blown to pieces. Meanwhile, overhead, strafing Stukas, Messerschmitts, and Dorniers pumped machine-gun bullets into the retreating army.

British troops, preparing their last line of defense with the French, were blowing up equipment to keep it out of the hands of the Germans; refugees, possessions wrapped in blankets and loaded onto baby carriages and wheelbarrows, mingled with the trudging lines of khaki. Leaning out of a window, Miller saw a thick coil of greasy black smoke hanging over Dunkirk.

A shell plowed into a vegetable garden beside the track. Clods of earth spattered the carriage, a tiny fragment of stone nicked Miller's cheek, drawing blood.

Gisella pulled at his arm. "Come back in, that could have been your eye." She held onto his arm.

Holding a handkerchief to his cheek, he said, "This is the worst part. One bomb, one shell, and the whole thing's been for nothing. I remember hiring a car once. I kept it for a week without damaging it; I hit a van in the driveway of the garage when I was returning it." He slipped his arm around her waist. "Don't worry, we'll make it." He pointed at the refugees. "Where can they go?"

She laid her head against his shoulder. He thought she said, "Perhaps they're luckier than me," but he must have been mistaken.

"What shall we call our jewelry shop?" he asked.

"Charlie's Place," she said. And then, "Kiss me, Charlie."

With his hand he tilted her head and kissed her on her lips, but for a moment he, too, was scared by some knowledge in her gray eyes that he couldn't identify.

The moment passed. "What's that in your hand?" he asked.

She opened her hand. The nugget of coal lay

warmly in her palm. "Twenty carat," she said and turned her head away.

The train stopped.

He said, "I'm going up to the footplate."

"Charlie . . ."

He turned.

"Just Charlie . . ."

Such a gentle, humorous name, she thought as he climbed down onto the track, and she returned to that arid land that lies beyond tears.

IT TOOK FIVE minutes to clear the debris tossed onto the track by a bomb. As 18 547 got up steam again, Miller said to Pritchard, "How are you feeling?"

Pritchard's bloodless lips moved. Miller put his ear close to them. "If I don't make it drive onto the ferry slowly. Here, like this . . ." He moved the regulator and brake with a shaking hand.

The bullet, according to the Medic, had made a clean wound with a neat exit puncture. The trouble was that, like the German soldier before him, he was bleeding inside. And he had lost blood from the wound on his arm.

Pritchard clawed at Miller's arm. "Listen. I know these ferries . . . Five rail tracks . . . One track will take the engine and two coaches, no more, so you'll have to uncouple the other three . . ."

And leave the wounded behind?

"Of course," Pritchard said, voice laboring, "you could shunt the other coaches on board. Shunting engines . . . small-time-engines . . . the sort I was born to drive . . ."

"Oh no," Miller said, "you were born to drive the best."

Pritchard smiled faintly, stumbled against the side of the cabin. Miller put his arm around his shoulders. When he took his hand away there was blood on it.

Two miles. And they were steaming into an inferno. A Dornier passed low over the engine; two bombs fell from its wings. They hit a row of shops. An old woman and a boy ran from one of them. They didn't appear to be hurt but they wore their fear like new, ill-fitting clothes, the boy trying to hold onto trust, the hand of the old woman.

Leaflets fluttered down from the smoke-filled sky. They were in English. Lay down your arms, they said. You are surrounded.

Miller asked Pritchard what guarantee there was that the track they were on would take the Rheingold direct to the ferry terminal.

None, Pritchard said. But if the points were set for them to join the main line from Paris, then there was a fair chance that they would steam direct to Dock Number 5. "I came here once," he explained, "with a railway club . . ." He pulled his goggles over his eyes and peered down the line.

Miller leaned out behind him. A maze of tracks gleamed brightly ahead. He supposed it was logical that the main line from Lille would link up with the main line from Paris. But not surely continuing in the direction of the ferry terminal.

Pritchard straightened up inside the cabin. He pushed the goggles onto his forehead. "We're on the main line to Paris," he said.

"Going in the right direction?"

Pritchard shook his head. "No the wrong direction—toward Paris," he said, chipped teeth bared in a smile. Had the internal hemorrhage affected his brain? "It's perfect . . . I hadn't worked it out properly . . . I'm sorry . . . You see, we can go into reverse . . . That way we can back the coaches with the wounded onto the ferry first . . ."

Leaving the gold to the last. Waiting on the quayside. The idea pleased Miller. He doubted whether it would have the same effect on the Governor of the Bank of England.

THE FINAL APPROACH to Dock Number 5 was across an articulated bridge built in two parts, with a pivot in the middle to accommodate tide levels and the rise and fall of the ferry determined by its load.

The ferry, churning water furiously, was 100 yards from the dockside when the Rheingold reached the bridge.

Miller leaped down and, with the help of the army captain and a sergeant wearing an eye patch, uncoupled the passenger coaches and dining car from the two head-end cars, the tender and the engine.

Troops waiting for the *Twickenham* and other rescue ships watched the proceedings incuriously, tunics unbuttoned, steel helmets and forage caps at careless angles. A pack of drunken soldiers brandishing bottles of wine and brandy lurched along the quayside.

Warehouses blazed, and over the sea brawling fighter planes knitted the blue sky with skeins of white. Immediately overhead the sky was black with smoke from burning oil installations.

The *Twinkenham* edged nearer.

Seventy yards, fifty, forty . . .

A soldier waving an empty bottle of Courvoisier challenged the German aircraft circling overhead to "come and get us."

They did. Three Stukas.

THE PILOT IN command of the three Spitfires flying across the English Channel toward Dunkirk was Pilot Officer Richard (Chummy) Hammond. He was just nineteen.

He was wavy-haired and keen-featured in a very English way and, having played rugby at a public school, was well attuned to the glorious brutality of aerial combat.

Chummy loved ragging and rugby and flirting, but above all he loved his Spitfire with its compact lovely lines, like a swallow with straightened wings. It was the first serious affair of his life.

His Spit was a Mark 1 powered with 1030 Rolls-Royce engines and armed with eight, wing-housed .303 Browning machine guns. Its wings and fuselage were camouflaged, its belly, apart from the red, white, and blue rondels, sky blue.

As usual he was thirsting for battle, but today he

was puzzled by his briefing: to look for a train, easily identifiable in purple, cream, and gold livery, approaching Dunkirk and to shepherd it to the docks, keeping a special lookout for Stukas.

According to the briefing at Hornchurch, where Chummy's unit, 74 (Tiger) Squadron, was based, Fighter Command had hinted that a secret weapon capable of changing the whole course of the war was on board the train.

What was it doing on a train that was obviously one of the crack European expresses, for heaven's sake? Ours not to reason why, Chummy decided and peered down at the molten blue sea.

It presented an extraordinary spectacle. A vast mongrel fleet, anything from hedonists' yachts from Henley to cockle boats from Southend and Thames barges, had been summoned to supplement the destroyers, ferries, paddle steamers, and Dutch skoots evacuating troops across Britain's moat.

The sea fairly jostled with them.

Dunkirk was a shock. Chummy had guessed it would be bad, but not this bad. A funeral pyre of black smoke from bombed oil tanks hung over the harbor and dock basins; only two moles of the harbor appeared to have survived the Luftwaffe *blitz*. The approaches to the port were spiked with sunken ships; fires burned all over the town, flames pale in the sunshine.

On the beaches, backed by dunes, stretching on either side of Dunkirk from Nieuport to Gravelines,

lines of troops were beginning to assemble, linking the sea with the flooded fields behind.

Chummy had no doubt that they would all get out. And that one day Jerry would pay for this. Meanwhile, the smoke was interfering with his mission, wasting time and fuel. Flanked by the other two Spitfires of his flight, he flew low, looking for the train and for Stukas.

Stukas, Chummy had to admit, held a certain fascination for him. With their bent wings, talon-like wheel shields, and sirens operated by wooden propellers on their undercarriages—Jericho Trumpets as they were known—they were the airborne epitome of Nazisms. *Sturzkampfflugzeug.* Once it had merely been a word describing dive-bombers. Now the abbreviation Stuka meant only the Junker 87, the screaming predator of the skies that had helped to bring Poland and now the Low Countries into submission.

Although the Stuka pilots hadn't quite realized it yet, they were now more than meeting their match. It wasn't all that difficult to dive-bomb virtually defenseless targets, with automatic dive brakes to stop you from blacking out, and return to machine-gun the victims. It was a different matter to shoot it out with a Spitfire or, to a lesser extent, a Hurricane.

The maximum speed of the Stuka was 236 mph. The maximum speed of the Spitfire at 19,000 feet 355 mph. And the maneuverability of the Spit compared with the egg-bound Stuka was magic.

Bring on the Stukas, Chummy thought as he

scanned the railway lines leading into Dunkirk and the meshwork of tracks beside the quays. Had the smoke delayed them too long? Supposing the Stukas had found the train first and destroyed it . . . "Hammond, you couldn't organize a piss-up in a brewery." He could hear the C.O.'s voice now. No gongs for Chummy today if he couldn't find the bloody thing, not for many a long week, come to that, because headquarters was taking the mission very seriously.

Then he spotted the train waiting on the dockside while a ship that looked like one of the old Channel ferries thrust its stern at the quay. The trouble was that three Stukas, a *kette*, had spotted it first.

THE STUKAS WERE lined up for a 70-degree dive like gulls swooping for food.

Their precision bombing of marching columns, vehicles, and trains had already gained them a fearsome reputation; but surely they would not be so precise, Miller reasoned, if the targets they had lined up for were suddenly shifted to one side.

Standing on the quayside he shouted to Pritchard, "Now, move them." The Stukas swooped screaming toward the Rheingold.

He didn't know if the *Twickenham* had closed the last few inches of the gap between her and the quay; he didn't know if the German coaches, not trimmed for the ferry like the French carriages, would even board her.

18 547, her tender, and the two head-on vans butted the two passenger coaches and the dining car. The first bomb bounced where they had been standing. Yes, bounced, Miller marveled, lying face down on the quay. It was a dud.

The plane climbed back into the sky, and the three coaches trundled toward the articulated bridge.

They won't make it, Miller decided. Too big by far. How stupid not to have thought about that days ago.

Fatalistically he heard the scream of the second Stuka. Would its bomb or bombs miss the target that had suddenly moved aside?

They did, hitting the quay where the engine had been standing. They were 50 kilograms each by the sound of the explosions, which were deafening but lacked the roar that bigger caliber bombs would have had.

Miller, who had crawled behind an overturned Citroën sedan, ducked as debris showered around him. Beside him, a kneeling soldier was loosing off an old Lee Enfield at the departing plane. The drunks seemed to have sobered up.

One more to come in this first attack. It looked as though the pilots had been ordered to cause minimum damage, one bomb from the first attacker, two from the second, and now the third.

The last Stuka pulled out of its dive and disappeared into the black smoke without dropping any bombs.

Odd, but Miller was convinced it would be back.

He stood up to see if the coaches with Gisella, the prisoners, and the wounded on board had reached the *Twickenham*. They were crossing the bridge but slowing down. As they reached the gaping mouth of the ferry they seemed to hesitate, then hurried forward and, as they passed inside, suddenly toppled to one side.

"They're derailed," Pritchard called from the engine.

"It doesn't matter," Miller shouted back, "they're in."

He shaded his eyes and scanned the pall of smoke for the Stukas.

CHUMMY HAMMOND HAD lost them too. The three Spitfires had been poised to fall on them when they had wheeled away into the smoke. Chummy shrugged and pointed the terrier nose of his Spit into the black soup. He spoke into his radio. "Keep your eyes peeled, chaps, we don't want any surprises." The soup engulfed him.

THE SOLDIERS WAITING for ships who had thrown themselves onto the ground when the Stukas attacked were getting to their feet, all except a handful who had been wounded by the blast from the bombs.

Miller shouted to them, "Get down, they're coming back."

Some dropped down again; others stared at him

uncomprehendingly. Who the hell are you, the stares said, a civilian giving us orders? We who've been through hell and back, fighting for you.

The North Countryman approached him from the direction of the engine. He was carrying a canvas bag. Why? Miller forgot about it as 18 547, the tender, and the two head-end cars began to move toward the *Twickenham*.

The North Countryman said, "We'd better get on her. She won't hang around once they're on board."

Together they began to walk toward the ferry as £500 million worth of gold trundled slowly across the quay, watched lethargically by unsuspecting British soldiery.

The head-end cars paused on the lip of the train deck, then accelerated inside followed by 18 547 and her tender. Wheels left the tracks, the *Twickenham* shuddered, but the gold was on board.

Miller and the North Countryman began to sprint toward the ferry. As the Stukas returned.

Seeing them, Miller knew that he should stop running. The *Twickenham* was a helpless target, and the bombs would hit just as he reached her. He ran even faster because Gisella was on board.

He heard the death rattle of machine-gun fire and thought, Strange, where are the bombs? He ran on, closing the gap, only 2 yards or so now, as the propellers of the *Twickenham* began to churn again.

"Christ, look." The North Countryman was pointing upward as he ran.

A Stuka was cartwheeling across the sky toward the open sea. There were the Spitfires. Those lovely pointed wings, the most beautiful sight in the world. The soldiers were cheering.

The second Stuka seemed to break apart just before it reached the low point of its bombing dive. Miller, slowing down, because if you didn't watch this you weren't human, saw the face of the pilot just before the cockpit plunged into the harbor.

The sky beneath the smoke seemed to be full of red, white, and blue rondels and the air full of coughing machine-gun fire and the cheers of men.

Where was the third Stuka?

The North Countryman yelled, "Look out," as it swooped low over the quay, black smoke streaming from its engine, MG 17 machine guns blazing from its wings.

The North Countryman leaped at Miller, knocking him sideways and felling him with the heavy canvas bag as bullets raked the quay. Miller felt the impact of a bullet in the North Countryman's body as, bag still tightly gripped in his hand, he fell on top of him.

The Stuka, skimming the water, throwing up wings of spray, flew toward the blazing oil tanks, finding one that hadn't been ignited and transforming it into a great ball of black-veined fire.

The North Countryman rolled to one side and said, "I didn't bloody leave you that time, did I?"

"Are you all right?"

"Copped it in the arm. I'll be okay."

They made it to the *Twickenham* just as she began to pull away from the quay. The Engineer was standing at the entrance to the rail deck as they leaped on board. "What kept you?" he said.

MILLER WENT STRAIGHT to von Ritter, who was still trussed up in a chair in the dining car, and took a clasp knife from the pocket of his leather jacket. "Can you swim?"

"Like a dolphin."

"A shark," Miller said, cutting through the wire binding him.

"Why are you doing this?"

Shrugging, Miller said, "I don't know. Perhaps because we're two of a kind."

Ritter nodded toward Hanna. "Can she go too?"

"Why not? After a swim you'll need someone to warm you up." He turned and cut the wire around her wrists and ankles. "You'd better get out quickly, before anyone realizes what's happening. Hide out until the rest of your army gets here."

Ritter said, "In a way I know why you're doing this."

"Then tell me, I'm curious."

"Because we're both on the same side."

Miller nodded. "Who's the enemy?"

Standing on deck, he watched Ritter, Hanna beside him, swimming strongly for the shore.

He turned to Gisella and said, "A pity, he could have been the best man at our wedding," but she didn't reply.

342

Watching the *Twickenham* leave the ruined harbor and steam toward England, her prow throwing up a sparkling arrowhead of water, Chummy Hammond congratulated his fellow pilots on the radio. "Good show, chaps. Now all we've got to do is wait for the relief effort."

17

May 26

THE REPORT FROM the pilot of a reconnaissance aircraft that the *Twickenham* had berthed at Dover was read over the telephone to Goering at the farmhouse.

Defeat. His anger and frustration were more savage than anything he had experienced since his aircraft had been shot down riddled with bullet holes in the last war.

Impotently he stormed around the living room. He hadn't even got the Rheingold!

At last, after a goblet of white wine, his true warrior instincts began to reassert themselves: the born fighter never gave up. Hadn't he taken to the skies again in the 1914-1918 conflict despite his wound?

He poured himself another goblet of wine. He could have given orders for the *Twickenham* to be dispatched to the bottom of the Channel if she succeeded in leaving Dunkirk, but the strategist in him had whispered, "Caution." What would have been the point? That way neither he nor the British would have got the gold.

As it was, with the way the war was going, he would soon be able to get his hands on it in London. At this thought, he brightened perceptibly.

And now he was free to concentrate on the annihilation of the British at Dunkirk. Historians, he thought, would wonder why his leadership had so far been so lackluster. They would never know that there had been other things on his mind.

The telephone rang. He picked up the receiver. Emmy.

"Are you all right, Hermann?"

"Very well, my dear." As well as could be expected in the circumstances. "I think I've shed a few kilos."

"Good news indeed, Hermann. And there's more to come. I've just dealt the cards. No doubt about it. Today is going to be your lucky day."

Goering hung up.

THE REACTION OF Franklin D. Roosevelt to the news that the bullion had arrived back in Britain—a delayed revelation because Grover's successor in the American Embassy in London had not picked up the threads yet—angered J. Edgar Hoover.

The President and the head of the FBI were sitting on a wooden bench on the lawn of the Roosevelt home at Hyde Park in New York state, overlooking the wooded banks of the Hudson.

"Hell, isn't that the news you've been waiting for?" Hoover demanded. He had traveled all the way from Washington in the hope that at last Roosevelt would come clean.

Roosevelt smiled that winning smile of his that seemed to wipe away the shadows under his eyes. "Of course it is," he said. "I always said that when the chips were down the British were as good as gold."

But Hoover wasn't convinced that his relief was genuine. He knew damned well that Roosevelt was holding something back from him with the charming lack of commitment that he employed when dealing with the press.

Hoover's anger intensified. He said, "You're not leveling with me, Mr. President."

"No," Roosevelt said. "This time I'm afraid I'm not. You see, you don't own the copyright on secrets. And now, if you will excuse me, I have work to attend to."

It was the most frustrating moment in Hoover's life.

MUNNION WAS EQUALLY baffled by Logan's reaction to the news.

Smoothing the teleprinter printout on his desk, Logan said, "So it's arrived."

"Thank God for that," Munnion exclaimed, relief flushing his cheeks.

"Don't let's get too carried away," Logan said. "This was a rescue operation, not a victory. Like Dunkirk, God willing."

Could anyone really be as coldly analytical as this? Britain's financial capital had been saved, and they had been working to that end for many harrowing days!

Munnion said, "I think it is a victory. We made the opening play. Goering chanced his arm. We won in the end."

"If you say so."

Logan looked bored.

Munnion decided to try and pierce Logan's frozen defenses. "I think Miller should get a knighthood," he said.

"Really? What for? I think His Majesty would find it most embarrassing to confer a knighthood on a thief who has been involved in an escapade that no one must ever know about."

"Then he should get some reward."

"And what do you suggest?"

Munnion told him.

Logan stared at him thoughtfully. After a while he said, "That really is the most preposterous suggestion I have heard of for a long while."

Munnion pressed home his attack. "And if you have any other ideas about Miller's future, any ideas that might shorten that future, then you should know that I have lodged papers giving full details about Operation Croesus to be published in the event of his untimely death. Or mine," Munnion added.

"Really?" Logan searched the pockets of his tweed jacket for his cigarettes. "Lodged with whom?"

"That would be telling," Munnion replied.

Logan said, "I've said it before and I'll say it again, you really are a most capable chap." His voice came from the Arctic. "Now get back to your roses."

"Cabbages," Munnion said. "I told you before. Don't you know there's a war on?"

18

May 26

PRITCHARD WAS FIRST off the *Twickenham*. He was taken by stretcher to the automobile examination hall on the ferry dockside where a casualty clearing station had been set up.

On the way, accompanied by Miller, he lay quite still, staring at the evening sky, unaware of the chaos around him. The harbor between Prince of Wales Pier and Admiralty Pier was a melee of assorted ships; the quays were crowded with disembarked soldiers, some of them still wearing life jackets, waiting for trains to take them inland. Many of them, stoic at Dunkirk, had lapsed into secondary shock. As they stood trembling, hands seeking the warmth of their bodies through disheveled khaki uniforms, determined women poured them mugs of tea.

A young RAMC medical officer examined Pritchard. "Nice clean wounds," he said. The sight of them seemed to give him considerable pleasure.

"Blood group?" Miller found Pritchard's papers in his combat jacket. "B negative," he said.

"Fine," said the MO, beckoning a Red Cross nurse making her way through the stretchers.

Miller returned Pritchard's papers to his worn pigskin wallet. In the wallet was a photograph of a locomotive. A very small locomotive.

"Is he going to be all right?" Miller asked the MO.

"With nice clean wounds like that? Of course he is." The MO moved on to the next casualty.

Miller touched Pritchard's hand. "You heard that?"

Pritchard's lips moved. Miller bent to catch the words. "Old Hercules did well, didn't he, sir," Pritchard said.

Miller departed through the organized confusion to the quay where the *Twickenham* was berthed.

As he neared the ferry he did his accounting. Of the nine men dropped in the Saxon Forest, four were dead—the Spotter, the Mailman, the Marksman, and the Chauffeur. The Prizefighter, Engineer, North Countryman, Medic, and Pritchard had made it.

As he walked briskly down the quay looking for Gisella to tell her that Pritchard was going to be all right, he saw her leaving the ferry. She was accompanied by two men in plain clothes.

THE TWO SPECIAL Branch officers, who had introduced themselves as Wilson and Macdonald, allowed him five minutes with her, keeping fifty yards away as he walked with her to the end of the jetty.

A soft, moist breeze was coming off the sea, and a single star had crystallized in the darkening sky. The rumble of distant explosions reached them from across the Channel.

He said, "I suppose I should have guessed."

"I love you," she said.

"Love? It was a lie from the beginning."

"No." She turned and stared out to sea. A rescue ship sounded its siren, and the note lingered, imprisoned in the mist rising from the water. "I loved you from the beginning."

"And betrayed me. What I don't understand is why. I thought we both hated what was happening in Germany."

She turned and faced him. "We did. But I hated it as a German. I had to fight the Nazis and save Germany. To you they were one and the same. The enemy."

She looked very German standing there in her seafaring clothes, blonde hair stirring in the breeze coming in from the sea. Why did I think we could fight together? Dear God, why?

She said, "That day in the village, that was when I betrayed you."

After we had made love, his look said. When else?

"Even then I hoped that you would understand. Would know, that I had to do it. I had sworn to the only other man I ever loved before you to carry on the fight. He died for a cause. I couldn't abandon it. I hoped you'd understand. Hoped . . ."

A sea gull wheeled above them, punctuating her words with cries of loneliness.

The stranger beside her said, "*You* were the enemy."

"What else could I do? Otto and I, we used to talk about Goering. To us he was the symbol of Germany's sickness. When I knew what he was going to do, I had to stop him. Do you understand that?"

"Go on," he said.

"My contact in London, he's a good man. Fifth Branch and indirectly *Abwehr*. He works for Admiral Canaris and believes in the same things I do."

"What things? Your ideals? To hell with them. You told the Germans where the train was. A lot of good men died because of you. Germans too. And that signal to the train that was following us. It wasn't Hanna, it was you. I should have realized when the Marksman tried to show me. Two hands above the head. It was in that old manual we found in the dining car. Did you set Ritter free at the same time?"

"I knew he was working for Goering. But he was my only hope. And they *were* SS following us. I knew they wouldn't hand over the gold to Goering."

Wouldn't they, he thought. Surely she must realize that all the troops that had been sent against them had been sent by Goering? He stared into her face, across which a strand of hair was blowing, and suddenly realized that she had thought nothing of the kind. To her they had been sent on orders of the *Abwehr*. And, strangely enough, as he thought that, his love for her returned.

The detective named Macdonald called out, "Please hurry up, sir."

She was in his arms, her tears were wet against his cheek, her lips dry against his, and he remembered when they had been one.

As the two Special Branch men approached she drew back. She pointed across the sea. "I couldn't have stayed over there, not without you. I hoped . . ."

"I know what you hoped," he said. "You hoped you wouldn't be caught," but the anger had left him.

"Here, take this." As the detectives stopped in front of them she handed him a tightly folded sheet of paper. "Perhaps when all this is over . . ."

"Perhaps . . ." But no, that would be wrong; there had been enough lies. He bent and kissed her. He said, "It's over."

She walked away between the two detectives. She turned once. She waved and was gone.

Standing there in the fresh, sea-smelling dusk, part birth and part death, he unfolded the sheet of paper and read her handwriting. *Remember that evening on the train when I was writing this in the exercise book. Remember it, my love, and remember me, the person you thought I was, because I have a terrible premonition that what is happening to us was never meant to be. If it is not, then just think from time to time when you stare into the night sky that we are looking at the same star.*

He looked at the single star and shared it with her.

As he turned on his heel he felt something break beneath his foot. He knelt and saw the shattered fragments of a piece of coal.

THE FOLLOWING MORNING Miller gazed across the docks from the bedroom of the guesthouse where he had spent the night. According to Munnion, who had telephoned him at dawn, more than 25,000 troops had been evacuated by midnight, but they had mostly been backup units who had already been on the coast. Today, the second day proper of Operation Dynamo, would be tougher because the Luftwaffe was attacking the beleaguered army with renewed venom, and Hitler had countermanded his order halting the attack on them from the west.

Munnion had also confirmed that Gisella's source in London hadn't been the idealist she had believed him to be: he had been working for the *Forschungsamt.* In other words, Gisella had been helping "the symbol of Germany's sickness." He hoped she never found out; the tortuous intricacies of Intelligence were such that there was always that hope.

Then, although there was no way he could stop her memory returning to him at unguarded moments, he applied himself to the present. Some of the original team dropped in the Saxon Forest were staying in the guesthouse, and it was to the room occupied by the North Countryman that he took himself.

The North Countryman was shaving in a handbasin in the cramped room, papered with the same cornflower pattern as Miller's. His free arm was bandaged.

Miller said, "All right, where's my share?"

The North Countryman turned, razor in hand. "What are you talking about?"

"The gold bars in the canvas bag."

The North Countryman's arm fell, and he laid the razor beside the handbasin. "I save the man's life and he wants my wages."

"Our wages. We both earned them. When did you pinch them? Just before we got to Dunkirk?"

The North Countryman nodded. "The crate that had the bullet hole in it." He bent and washed his face, picked up a towel, and began to dry himself.

"Two big bars, judging by the size of the bag. One for you, one for me. A nice, tidy arrangement."

The North Countryman put the towel back on the rack, bent down, pulled the canvas bag from under the bed, and opened it.

Miller picked up one of the ingots. It felt just a little too light. He frowned. He picked up the other. He struck the two together. The sound was metallic. Golden, never.

He replaced the ingots in the bag and, watched by the puzzled North Contryman, walked to the window and stared across the Channel toward France. Toward Belgium and Germany.

He knew that it wasn't just the two that were counterfeit: there had never been an ounce of genuine gold on the Rheingold all the way from Hamburg to Dover.

He began to laugh but, when he explained, the North Countryman didn't see the joke.

As the train taking him back to London—back to Vic and his parents—passed through the Kentish countryside, he still laughed from time to time. The beaten troops packed into the compartment sensed a crazed note to the laugh and stared at him with hostility. What right had a civilian to seek refuge in madness? He hadn't seen anything.

EPILOGUE

19

STORY SHIFTED HIS aching bones around in the leather armchair and said to Shaw, "Are you trying to tell me that the gold in the Bank of England is counterfeit?"

What an incredible proposition. Could it really be possible that the bulk of the bullion in the vaults of the Old Lady of Threadneedle Street was phony? He saw the headlines: ALL THAT GLITTERS . . . He would make a killing. But what sort of a killing?

If I break the story, then the Western economy could collapse. What if I were offered money—a fortune—to suppress it? Get thee behind me, Satan. My whole career has been based on integrity, the stone on which I've sharpened the knives with which to attack the manipulators of high finance.

But, as he had brooded only that morning—morning? it seemed like a week ago—the Bank of England was fraudulent. One of the foundation stones of the system was ready to crumble.

I would become a multimillionaire. I would join the elite.

He realized that the suave, silver-haired man sitting opposite him was observing him closely.

"Not quite, Mr. Story, not quite," Shaw said, in answer to his original question.

Story stared speculatively at the Bank's head of security. So there was still more to this story? Somehow he didn't think he'd come up a loser whatever the final solution was.

Shaw stood up and gazed through the window. The storm had spent itself, and the evening was gray and dripping. "Come on," he said, "let's take a walk. We'll have a pint in a City pub."

Outside, the City was emptying, servants of the pound, dollar, mark, yen, scurrying home to the domestic terminals of their lives, leaving their square-mile sorting house to its custodians and cats.

They walked against the rush-hour tide, Shaw prodding the pavement with the spike of his rolled umbrella as though it might conceal landmines. After a while he said, "The *gold* was lead electroplated, with a 10,000 part of an inch of the real stuff."

"Go on."

"All this, of course, is classified information."

"Not outside Britain." Story dodged a gang of office girls running to the subway. He stepped in the gutter and water spurted up his trouser leg. "In any case, there's a time limit to your official secrets."

"That's what the public is encouraged to think. *Now it can be told* . . . all that. But those are only the secrets that British Intelligence consider harmless. Sops. The mind-boggling stuff never gets published."

"Why not get to the point, old man."

Shaw prodded a piece of sodden cardboard with the intensity of someone trying to spear an errant banknote.

"Very well," he said. "The *real* gold was dispatched to New York on a naval cruiser, HMS *Emerald*, from Greenock, the same port in Scotland from which the *Alaska* sailed. But the whole operation on the *Alaska* was a diversion. Logan knew there was a leak somewhere at the top. Grover, as it happened, but at that stage he didn't know who."

"Who knew about the diversion?"

"Three men. Logan, Churchill, and Roosevelt. The Governor of the Bank of England, himself, thought that that was his gold in transit across Europe."

"I don't understand," said Story. "The diversion would seem to have succeeded."

"It was supposed to be a temporary diversion. The Luftwaffe, U-boats, whatever, would throw everything they'd got against the *Alaska,* while the *Emerald,* with its escort, slipped across the Atlantic."

"And what altered the temporary nature of the plan."

"There was an imponderable."

"There always is," Story said, feeling cold water seep into his shoes.

"Not much farther," Shaw said.

"To where?"

"To the pub where we're going."

Story said tightly, "The imponderable, Mr. Shaw. What was it?"

"The *Emerald* broke down. So it became vital that the charade be continued while she was repaired. If Goering had suspected that the cargo on the Rheingold was fake, he would have gone berserk. He could have covered up his own interest in the bullion—he was Hitler's deputy after all—and told Raeder to get the German Navy to scour the Atlantic for the *Emerald*. She would have stuck out like a sore thumb."

"And there was a bonus. Logan wanted to nail Goering's source in London."

"Precisely. Until he was caught, the whole British war effort was at risk."

Shaw led the way across a narrow street shining wetly in the evening light. Story could see the dome of St. Paul's. Somewhere a clock chimed.

Story said, "And the gold was really intended as payment, or part payment, for Roosevelt's contribution to that war effort?"

"Intended, yes. But I doubt if either Churchill or Roosevelt really believed that. If Britain had gone down in those dark days, then Churchill would have said, 'Look, we've entrusted our capital with you.'" Shaw's imitation of Churchill wasn't at all bad. "'Now we must fight the Hun together.' If, as happened, Britain survived, then he could say, 'We paid you in good faith.'" Now Shaw *was* Churchill. "'But if democracy is to survive, then you must return that golden heritage because it must never be known that Britain so lacked faith in her ability to defeat Corporal Hitler that she shipped that heritage to America.'"

"Very good," Story said. "Move over Sir Laurence." They were approaching a pub; Story hoped it was *the* one. "So the gold did reach New York?"

"Correct."

"And was shipped back here after the war?"

"Correct."

"So the Bank of England isn't bankrupt?"

"Sorry to disappoint you, Mr. Story."

It *was* the pub, a warm-mouthed, Edwardian-styled establishment called the Magpie and Stump. It was pleasant enough, crowded with City workers imbibing the courage to return home. Shaw ordered a pint of bitter, Story a large Scotch—an ordinary British measure evaporated on your tongue—on the rocks. While the bartender poured the drinks, Shaw led Story down to the quiet end of the bar.

Story swirled the ice in his glass—the bartender had suffered an aberration and given him two cubes—and considered his options. So the Old

Lady wasn't bankrupt after all. It was still a hell of a story, but, the more he thought about it, the more he was convinced there was something he hadn't figured out.

"You've collected an amazing amount of detail about this operation," Story said. Shaw put his bitter down on the bar. "What happened to Miller, Mr. Shaw?"

"Miller is the reason I know so much. I met him once. When I became head of security I made it my business to find out everything about the bullion episode."

"And he talked?"

"Why not? He was very bitter and said he didn't give a damn about the Official Secrets Act. Anyway, I was hardly likely to let the cat out of the bag, was I?"

"Weren't you?" Story stared at Shaw over the rim of his glass; the blue eyes stared back. "How was he doing?"

"Prospering as a matter of fact. For the rest of the war he worked as a demolition expert. Then he got a good job in the City. It was part of the deal Munnion extracted from Logan. Logan hated it but Munnion had lodged papers with a lawyer that could have blown the whole thing."

"A good job in the City?" Shaw ordered another bitter and downed it almost as fast as the first one. "I hope the firm he worked for checked the till every night."

"He was a reformed character," Shaw said.

"Really? I doubt it. Not after what he'd been through. Not after he'd been betrayed twice."

I'm inching toward knowledge, Story thought.

"Betrayed? Yes, he was betrayed all right. But there was worse." Shaw picked up his pint. "Vic and his parents were killed in an air raid in 1944. A V-1 rocket. They had just moved to a semi-detached in Epping Forest."

"Poor bastard," Story remarked. "A loser."

"Loser? I doubt that." And he called for another bitter, a small one at last.

"And Pritchard?" Another circumspect approach; that was the only way with a man like Shaw.

"According to Miller, he was invalided out of the army. He went back to the Romney, Hythe, and Dymchurch Railway. They had mobilized it by then, miniature armored trains patrolling that stretch of the Kent coast, so he went on doing his bit. Miller went to see him. He was quite happy, and he told Miller, 'At least I've driven a crack express. If it's always like that, once is enough!' Something like that."

"And Gisella Hessen?"

Shaw sipped his beer. "She married the other *giant* in the story, Max von Ritter. A wonderful match, I believe. You realize, of course, that Schleicher, the man you robbed in Gernsbach, is von Ritter? like most Germans he couldn't resist keeping records, and he put it all down in the leather-bound book."

"And the gold ingot in Schleicher's house?"

"Gold ingot?"

"There was a gold ingot in Schleicher's house. I didn't know what to make of it when Meyer told me about it. All of a sudden it begins to interest me very much." Story stared at Shaw, his third degree look, as a financier had once described it. A feeling of exultancy possessed him; he knew he was on the scent.

Shaw looked pensive. "Miller swore me to secrecy."

"Don't give me that. You were sworn to secrecy about everything you've told me today. For some reason you think I won't write this story."

"It doesn't matter anymore, I suppose," Shaw said. "You were right about Miller up to a point. He wasn't a totally reformed character. Not to start with, anyway. He pulled one more big job. One very big job."

Story waited.

Shaw put down his tankard unfinished and said, "Come outside for a moment."

When an Englishman leaves his beer it's got to be important, Story thought. They stood outside, gazing across the street at the Central Criminal Court, the Old Bailey, and, on top of it, the Scales of Justice that were silhouetted against the darkening sky. He felt close to what was eluding him.

Shaw said, "Miller was given the job of supervising the return of the gold from the United States. What better choice? He had snatched the fake gold from the Germans—he never let on that he knew it was counterfeit—and British Intelligence wanted as few people as possible to know that the bullion had ever been shipped to America."

"And not all the real gold got back to the Bank of England?"

Shaw smiled thinly. "A considerable amount didn't. At today's prices he's as rich as Croesus. You can't blame him, can you? He deserved something."

"My God," Story said, "it's not possible."

"*Possible? Is anything impossible? Read the newspapers!*' Wellington."

Story was thinking aloud. "Then the ingot that was stolen from Schleicher's—Ritter's—house was part of Miller's haul when he brought the gold back from New York."

"A wedding present. And so, although the Old Lady isn't exactly bankrupt, she's short of a carat or two."

Story looked away from Shaw toward the blue and black clouds that were moving and shifting in the sky beyond the Old Bailey. At last he said, "That's an interesting story, Mr. Shaw."

"Not one I'd like to share with the world."

"Then correct me if I'm wrong. You're prepared to do a deal on Miller's behalf. To save him from justice, for want of a better word."

"Correct."

"What makes you think I'd give up the story of a lifetime?"

"One million pounds," Shaw said softly. "He

can afford it. You see, he knew that once you got hold of that leather book you'd track down the whole thing."

Story felt the foundations of journalism shaking beneath his feet. And he had thought it was the Bank of England that was going to fall. "Done," he said, and shook Shaw's hand.

A crowd of office workers brushed in front of them. Staring at Shaw almost shyly, Story said, "That chain across your waistcoat—is there a gold hunter on the end of it?"

Shaw took the watch out and weighed it in his hand. "Miller gave it back to Munnion as he promised. But Munnion left it to him in his will. Munnion died twenty years after the war, in his garden."

"Pruning roses?"

"Planting cabbages. Apparently he got to like vegetable gardening. The war changed everyone. The bequest to Miller in the will said *For Services Rendered*."

"And Miller gave it to you?"

"I think you know," Shaw said.

"The job in the City that Munnion arranged for Miller. It was a *very* good job, wasn't it?"

"Very. But he had to work his way up. And change his name."

A single star had appeared in the sky above them, and for a moment the breeze coming off the Thames smelled of the sea.

Story pointed across the street at the Old Bailey.

"Do you still dream about the day you stood in the dock and heard yourself sentenced to death?"

"I also dream about the scaffold. But when they open the trapdoor these days, I fall into a crock of gold," Miller said.